'Get out! You're all the same,' Blanche exploded.

'My dear . . .' he murmured, coming forward.

'I'm not your *anything*!' A heavy paperweight crashed against the wall, missing him by inches.

'That's enough!' With a spring, he captured her hands, bringing them behind her, lifting her off her feet, holding her hard against him.

'Let me go!' A slippered foot cracked into his shin, and he gave a soft curse.

'I said, that's enough!' He threw her on the bed, holding her wrists captive, his hard body preventing her struggles until the flashing eyes suddenly changed as she realised her helplessness and felt her own anger in him.

He kissed her, then, with a sensual expertise, bringing her hard against the taut length of his body, and a soft moan was torn from her throat as she felt his need of her. His mouth had travelled down over her bare shoulder, then lower to the silken fullness of a breast, and Blanche shuddered in exquisite torment as his lips and tongue brought waves of sensation up from her stomach, and lower.

'No!' she murmured, yet clung to him as if drowning. 'Please, no!' But she knew she was lost as she felt his husky laughter against her throat.

'I'm not going to rape you, woman. I'm going to change your mind!'

Hazel Smith was born in Loughborough, but spent her early life in London and the Croydon area. She now lives in Coulsdon, fitting in writing with keeping a ten-roomed house in an acceptable degree of chaos, and coping with a hectic book-keeping job and an active fourteen-year-old son. She has been writing short stories since her teens, and *Gypsy Royal* is her third Masquerade Historical Romance. Her first two are *Master of Moonrise* and *A Cast of Hawks*.

GYPSY ROYAL
HAZEL SMITH

MILLS & BOON LIMITED
15-16 BROOK'S MEWS
LONDON W1A 1DR

First published in Great Britain 1986 by Mills & Boon Limited

© Hazel Smith 1986

Australian copyright 1986 Philippine copyright 1987 This edition 1987

ISBN 0 263 75670 X

Set in Linotron Times 10 on 10 pt. 04-0287-79917

Typeset in Great Britain by Associated Publishing Services Made and printed in Great Britain by Cox & Wyman Ltd, Reading

CHAPTER ONE

IT WAS COLD, cripplingly cold in that winter of 1832. The rich drew on their ermine muffs and heavy cloaks with fur-lined hoods, and the poor died. In the 'rookeries' off St. Giles and the slums from Soho to Stepney they huddled beneath their piles of rags emerging only to beg—or steal—their meagre survival rations, returned to beat their wives or children out of fear and frustrated anger, crawled into dark alleys where a packing crate lined with newspaper served as a nest for one more night of frost, and prayed to, or cursed, the unseeing, uncaring God who had made all men equal! Some were luckier than others. Some in that area of St Giles, where a group of high-born ladies came two or three times a week to a draughty, bare hall and dispensed soup and sympathy, receiving nothing in return except the knowledge that a few less would die that night.

A ragged cheer went up as the carriage drew to a halt outside the crumbling building, and the long and patient line of scarecrows rippled expectantly 'We'll be all right today,' said one man to his mate 'The White Lady's here.'

'Ruddy toff!' objected the stranger in front of him. 'Showing off her finery to us wot ain't got none!'

'She's all right, that one,' the first man growled, his very size preventing any argument. 'When my Meg was sick after our eleventh—'course, seven of 'em 'ave died b'now—she brought soup and fresh bread still hot, and she fed my old woman and the young 'uns wiv 'er own 'ands. We ain't never going to forget that.'

'I'm on first name terms wiv 'er,' boasted a skeletal little prostitute barely into her teens, her tattered dress and filthy crimson shawl throwing her cavernous, colourless features into pathetic relief.

'G'wan!' scoffed the stranger. 'She wouldn't even look at the likes of you!'

'She would, too, y'old rat-bait! I 'eard one o' 'em others call 'er Blanche one day, so I called her Lady Blanche. "Fanks awfully, Lady Blanche," I sez, putting on my best voice, an' she smiles like an angel out of 'eaven. "It's my pleasure, my dear," she sez, so now when I sees her, I sez, "How do you do, Lady Blanche." So don't you dare say I'm not on first name terms!'

The others looked suitably impressed, then a young urchin, eyes widening, breathed, 'Cor! Ain't she beeootiful!' as the vision stepped from the carriage, smiling and nodding as she swept into the cold, cheerless hall.

She crossed to the far end at which three long tables had been set up to hold steaming cauldrons of soup and wooden platters of roughly chunked bread. As she approached the four other women already at their places, she was swinging off the long, voluminous cloak and removing the beribboned and feathered bonnet to reveal smoothly-parted hair coiled into honey-gold plaits about her ears. From head to toe she was dressed in white, the only relief shown in the black tips on the tiny ermine muff, but the impression of fragility, accentuated by the wide gigot sleeves and tiny waist, was totally dispelled by the long stride and thickly lashed grey eyes that twinkled from an unfashionably healthy complexion. 'Forgive me!' she exclaimed in tones that knew she would be forgiven anything. 'I had to stop off at the Marquis of Asherleigh's—a small matter of a donation to our cause. Priscilla, you really shouldn't be here with that awful cold!'

The young woman so addressed gave a delicate shiver. 'I should have spent another day or two in bed, but I felt that an ordinary cold didn't warrant letting down these poor wretches. They do rely on us so.'

The newcomer gave a snort. 'You never were blessed with a surfeit of sense. These people certainly need our help, but they won't appreciate your collapsing into the soup! Still, now that you're here . . . Open the door, then, and let's see what the good Lord has provided us with today.'

''Pon my soul, Lady Davenport, you actually seem to enjoy this weekly crusade of yours!'

The cool grey eyes turned to the woman at the far end of the table, and she gave a decisive shake of the head. 'No, Mrs Hartington-Smythe, but it's a challenge I accept. I can even accept the late Regent's desire to create his 'Royal Mile' between his Carlton House residence and his summer retreat back in '17, and the Circus is quite lovely now and a perfect solution to that awful problem of crossing Piccadilly, though I can't imagine our starchy William wanting anything so grand. What I have difficulty in accepting, however, is that quarter-mile up to Oxford Street that demolished over seven hundred of these poor wretches' shops and homes. The rookeries are terrible slums, and their clearance would be a blessing to mankind, but there are still human beings living there.'

'But you must consider the hundreds, not the individuals,' argued the older woman. 'Why, I don't even see faces any more; all I see are dozens of filthy hands clutching bowls which I fill.'

Any further discussion was prevented by the appearance of the first of those dozens, but as the suprisingly disciplined line filed by, the fourth member of the band gave Blanche a broad wink. 'You stick to your guns, my girl! You keep fighting, and keep the tears for the bedroom!'

Blanche returned the other's smile. She had known Alexandra Fitz-Hugh for over two years, and the warm affection she felt was mutual, based on an intimate knowledge of each other's lives that neither would trust to any other. 'Beatrice, the Lady Davenport, *never* cries!' she stated firmly, using her real name, rather than the one she had been given because of her idiosyncrasy of wearing only white, but turning her attention to the work in hand, she wondered how she managed to prevent those tears that she must never shed.

The derelicts of the neighbourhood appeared to be more like creatures from Dante's imagination than human beings. 'It's all very well to dispense charity,' she thought bleakly. 'We can all do that. But when it comes down to cold hard facts, what counts is not the faceless mass but the face before you . . . and how much that particular crippled child means to you.'

She closed her eyes for an instant as one typical waif held out her bowl with trembling hands, hands that were blue with cold and raw with the effects of lye soap and hours at the tub. Blanche noticed on the child's legs the freshly healed scars from bites of rats in the crate in which she slept. From a small pouch at her waist she took a new shilling. 'You must get off the street, Liza,' she admonished. 'I gave you an address to go to where your stepfather wouldn't find you. The couple there would have been only too glad to take you into their kitchens, even though, Heaven help us, I've already overstaffed them!'

The girl gave a crooked smile and her eyes bore the wisdom and pain of one twice her ten years. 'I gave my baby bruvver to that lady, and got 'im some warm clothes wiv the other money you give me. We won't be beholden to anybody . . . 'cept you. Me dad broke Billy's arm, you see, when he tried to stop 'im 'itting me ma. Billy's only seven, and 'e ain't as good at sleeping in the alleys as wot I am, not wiv a broken arm, any'ow.'

Blanche felt her throat tighten. She would never get used to this, never! But already the child was moving on, secreting the precious coin beneath her rags and taking her bread and soup to a far corner of

the hall where one of the two small, totally inadequate
fires was ringed about by several dozen people, old
and young, crippled and whole, some with rapacious
fingers eager to steal another's bread, others gladly
sharing theirs with their still hungry babies.

Just as the queue thinned to a trickle and the soup
cauldrons were being scraped for the very last morsel,
Blanche happened to look toward the door—there
were always more beggars than food, and in the last
few minutes she had to choose the worst cases to give
that last mouthful to—and saw a man standing there.
He was not of that area, for he wore the garb of a
dock-worker and, although his clothing was as full of
holes and patches as any in the rookeries, his stance
did not betray the stooping, hopeles gait of those
about him. He was looking directly at her, she knew,
and there was an intensity in that regard that Blanche
found unnerving . . . and what Blanche had cause to
fear, she faced.

With a murmured word to Priscilla on her left she
crossed the hall toward him, at which the stranger
immediately turned to leave. 'Wait!'

He halted, lowering the grimy cap that covered his
hair and pulling up the scarf flung round his neck and
concealing the lower part of his face. He said nothing,
keeping his head averted until, exasperated and not a
little nervous, Blanche commanded, 'Please be so
good as to look at me when I'm speaking to you.'

At which he turned, and Blanche took an
involuntary step backwards for the eyes that held
hers were clear and thickly lashed and of the strangest
shade of green—a cross between dark jade and sage—
and were sparkling with laughter! At the same time
she noticed the fingers that held the scarf close about
his face. They were long and slender . . . and with
manicured nails!

'You imposter!' she exploded, grey eyes flashing
fire. 'You're from neither the rookeries nor the docks.
You aren't even a man! You're just a bored, spoilt
blue-blood, one of society's parasites coming down

here to feed off the misery of others! Well, I hope you've had a good meal—which is more than they have!'

The amusement had died from those eyes as she spoke, and as she paused for breath he stated quickly, 'You're wrong, my lady. One day you'll know just how wrong!' Then, before she could continue her tirade, he gave a low courtly bow and left, a few long pantherish strides down the cobbled street then, miraculously, falling into a bent, shuffling gait that blended him instantly into the crowd.

Frustrated at his retreat, anger vying with curiosity—she would have given anything to have seen the rest of that aristocratic face—Blanche returned to the avid interest of her companions.

'Who was he?' Priscilla asked eagerly. 'Why, Blanche, you're absolutely furious! What did he say to you?'

'Are you well, Lady Davenport? Your colour is quite unusually high, even for you?'

'I'm quite well, thank you, Mrs Hartington-Smythe, and yes, Priscilla, I *am* furious. Would you believe that creature was nothing more than some brainless, parasitical popinjay who affected a disguise in order to gain amusement watching these poor devils finding a moment's respite from the cold. He hadn't even bothered to dirty his face, and his manicure was so new that his buffed nails positively gleamed!'

'Well, I'm sure you saw him off,' Priscilla stated, her streaming cold forgotten for a few moments as the others echoed Balanche's own indignation.

The queue had died now and, seeing that there was no more charity forthcoming, the scarecrows drifted away, leaving the hall littered with an assortment of wooden bowls—though many had brought their own—and newspaper, too torn to be of use even for the lining of shoes. Paper was a much-sought-after commodity, as it could give considerable protection when worn beneath layers of rags or put beneath one when sleeping in cobbled alleys, and Blanche always made sure that her coachman brought a large pile. She unashamedly begged from her friends and foes alike—the latter donating the odd rag for the simple pleasure of imagining that five-foot frame bending over lice-ridden denizens of some Soho slum, bowed by the weight of the sack of rags she carried.

What they were unaware of, that her friends knew all too well, was that the White Lady, for all her diminutive size and mere twenty-three years, was regarded as little less than an angel among the poor, and when she did venture abroad there would always emerge a large figure from the shadows—sometimes two or three—with faces like gargoyles and fists that could fell an ox, and gently relieve her of her smallest package before falling in behind as bodyguards. Blanche—Beatrice, Lady Davenport, in white cashmere and furs that would keep a family for years—was incredibly as safe in the rookeries as in her own drawing-room.

'Don't think of such unpleasantnesses,' Alexandra Fitz-Hugh smiled. 'I'm holding one of my little dinner parties next week—not Saturday, because simply everyone will be at the Countess Vandaneuve's, so I want mine to be on the Friday afternoon.'

Blanche gave one of her rich chuckles. 'You're cruel, Lexie! If I attend what you so modestly call your 'little dinner parties', which usually include at least twenty of the cream of society, I shall be quite unable to face another glass of champagne or morsel of pheasant for at least a week, and I doubt that I'll be alone. Why do you dislike the Countess so?'

The older woman gave a grim smile, pulling on her grey kid gloves with remarkable ferocity. 'I have no time for one who is so blatantly an impostor and who treats her King Charles spaniel better by far than her servants!'

'I know she has no blood-line,' conceded Blanche, 'and I abhor her attempt to become an aristocrat simply by marrying older and older titles, both in blood and age . . . Why her last husband, dear

Vandaneuve, must have been sixty at least. No wonder he lasted a bare year! However, I do agree with your views on the dog; that pampered pet of hers is a parody of its hunting ancestors. The servants, though, appear to be in the best of health.'

'I dare say, Blanche.' But then Alexandra gave a gentle smile that still did not quite reach her eyes. 'Enough of such talk! You *must* come to my gathering, for there are one or two quite interesting young men I've a mind to introduce you to—one in particular . . .'

'No more!' laughed Blanche. 'I know you Lexie. You've that matchmaking light in your eyes,' and then, as the other made to protest, 'I know . . . I'm a fast-ageing spinster that should have been wed years ago, but please, dear Lexie, consider the choices I've had! With my character, I can't see myself like the Countess as the wife of some elderly Count, sitting in some icy, crumbling mausoleum with my embroidery, nor married to one of those delicate dandies that follow Brummell as if he were some prophet of fashion. I know you mean well, but I've many more places to see and a thousand people to meet before I settle for marital monotony.'

Alexandra gave a smiling shake of her head. She had been married to the gentle, portly Fitz-Hugh for ten years, since her twenty-fifth birthday, shortly after her first husband, an ailing, geriatric earl, had died and relieved her of an arranged marriage. Although Fitz-Hugh was also almost old enough to be her father, they had been blissfully happy from the first. But then, she reflected, she was not one of the 'Butterfly People', as Blanche called them, including herself in that flock of shifting, lifting, settling and moving on again people for whom a stable relationship was something to be feared rather than sought. Yet still Alexandra tried to give Blanche the opportunity to meet that one person with whom she could find Alexandra's own happiness, so she persisted, 'You simply can't afford not to meet my Lord Hunterton.

He's been over from Paris for almost a year, but has only just come into circulation this season and every mother in London is positively hurling her little darling at his head.'

'No doubt a very swollen head, then!' remarked Blanche caustically.

'Not at all. He has the manners of a true aristocrat and shows no favouritism at all. He's the greatest wit, and out-dandifies even Mr Brummell himself, though in quite a different way, and his attire is always a surprise. But then, being half French on his mother's side—a duchess no less—what can you expect?'

'Doesn't sound at all my kind of man,' Blanche exclaimed.

'Oh, but he also rides like a dream and drives that black carriage of his as if the very devil were beside him. Doesn't *that* sound like your kind of man? I'd wager *he* could give you a run on the Brighton road!'

Blanche refused to show interest, yet her curiosity was indeed aroused, for her own superior horsemanship and reputation as a whip had, until now, been unsurpassed, and many had been the young buck who had ruefully admitted defeat in the wake of her dustcloud. 'Well, of course I'll come but only because your dinner parties are quite the best in London. Now, however, I really must create some semblance of order about us. I refuse to leave it all to the servants, who should be arriving at any minute. I do declare they put on such airs that you would think they were above a little dirt!' With total disregard of the effect on that dazzling white merino skirt, she bent to gather the scattered soup bowls from the floor.

CHAPTER TWO

THE FITZ-HUGHS' terraced house overlooking St James's Park was ablaze with light, and even from the street, as Blanche's carriage drew up outside and she paused a moment to shake her head at the pretentiousness of the stuccoed columns and surfeit of sculpture, the laughter and music could be heard. She much preferred the simplicity of her villa out at Park Village East—a relatively new project of Nash's similar to those on the Eyre Estate in St John's Wood—but always enjoyed the Fitz-Hughs' parties, so gladly forgave them their touch of ostentation.

Slipping her fur-lined cloak from her shoulders and handing it to the hovering maid, she adjusted the multiple bouffants of her sleeves that had been crushed a little by the cloak, before allowing the butler to announce her. Alexandra saw her even as she entered and immediately crossed to her side, resplendent in rose satin bordered with cream lace, but her admiration for Blanche's attire was fulsome and quite genuine. 'My dear, you look devastating! That velvet must have cost you at least a kiss!'

Blanche laughed good-naturedly, tossing back the ringlets that swung over her ears, her grey eyes already scanning the crowded room. 'An insignificant earl that simply insisted on repaying me for bringing him luck at whist. I see Mr Brummell is here again? He really is out of favour now with the "ton". Only he would wear those pale violet pantaloons with a scarlet waistcoat, and that white satin cravat must have taken him at least a half-hour to tie. He was far more circumspect in his youth.' Then her gaze sharpened. 'But who is that who has just joined him? Surely no one should be attired like that, even in our eccentric society?'

'You are, my dear.'

'But for a *man* to be dressed entirely in white . . .'

'I told you that my Lord Hunterton always produced a surprise,' Alexandra stated, looking smug. 'Won't you allow me to introduce him?'

Intrigued in spite of herself, Blanche accompanied her friend through the milling crowd, stopping over and again to pass a word with old acquaintances or to jest with young dandies in gay satins of purple and sky-blue. Only once did her smile fade. It was as she nodded to a group and caught the words, 'rabble' and 'slums demolished'. 'They really should just set fire to that place,' a young exquisite was saying in carrying tones, touching his fine lace-edged handkerchief to delicately flared nostrils as if the very subject brought an unpleasant odour to the room. 'The vermin, both two-legged and four, would, one might hope, flee into the countryside and leave us a far cleaner city, what?'

Alexandra held her breath, waiting for the explosion which never came. Instead, Blanche readjusted her smile; yet there was ice crackling across her words as she enunciated clearly, 'Sir Anthony . . . if your brain was one-half the size of your mouth, I might deign to answer you. Instead, I merely pity you.' With a nod to the other members of the group, she turned her back on him and continued her leisurely stroll.

Eventually she found herself behind the stranger whose raven hair clung in crisp curls to the back of his head, even shorter than was fashionable, being well clear of the rolled collar. His broad shoulders threatening to split the tailored dress coat obviously needed no padding, nor, she suspected, did he wear the tightly-laced stays that the dandies often employed to accentuate the close-fitting waistline. But then Alexandra was saying, 'So nice to see you again, Mr Brummell. Lord Hunterton, how good of you to come. Will you allow me to introduce you to my dearest friend, Beatrice, Lady Davenport? Blanche, this is Jason, Lord Hunterton, the infamous whip?

Blanche raised her eyes slowly—a trick she had perfected and one which usually had a devastating effect on the object of her scrutiny. She took in the dazzling white embroidered silk stockings, and trousers so tight over muscular thighs as to appear like a second skin, the satin waistcoat and frilled shirt in which a large diamond pin set in gold caught the light from the chandeliers and shot rainbow sparks over the dress of those about him.

A deep, rich voice said, 'I had heard that the famous White Lady would be here, so thought to dress accordingly.'

Then she met his eyes—eyes of a rare deep jade touched with sage, heavy lidded and deceptively languid and her own went glacial as she turned abruptly to her friend. 'Lord Hunterton and I have met,' she stated coldly. 'Please forgive me if I choose not to renew our mercifully brief acquaintanceship. I do hope *we* may speak later, Mr Brummell.' Spinning on her heel, she left them speechless and stalked into the throng.

Crimson-cheeked, Alexandra spluttered, 'My lord . . . I . . . She . . .'

'Please don't distress yourself, Mrs Fitz-Hugh,' the stranger smiled. 'Lady Davenport has gained quite the wrong impression, and it is my fault entirely. Under the circumstances her attitude was quite understandable. If you'll excuse me, I'll make amends.'

'Take care, my lord,' laughed Brummell. 'In spite of her size, that particular kitten has surprisingly sharp claws!'

'Oh, please don't gain the wrong impression yourself, Lord Hunterton,' Alexandra begged, nearly in tears. 'Blanche is really the sweetest soul; it's just that she is . . . er . . . a little lacking in diplomacy. I'm sure that when you explain whatever it is you have to explain . . .' She trailed off before the twinkle in his eyes as he took her hand.

'You are a true friend, and Lady Davenport is fortunate indeed.' He bowed over her fingers, and with a flash of even white teeth said, 'You know, you have the most incredibly beautiful hands, Mrs Fitz-Hugh: your husband is a lucky man, and I shall try to refrain from disliking him intensely.'

Alexandra blushed and gave a choked giggle—she who hadn't giggled in twenty years—but with a broad and positively wicked wink he turned and followed in the wake of the White Lady.

Blanche felt his presence even before he spoke, but refused to turn, irritated by the glazed look of admiration that had washed over the face of the young dandy with whom she had been speaking, a look that a moment earlier had been bent upon her.

'Lady Davenport, I feel that I have offended you, and beg you to accept my apology.'

The young man gulped and made some excuse to leave, but neither noticed him go. Blanche turned slowly, raking him from head to toe and back again, and a flicker of a frown touched her brow. How could anyone with so much animal virility sink so low as to take his sport from the suffering of others?

He noticed the quickened breath that caused her full breasts to strain at the extreme *décolleté* neckline, and his throat went dry. 'I should have introduced myself at once,' he continued, holding those stormy eyes, willing her to show some small sign of softening, unaccustomed to such inflexibility from the fair sex. 'I was not there, I assure you, to alleviate the tedium of yet another party, nor to seek any amusement from the despair of those poor devils. I don't need to live vicariously, Lady Davenport.' He spoke quickly and earnestly, entirely without the affected drawl of fashion, and saw the very slightest spark of doubt behind that cool regard. 'Allow me to explain. We have time. Mrs Fitz-Hugh in her wisdom has made us dinner partners. That is, unless you would like to request a change of place . . .'

The slightest flicker of a smile touched the softly rouged lips though the eyes remained cool. 'Not at all, Lord Hunterton. For if you do not convince me of your good intentions I shall take the greatest pleasure in ignoring your presence totally, and how would you and my friends know that I was deliberately ignoring you if we were seated apart?'

His laugh startled her, but at that moment dinner was announced and her icy retort was forestalled. Carefully she placed her fingertips on his extended hand, accompanying him into the ornately decorated dining-room with its wall tapestries and rich velvet curtains, its surfeit of silver candlesticks reflecting the brilliance of the three heavy crystal chandeliers.

The light conversation of the other guests had not ceased with the transition from the salon, so effortless was the Fitz-Hughs' hospitality, and even the musicians were replaced by a second group that would play softly throughout dinner without anyone noticing the changeover. It would be noticed only if the discreet music did not continue until past nine-thirty. With pleased surprise, Blanche turned to the young man seated to her left. 'Jeremy, how nice! How long have you been back? How was Paris?'

Jeremy Montague Linton, 2nd Viscount Carlysle, gave a bored yawn. 'Usual round of *ennuim*. If this hadn't been one of the Fitz-Hughs' little affairs I confess I'd have cried off.' Then the brown eyes gleamed and the accent changed entirely at the sight of Blanche's quivering lips that she tried unsuccessfully to keep from curving upwards. 'Deuce take it, Blanche, you're not in the least impressed! Oh, I surrender! Paris was wonderful, exciting, and more than I ever dreamed of.' He leaned forward eagerly to include Lord Hunterton in his pleasure. 'You were so right, Lord Hunterton. All those places you mentioned, the people you sent your card to . . . The people you didn't!' He gave a gay laugh. 'Blanche, he must know a hundred people at the very least from princes to paupers . . . Especially the paupers! It was only when I realised how much he did for *them*, and then after speaking to dear Alexandra on my return, that I suggested that he meet you.'

'Thank you!' replied Blanche caustically, but the young aristocrat was enthusing, 'You should just hear the gossip, Blanche. His lordship has done some wonderful charity work in the dock area since his return to England. I don't know what he has done to gain such a following, nor, looking at him now—and you really must recommend me to your tailor, my lord—can I imagine how he could possibly move among them to the degree that he is taken as one of that tatterdemalion rabble, but I *do* know from unimpeachable sources that he's loved and trusted by people who don't even trust the local constabulary. Lord Hunterton, I am honoured, sir, to know you.'

The stranger gave him an answering smile and made some inconsequential disclaimer, but his eyes were on the woman beside him as the slow flush crept up her neck to suffuse her cheeks with the warmth of wild apricots and even spread downwards to the exquisite curves revealed by the low-draped neckline.

Blanche could feel his eyes on her but could not raise her own for several seconds, grateful for the timely arrival of the first course, but then drew a deep breath and faced him squarely. 'Lord Hunterton, I owe you an apology.'

He raised his hand with a smile. 'It is I who should apologise, Lady Davenport, for not having introduced myself immediately. When I saw you at St Giles I had just come from St Katherine's Dock, and the garb I wore seemed equally in keeping. I had thought to come to you directly, but when I saw you with those people—the way they reacted to you, joked with you, yes . . . *loved* you, even knowing that you were a lady of undoubted quality, I could only stare. There was no resentment of your finery, no sullenness over accepting what was so obviously charity. I watched your face, alight with laughter, quick with a jest, or changing on the instant to sympathy and concern, never still, never bored or condescending. My original plan was driven from my mind, but then you saw me and came to the door. I knew at once what you would think and it was neither the time nor the place for explanation. I knew, too, that we would meet again. We had to'.

Blanche watched his strong features as he spoke, read the sincerity in his voice and caught something deeper in the eyes that moved caressingly over her face. This close to him, unable to move away, she realised that here was a man whose animal magnetism could draw her as a moth to a flame . . . or a butterfly to a spider's web . . . and reacted instinctively. '*Jason*, Lord Hunterton? What kind of name is that for an English aristocrat?'

He smiled at the slightly interrogative tone, reminded of a pure blood Arabian mare he had once purchased—she, too, showed her mettle by snapping when all she wanted was love and the reassurance that no harm would befall her. 'It's the kind of name one inherits from a father who absorbs Homer as others breathe air. I have a sister Helen and a brother Hector.' His smile widened. 'It could have been worse. You might have had a dinner companion named Agamemnon or even Achilles!'

Blanche was diverted, embarrassment forgotten, and she gave a gurgle of laughter, raising her knife. 'And this the spear that wounds you in your only vital spot . . . The heel, wasn't it?

'My lady, your glance earlier served that purpose, and, no, it was not my heel that you caught; so unless you would have me expire on the field of battle—or collapse face down in this excellent turtle soup which neither of us has touched—you must bind the wound and make amends.'

Deliberately Blanche took two spoonsful of the now cool soup, appreciating its tang of vintage sherry, before asking, eyes ingenuously wide, 'And how would you suggest I do that, my lord?' and realised that she had fallen neatly into a trap at the sudden flame in the dark eyes.

'Come to visit my people as I visited yours. Come to St Katherine's dockland with me, but not hiding behind the protection of the White Lady, for it would serve you for nought there. No, come in disguise. Accompany me, if you dare, on one of *my* forays.'

'I couldn't!' Then, as her plate was cleared, the Fitz-Hughs using the new French method of sending the servants round with the plates rather than everyone helping themselves from the centre of the table, she declared, 'By Jupiter! Yes! I will! Her eyes were alight with challenge. 'When?'

Jason's breath caught at her loveliness. He had never known a woman so alive, so in love with life and all it offered, so sure of herself that she would accompany a virtual stranger into the slums, the kingdom of cut-throats and thieves, harlots and harridans, and light up as a candle in the darkness at the very challenge of emerging unscathed. 'Next Friday morning. I shall bring my carriage for you to take us at least away from the sober respectability of Park Village. It will take a little planning. How will you come?'

She did not even question how it was he knew her address, for she realised that this man would be able to charm a bird from a tree, and the well-meaning, matchmaking Alexandra Fitz-Hugh was certainly no challenge. Her grey eyes moved beyond him to some distant place in her past, and a tiny smile curved her mouth. 'Don't worry about me, my Lord Hunterton: you will be hard put to recognise Beatrice, Lady Davenport, or Blanche, the White Lady.'

He nodded, then asked a question that had puzzled him since the first time he had heard of her. 'Even your oldest friends call you Blanche. Is there a reason why you always wear white?'

The second course was served, a delicately decorated

sturgeon with cucumbers in Canary wine, and
Blanche's eyes echoed the appreciative murmurs of
the other guests, but then that sparkling gaze looked
full into his. 'Oh yes, my lord . . . But I'm always
open to change!'

In the instant it took him to recover, Jason's shock
at her choice of words and totally sexual innuendo
registered in his face, and Blanche gave one of her
involuntary bursts of laughter, immediately joined by
his. Heads turned, and Jeremy Montague Linton
expostulated. 'Deuce take it, Blanche! Can't you
control that merriment? You know how unfashionable
it is!' At which the couple dissolved into choked, lip-
biting, silent laughter that shook their whole frames
and only subsided by Blanche taking a deep breath
and engaging the discomfited Jeremy in the kind of
conversation that could be conducted in a fashionable
drawl, beginning, 'Do you not think the fish exquisite,
Jeremy? Almost on a par with a design of Carême's,
don't you think?'

He laughed, reassured. 'The late Regent's chef may
well have created such a design. Why, I saw a sugar
windmill that he designed when in Brighton that
would have done credit to the finest sculptor, but I
happen to know that the Fitz-Hughs' chef is also
accustomed to serving the French aristocracy and
came over after the war.'

Through it all Jason watched her, taking in every
shade of the honey hair that gleamed beneath the
lights, every movement of her head, every shrug of
her shoulders. At the succulent slices of *filet de boeuf
Masséna*—strips of beef on a bed of artichokes with a
rich perigourdine sauce—his mesmeric regard brought
her attention back to him—as if it had not been there
at every minute—and she gave him the benefit of a
direct look coupled with a slow smile that had brought
others, literally, to their knees. 'You are staring, my
lord, and have been for some time.'

'I was wondering,' he said in all seriousness, 'what

you would do should I be unable to resist an almost overwhelming impulse to kiss you.'

Blanche gave a gurgle of laughter, quite incapable of reacting with the shocked protestations of a woman of her time. 'Why, I should probably enjoy it, my lord! However, the rest of the table would undoubtedly be so scandalised as to exclude us from every invitation throughout the season.'

He gave a sigh. 'Then with extreme reluctance I shall perforce wait until we're alone.'

Blanche lifted her glass, took a tiny sip of the Madeira and delicately ran the tip of her tongue round the rim while holding his eyes: sensual provocation personified.

As before, Jason felt his throat go dry. This was a woman who was all woman, a woman he must have at all costs!

Blanche read his eyes, and warning bells rang. She was accustomed to flirtatious repartee but also knew when to bring it to a close. This raven-haired stranger might dress as a dandy, but undoubtedly there was steel beneath the satin. This was a man accustomed to taking what he wanted from life and she had no illusions at all as to his present desires. 'Lord Hunterton, you'll have me worrying for my safety when I visit the docks with you. Do you not think I'd be safer without your protection?'

Jason smiled, recognising the strategic withdrawal and content to accommodate her—for now. 'You'll be as safe as you wish to be, Lady Davenport.'

'Of course I shall,' Blanche agreed with a twinkle. 'But won't you please tell me more of your crusade?' She became suddenly serious. 'I know that many were made homeless when the docks were built . . . a terrible thing.'

His eyes were bleak and the fine lips tightened. 'Twelve hundred homes were demolished and well over eleven thousand made homeless when St Katherine's was created out of a Stepney slum four years ago. Did you know, Lady Davenport, that the average age those people are normally expected to reach is two-and-twenty? Typhus and smallpox kill thousands every year, where the overcrowding encourages infection, but now, with families taking in friends and relatives, it has risen to epidemic proportions.'

'But what can *you* do?'

Those remarkable eyes suddenly darkened, and a slight frown creased the broad forehead. Almost to himself, he said, 'I came to England on another quest . . . a quite different affair . . .' But then, with a shake of the head, 'I realised, getting to know and care for these people, that there was very little I could achieve for the masses. I have a small amount of money to lose. I move among them and find out their needs, but that helps only one family at a time. Most of the time I gain their confidence and just talk to them. Despair, you see, is the greatest killer, and if one person should die . . . or even worse, take his own life, because I was unable to give him a reason for living, then that is by far a worse crime than that committed by unseeing officaldom that is unaware of its neglect.'

Blanche stared at him, seeing a new man beneath the satin-clad façade. 'You really care for them.'

He returned to her with a wry smile. 'Yes, quite unfashionably so. And you? You also care, or you'd not have created such a legend in so short a time.'

'Sometimes I wonder whether I do it for the purely selfish pleasure that their adulation gives me. It's a heady feeling at times. But then I know that it's not the hundred that count but the one child facing me, and the pain I feel *is* a genuine one. As you say, quite unfashionable in our society of carefully calculated *ennui*, but then I've always been my own person.' She gave an expressive shrug. 'I must, I confess, taste all of life, both the wormwood and the wine. But you mentioned another quest that brought you here?'

He nodded, his eyes suddenly intense. 'A boy . . .

I'm looking for a French boy, the son of a . . . a friend, who was kidnapped by gypsies five years ago. Gypsies travel all over Europe, and I fear that my search is an endless and quite vain one, but,' he gave a totally Gallic shrug, his eyes losing their fire, 'I cannot abandon the search. It was a death-bed promise, and I mean to do all in my power to honour it. I don't even know whether he is still with the band who took him, or even with gypsies at all. There are many French *émigrés* here in London now, especially around Soho. Perhaps you may remember a child with a large birthmark, a circle on the back of his left hand . . .' Blanche shook her head, and felt the almost imperceptible sigh. 'No matter. One day . . .'

Easily he changed the subject as their glasses were removed and the claret poured as the first dessert was served, a multi-coloured jelly, rum-flavoured, with exceedingly rich tarts, then a trifle flavoured with white wine and decorated with slivers of preserves. And still they talked on, Jason occasionally finishing a verbal thought she had begun, Blanche catching at a thread of argument and expanding on it until finally, as a frustrated servant again removed barely touched food, Jason said, 'Enough!' softly, then reached for a spiced grape from one of the silver epergnes along the centre of the table and held it to her lips.

After only the slightest hesitation, Blanche took it. 'Do you think to have me eating out of your hand, my lord?'

'Not . . .yet, my lady. I sought only to break our serious mood, for this is neither the time nor the place to speak of that part of us which belongs to a world so far removed from this gathering as to border on fantasy.'

'You are right. We have already incurred the speculation of our friends and the disapproval of our host and hostess by eating so frugally of such a wonderful repast. I wouldn't wish to ignore the company as well as the food. Do you think we should circulate?'

'The evening has reached that point,' he agreed, but as their eyes caught and held, both knew that, however much they might mingle for the remainder of that evening, their thoughts would not stray for one moment. The party rose like a cloud of multi-hued butterflies and fluttered into the adjoining salon for coffee and to be entertained by several of the ladies, who played the harp and the piano and sang until liqueurs were handed round to signify an end to the evening.

'My dear, you've caused a sensation!' Alexandra gushed the moment she had Blanche alone. 'I knew you'd like him, but whatever happened at the first? I was so mortified!'

'Forgive me, Lexie. I sincerely apologise. It's only you I could trust with the truth. But, you see, I instantly recognised Lord Hunterton as the man outside the soup kitchen.'

'No! That puffed-up parasite whom you saw off?'

'The same, only I was terribly wrong about him. Just as you know much of my youth that I've revealed to no one else, so does his lordship possess another side to his life which you mustn't even hint at or he'd be completely ostracised. He apparently does as much charity work in the dock area as we do here, but, unlike my bodyguards and I, goes in disguise and mixes quite freely with the people as one of them.'

Alexandra's gentle eyes gleamed. 'So you're kindred spirits in more than your mutual love of horses.'

'We have shared interests,' Blanche admitted, not wishing to reveal just how drawn she had been to the sable-haired stranger. 'But nothing more, so you can take that speculative glint from your eyes. Now, I strongly suggest a change of subject. There are, after all, some very old acquaintances whom I've totally ignored and you, as a perfect hostess, should never have allowed such a thing. I'm going to be extra kind to Jeremy.'

'That will make a change; he's the one person you

appear to take a delight in tormenting! He's obviously in love with you.'

Blanche laughed. 'Jeremy? Oh, I think not. He's in love with love, and I'm on the nearest horizon at the moment. Of course I tease him; he's one of those men—the greater majority in my experience—who will never grow up but simply grow older. There he is now with Horsehead Harrison. Whatever possessed you to invite *him*? I must rescue poor Jeremy.'

Alexandra regarded the long-nosed, cavernous-featured Percival Harrison with a tolerant smile. 'Oh, he's not so bad once you get to know him. He does vaguely resemble that sad-faced roan he rides, but he's quite vulgarly rich, and there are several young ladies who would not in the least mind a life of boredom in the kind of comfort he could provide. Very few are as difficult to please as you, my elusive friend!'

'My friends please me.'

'It's a husband I was referring to. Each time I invite some eligible young man—or two or three— you allow, no, positively encourage, them to be whisked away by some predatory mother with a totally unmarriageable daughter in tow. I despair of you, really I do!'

'Good! Now everyone's happy: all the pretty bucks and does go in two by two and I am allowed to circulate without some jealous husband telling me how to behave myself. Which is exactly what I intend to do now, if only to escape my Lord Hunterton's unwavering stare. He really is the most ill-mannered of men!'

'Or the most persistent of suitors. Take care, my dear: Jason Hunterton won't take to teasing as easily as young Jeremy. Touch that flame, and you'll be burned with more than his eyes!'

'Fiddlesticks! My heart's my own, Lexie, and my body most certainly is . . . But you're an angel to care so. Don't worry about me—pity his lordship if anyone.'

Blanche moved through the throng toward Jeremy with a quiet word here, a soft jest there, but aware that, through it all, the heat of those green eyes never left her, and as she finally moved to her carriage, he was there before her. There was little they could say amid the laughing, chattering throng calling their thanks and farewells, but he took her extended hand and raised it to his lips, his tongue briefly caressing her fingertips.

'This is only the beginning, my lady.' Then, as if she were made of the rarest porcelain, he handed her into her carriage. 'I shall come for you at nine.'

'I'll be ready.' It was enough.

CHAPTER THREE

JASON TURNED HIS cabriolet into Park Village East a good ten minutes earlier than he was expected. Drawing up before the house, he found its utterly simple lines a little austere for his taste but noted with approval the tiny, immaculate front garden and the gleaming perfection of the brass furnishings on the front door. With a quick glance along the street, he pulled the heavy cloak about him and alighted. Even the most casual passer-by could not fail to notice the shabbiness of his cloak and the ragged and scuffed boots beneath, and Jason had no wish to cause either Blanche or her neighbours any embarrassment. The liveried 'tiger' who leaped from his stand behind to take the chestnut's head, however, would have passed muster in any society—except the one they were about to visit—so they would leave the carriage on the outskirts of Stepney and walk in. 'I may be a while, John. You know what ladies are!'

'Yes, my lord.' There was a twinkle in the young groom's eyes. During this year in his lordship's service there had been innumerable hours spent outside innumerable houses from Belgravia to Brighton, and always a fat purse at the end of it. A popular man with the ladies was our Lord Hunterton. However, this day was dank and cold with a fine mizzle in the air, and John hoped that this particular lady would not keep them waiting for too long.

All that concerned Jason at the moment he raised the knocker was the lady's attire. 'If she's in white, I'll wring her lovely neck!' he muttered.

The door swung open and Jason froze, staring in

disbelief at the slut before him, her garish red skirt a
full three inches too short, the once-white gypsy
blouse a dingy grey and in constant danger of slipping
from one grubby shoulder. Her hair was loose, falling
about her shoulders, its rich colour dulled by grease,
a red bandanna keeping it from her face . . . a face
scrubbed clean of paint and powder and resembling
that of a sixteen-year-old. Only the eyes remained
the same, a clear cool grey and alight now with
laughter as she said, 'Me name's Trixie Devine,
m'lud, an' I used ter tread the boards, I did. It
shows, don' it?' And she struck a pose, one hand on
her hip, one raised over her head, hip forward and
legs slightly apart, then wobbled slightly and, at his
still stunned expression, collapsed into laughter. 'Oh,
my lord! Your face!'

Jason swallowed with difficulty, then, with a shake
of his head, choked, 'I don't believe it! It's incredible!'
finally joining in her laughter.

'You're not exactly playing the swell cove either,'
she accused.

Eyes gleaming, he made a leg. 'Jayce Hunter at
yer service, m'lady. And your pseudonym: I can
understand the diminutive of Beatrice, but why
Devine . . . A certain understandable vanity?'

'I'll tell you one day, but suffice to say it's a name
I'd answer to if called.' She looked past him. 'The
covered cabriolet will serve well in transporting two
scarecrows from the neighbourhood, but shouldn't
you have advised your tiger of our destination?'

Jason laughed. 'Oh, we'll leave John somewhere
secluded and utterly respectable with instructions to
meet us at the end of our journey. The poor man has
taken too many pains in acquiring his accent to allow
it to slip now. By the by, do you not know that it's
fashionable to keep a gentleman waiting? I believe
any time up to an hour is considered acceptable.'

Blanche gave a snort of disgust. 'What nonsense!
I've never allowed fashion to dictate my behaviour—
least of *all* my behaviour!' then, with a twinkle,

'Apart from which, I see no gentleman but John, and I'm sure he'd appreciate my punctuality.'

'Careful, woman!' Jason warned with a mock scowl. 'No skirt's yet accused Jayce Hunter of ungentlemanly conduct, so don't try yer arm!' Then a low court bow. 'My Lady Davenport, your carriage awaits.'

Swirling a thick shawl over her shoulders, Blanche allowed him to lead her to the waiting vehicle, throwing a wicked wink at the gaping groom before climbing aboard, knowing that it would take him some time to recover.

'Come, man!' laughed Jason, 'Don't just stand there. Loose the horse, or I'll be forced to drive over you. My Lady Davenport mustn't be kept waiting!'

'Lady . . . Lady . . . Oh . . . Yes, my lord! Certainly, my lord!' John leaped to his platform with alacrity. Lady Davenport? . . . The White Lady? No . . . Surely not . . . It couldn't be! He'd heard his master talk of nothing else for at least two weeks. Why, they had not even visited a certain address in Belgrave Square, or the other dazzler in St John's Wood, a rich merchant's daughter whose ample charms had brought his lordship to her door on at least three occasions. No, John sighed, his lordship was undoubtedly suffering from some malady brought on, no doubt, by the odoriferous air of the slums he frequented. This little kitchen slut could not possibly be the elegant, exquisite 'diamond of the first water' his master had talked of. It was with some difficulty, therefore, that he managed a sketchy bow as his lordship lifted . . . the woman . . . from the carriage. 'I trust the weather will clear . . . m'lady,' he murmured, and was startled to hear a low, melodious voice say,

'Why, thank you, John; I hope so, too, though in all truth it goes well with our surroundings.' He lifted amazed eyes to meet a warm, clear gaze and a gentle smile. 'I did not mean to discommode you earlier, John, but I was quite unable to resist the impulse. Do forgive me?' The dusk-rose lips parted to reveal even white teeth, and a soft laugh stirred the air between them as he stammered something unintelligible, but then she had turned to take his master's arm.

They moved off, and Jason gave a low chuckle. 'I fear poor John will never be quite the same again.'

'And you, my lord?' she teased. 'What of you?'

'I knew that the moment I saw you,' he said and there was a seriousness in his tone that she shied away from, changing the subject and glad when they had reached their destination, moving through mean streets to a crumbling tenement in Limehouse.

Jason moved surely up the dark stairway, ignoring anonymous doors behind which babies wept fretfully and the stench of boiled cabbage mixed with that of damp, fungus-covered walls. A woman's voice was raised in whining objection. There was a slap, a cry, and silence. Blanche shuddered, and Jason took her arm reassuringly. They reached a door, no cleaner than the others, but from behind it, incredibly, the sound of a woman humming. Jason knocked. Silence.

Then, 'Who is it?'

'Jayce Hunter. Will you keep me out here all day?'

The door swung wide and a young woman, a little younger than Blanche, held out a welcoming hand. 'Come in. Come in.' Pushing back curly brown hair that not even the heavily woven turban could restrain, she gestured them both inside. 'I'm Bridie,' she introduced with a gap-toothed but infectious grin.

'Trixie. Friend of Jayce's.'

'I'll bet you are!' And Blanche could not resist returning that knowing grin.

'Behave yourself, Bridie,' Jason ordered good-naturedly. 'I came only to see how young Sean was faring.'

The hazel eyes glowed as if a candle had been lit behind them. 'Thanks to you, Jayce Hunter, he's got a good life and hopes for a better one. The Society wrote me last week, and I got the Jew letter-writer to read it to me and pen an answer for a penny. It's hard work, mind, but the food's good, and Sean says there's land for the taking after he's free.'

'Transportation?' queried Blanche, wondering at the woman's apparent cheerfulness.

'Oh, no, Trixie. My brother was just off the Floating Bastille when Jayce came in on our lives.'

Jason had marked Blanche's puzzlement, and elucidated. 'It's the name some call the *Euryalus*, the prison ship at Chatham for boys under sixteen. It's better, I suppose, than putting them in with hardened criminals in Newgate, but the food's pretty poor—usually just porridge and bread—and with bad overcrowding the bullying can be too much to bear for some like Sean. I'd met him while visiting another young delinquent in hospital. Sean had deliberately broken his own arm to get sent off, and vowed he'd rather die than return.'

'He was a poet at heart, you see,' Bridie explained, continuing the story. 'And it was for stealing two reading-books that he was convicted. He was so sure he could teach himself to read if he learned the poems from the Jew, then followed the words. Thanks be, Jayce found him and put him in touch with a society called The Children's Friend who helped him get to South Africa as an apprentice on a farm there. They keep in touch with their children and, as I say, they've written me he's fine.' She broke off at a heavy tread on the boards outside, and those warm eyes lit up again. 'That's my man home!'

The door opened and a large, bearded man appeared, the tang of the docks bringing a clean saltiness to the air. 'Hey, let me get my coat off, ye hoyden!' he roared as Bridie hurled herself into his arms. He grinned over the top of her head, encompassing Jason and Blanche both. 'Ye'd think she'd behave in company! No lady would carry on so, I'll be bound.'

'Possibly not,' laughed Blanche. 'But that would be her loss; and we're not company, we're friends. At least, I know Jayce is and I'd like to be. Me name's Trixie, Trixie Devine.'

'You surely are. Jack O'Brien, at your service. Well met, Jayce. You'll stay for some porter?'

Jason glanced at the woman clinging to the giant's arm. 'Thank you, no. I came to ask of Sean, no more. If I stay, we'll start swapping yarns, and I've a feeling Bridie has other plans for you before lunch!' He laughed at her blushes and signalled to Blanche that they were leaving.

Having returned once more to the mist-laden street, Blanche was silent for some moments before musing, 'Such happiness in such grinding poverty.'

'They're not poor,' Jason smiled. 'They simply have no money. There are hundreds of Irish immigrants on the docks, mostly around Wapping, where we're headed. They're treated badly and as cheap labour for the most part, but yet it must be better than the conditions they run from, for still they come.'

A figure detached itself from the shadows, a woman of indeterminate age in a thin silk dress several sizes too large for her. 'A shilling, dearie. A shilling, an' yer lady can watch, too, if yer wants.'

Blanche felt her fists clench, but Jason laughed easily and tossed the woman two pennies. 'Buy yourself a meat pie, and not a tot of gin. Fill out to fit that dress, and perhaps I'll think about it next time round.'

The prostitute caught the coins expertly and gave a cackle of laughter. 'Didn't recognise you in this mizzle, Mr 'Unter. Fanks for the tip. One day I might surprise you.'

'I'll look forward to that!' He grinned and made to move off, but was detained by bony fingers on his arm.

''Ere, there's a new girl took Rose's place. You know Rosie; the one wot got took off wiv the coughing sickness. Well, this 'n's only a kid. Black Jack ain't broke 'er in yet. 'Ave a word, Mr 'Unter.'

Blance sensed his tenseness, and he nodded

brusquely. 'No promises, but I'll talk to her.'
Without further word or explanation he hurried
Blanche away, twisting and turning with sure
familarity through the narrow cobbled streets and
dingy back alleys. Even his haste and the strain in
him failed to warn Blanche until she saw the girl
leaning against a rough brick wall, and then
everything cried out in denial within her.

The child was barely into her teens, her boyish
frame accentuated by the threadbare shift she wore
beneath a tattered shawl. Under several layers of
accumulated dirt her long hair still held golden
glints, and the cornflower-blue eyes were wide and
thickly-lashed, holding no little uncertainty as she
approached the strangers. Her little mouth was
slashed with crimson, and a blot of colour had been
applied inexpertly to pale cheeks, giving her a
slightly clownish air. 'I can give you a good time,
sir, an' you, too, lady, if'n you want. I'm untouched,
I am . . . Well almost,' She smiled, but it was a
poor attempt, and never reached her fear-filled
eyes.

'How long have you been here, child?' Jason
asked, a deep richness in his voice, a tenderness,
even, that Blanche never thought to hear even from
this enigmatic man.

'Only a couple of hours, sir. Why? Was you 'ere
before? I can come earlier tomorrow, if you like,'

Jason reached out a lean hand, and Blanche
noticed the instinctive reaction, the body leaning
into the warmth of the fingers that curled about her
shoulder, yet still the bright, false smile. 'No. How
many times have you come to this spot? Rose died
two weeks ago.'

The cornflower-blue eyes widened endlessly. 'You
knew Rosie?'

He caught her panic. 'Not in that way; only
as . . . a friend.'

'I . . . I don't understand, but . . . Well, I'm near
as good as Rosie. I know you're not a toff. You'll

deal decent with me. Some o' them toffs wot come down 'ere in them black carriages . . . Well, I know you won't whip me or shiv me after yer pleasure.'

'Shiv?' Blanche choked out, and those strange green eyes tore away from the child and swung to hers.

'Shiv . . . Knife . . . cut up,' he translated with absolutely no expression. 'Apparently, unlike some clients of the . . . highest water, I can be trusted to take my pleasure straight and not use bonds or a knife to give it that extra fillip.'

'Oh, Jesus!' Blanche choked. 'What can we do?'

The eyes were of the deepest, darkest, sea depths, where the green turns almost to black. 'You've now learned the law of the streets, my lady,' he murmured.

'We can't leave her here . . . I *won't*!'

He sighed. 'I had no intention of doing so, not this one, but you can't adopt all the strays.' He turned back to the girl, who had been following the low-voiced exchange with troubled eyes and was now edging away. 'Stop that!' Jason ordered, and she froze.

'You ain't gonna bag me, mister. I 'eard of girls disappearing and turning up in Araby or China . . .'

'I'm not going to sell you,' he smiled, though there was a catch in his voice. 'Where do you live? Where are your parents?'

'I do all right! Ain't got no father—'e went off after me brother Mickey was born—coupla years ago now—nor no mother neither. She took sick wi' the fever. When the tide rises too 'igh, the water comes into the cellar where we lives, and sometimes even the bed gets wet. Well, anyway, she got took off a month ago. She 'ad five shillings saved, so me and Mickey did all right, but . . .' She faltered, then took a deep breath and finished in a rush, 'But I don't want Mickey to stay wiv the woman who took 'im when me ma got sick, cos I smelled gin on 'im a couple times and I know she feeds it to all them wot she looks after, and 'e ain't 'avin it!' She stood defiantly, daring them to prevent her earning enough to put her brother into care in the only way she knew.

Blanche felt the hot, angry tears behind her eyes, but it was a feeling she had grown accustomed to in her work. Already Jason was saying, 'It's going to be all right, child. I told you I was a friend. I'm going to help you *and* Mickey to find a better place; though, God knows, anywhere would be better than this. I want you to go to a couple I know, the woman's name is Bridie. I want you to tell her Jayce Hunter sent you. Got that?'

'Bridie. Jayce 'Unter.' But her eyes were still wary. 'Wot's she going to do to me?'

'She'll feed you and remove a few layers of dirt, I imagine, Tell her I'll come for you this evening. When do you pick up your brother?'

'Six . . . sometimes eight . . . I'm not sure . . .' Then her voice fell and she lowered her head. 'Yesterday was my first time. Only one cove came by this way in the morning. 'E wanted it over there in that alley. It 'urt something awful, but 'e said I didn't know nothin' so wasn't worth nothin'. Two came in the afternoon. It didn't 'urt quite so much then, and I didn't bleed any more, so I got a shilling. Nobody's come by yet today . . .'

'You'll get your money and more besides,' Jason promised. 'In fact, if you do exactly as I've told you, I'll see you have a new guinea. Now, this is the address.' Carefully he gave the O'Briens' address and made the dumbfounded girl repeat it twice. 'Now off with you. I'll collect you at six.'

With a quick nod the child hurried off, and Blanche gave a shake of her head. 'Now who's collecting strays?'

'I don't collect them; I re-direct them. She and her brother will go to a place in Southwark, and the girl will be taught a trade if not as old as the one she's plying, at least a more respectable one.'

'The Philanthropic Society, you mean? I've put one or two in their homes. At least they're assured of meat several times a week, which is far more than they'd get on the streets, but are you usually so generous? She's probably never seen a guinea in her life, nor ever will again.'

'A little bribery goes a long way, and I wanted to make certain she'd reach her destination . . . Besides . . . my last cravat cost fifteen times as much, so I hardly feel generous.'

They walked on towards Wapping, cutting into the busy High Street, and Jason shook his head. 'This area must be the filthiest, most disease-ridden, spot in the whole of England! You name a vice, and they have it here. Our young friend back there wouldn't be expected to live much beyond twenty, and then only if she stayed away from the near two hundred taverns, grog-shops and gin parlours in the area. She may . . . Hey, wait a minute!'

Before Blanche could react, he had gone running into the crowd, then turned and vanished down a side alley. 'Jayce?' Blanche called, hurrying after him, not at all happy to be deserted in this dehumanised sailors' town where murder was a common daily occurrence and a woman walked alone at her peril. But as the first prickle of panic iced the back of her neck, he was there again, dragging a filthy young urchin by the collar.

He gave the wriggling youngster a hard shake and the boy became still, glaring at him. 'Trixie, meet Ned, the best water-rat on the river. He's got the eyes of a hawk and could find a needle in those mud flats at low tide. Once found a Spanish doubloon, and was stupid enought to sell it for a bottle of gin for his ma and five shillingsworth of pie-and-eels for the kids. That's what you are, Ned Beldon, stupid!' His voice had roughened since his return with the boy, and Blanche realised that even Jayce Hunter moved in several strata of this society. 'You're stupid,' he repeated. 'Because, if that cove

had caught you cutting his purse instead of being
too drunk to care, he'd have called the Peelers and
you'd have got seven years' transportation at least.
It was six months' hard in Newgate last time, and
you got off light because it was your first and you
were only eleven. You're turned thirteen now, so
it'd be the colonies.'

'Garn!' the boy shot back, unrepentant. 'We don't
get the Blue Devils within a mile o' this place; we
got our own laws, and they ain't laws dealt out by
no paid lackeys o' the govermint.'

'Sounds like your father's words.'

'There ain't nothin' wrong with me dad. He'll do
in anybody as easy as look at 'em!'

'When he's sober, he's more trouble on the docks
than anyone else on the river, always telling the
gangs not to obey orders, not to let in outside
labour, stirring the men up—as if they're not restless
enough—and when he's drunk, he does more
damage than any ten men put together. Now . . .
How much did you get?'

Reluctantly the boy handed over the leather
pouch whose strings he had cut from the merchant's
belt. 'But it's still mine! You've said yerself that the
toffs wouldn't suffer if they had a bit less.' He
grinned. 'That's a bit less!'

Jason, now that he had the money, could afford
to let the boy go as he counted the coins into his
hand. 'Two pounds plus. A fair haul. What were
you figuring on doing with it?'

'Throw it in my brother's face and tell 'im 'e can
leave any time 'e likes, 'cos I can earn or beg or
steal enough to keep us all!'

A twitch of the lips was all that betrayed Jason,
as he said, 'Bill's two years older than you and
earning near as much as your dad. With seven of
you, and your mother . . . sick . . . you need his
money.'

The boy's fists clenched suddenly and there was a
sudden change in him as he aged before their eyes.

'Six on us,' he corrected. 'The new baby died. Don't know why. She was feedin' all right. We just got up one mornin' an' she was dead. Ma's drinkin' all the time now and our Bet says she's going to find some toff—she copies the way they talk real good—says a lot of 'em like 'em real young, and in a couple of years—when she's my age—she'll know 'ow to be a proper lady.'

'She's . . . eleven?' choked Blanche, and the boy gave her a surprised stare.

'Turned. Ma let her out last year. Oh, not for the real game, but just to sit on gents' laps and let 'em . . . well . . . We all put in for a silk frock from the pedlar. We did right well, so we know she'll be all right and she'll bring in nigh as much as Bill— maybe even more!'

Jason gave a sigh, and dropped the money into the boy's grimy palm. Instantly it vanished into one of his innumerable pockets, the mark of an experienced cut-purse. 'You're a gent, Mr 'Unter, a real swell!'

'But no throwing it at poor Bill, who's doing his best while still longing to jump a ship for the Americas, and no gin for your ma. Try to talk your sister into looking after the nipper and yer ma for a while longer. I'll send a girl on by who's worked for the toffs. It won't cost you.' He gave a smile tinged with a bitter knowledge of his own society—and theirs. 'Not all toffs prefer them quite as young as Betty. She might make a fortune if she took to my . . . friend's training and waited a couple of years.'

'I'll tell 'er,' the urchin promised. 'A fortune? You reckon?'

'At least.'

'Cor! Fanks, Mr 'Unter.' Within seconds he was gone, melting into the crowd like the mist about them.

'She'll still be only thirteen,' Blanche whispered.

Again that smile. 'And two years older and wiser.

The girl I know is a "tweeny", a good sort and only fourteen. I'm a great believer in miracles. They come in all sizes! Come, there's one more call I must make, and then we'll have a well-earned mug of ale at the Prospect.'

'No champagne?'

'Not for Trixie Devine and Jayce Hunter!'

CHAPTER FOUR

THE LIGHT RAIN had ceased but the mist had turned to a thick yellow-grey fog, rolling in off the river and blanketing the streets with a dangerous pall. Murder could be committed in the fog with no one the wiser. Almost imperceptibly Jason lengthened his stride, moving away from the busy thoroughfare and once more into the cobbled streets. They rounded a corner, and he cursed softly beneath his breath as a giant figure detached itself from the shadows. 'As you value your life, allow me to call the play,' he commanded *sotto voce*, and for once Blanche had no desire to argue.

The man that confronted them was living proof of Darwin's theory of evolution. He was over six feet tall with thick, greasy hair falling in a tangled black mane on to wide shoulders. His low simian forehead ended in heavy brows that slashed an unbroken line above eyes that bore no more intelligence than the beast he resembled. His broad nostrils flared as they caught the scent of the cheap perfume Blanche wore, and he ran an appreciative tongue over full red lips. His hair-covered hands, dangling almost to his knees, moved up and down the bulging thighs as if in anticipation, and she felt herself go cold.

'G'day to you, Jack,' Jason said easily, though Blanche could sense the leashed tension in him. 'This is my old woman, Trixie. Used ter be Trixie Devine when she trod the boards.' He turned to Blanche, putting a proprietorial arm over her shoulders. 'Trix, this 'ere's Black Jack. He owns this territory,' and carefully he instilled a note of pride into his words.

'Trixie, eh?' Black Jack grinned, revealing black and broken teeth. 'Well, she could turn a few tricks in *my* stable.'

'Jack also owns the brothels from Wapping to Limehouse, and you'll not hear a word of complaint from *his* girls.' Blanche remembered the old prostitute saying, 'Black Jack ain't broke 'er in yet,' when speaking of the child who had taken Rose's place, and felt physically sick.

'Not a word,' Black Jack was agreeing, eyeing her up and down. 'Keep 'em sweet I do. What say, Trixie? Jayce might be the best gentleman of the road since Turpin, but down 'ere I'm king, and I can see 'e don't tog you out right. I'd not put you on the streets. You'd 'ave yer own room and wear silk next to yer skin.'

'No, thanks,' Blanche said, then, feeling a warning pressure from the hand curled negligently over one shoulder, added, 'though if I 'adn't met Jayce first, I might 'a been tempted!'

'She's my old woman, I told you,' Jason put in, but the other was not going to release this prize so easily. He had seen Jason use his fists and knew that he carried a knife beneath his cloak. He knew that Jason gave away a fair amount of the money he took from the toffs who were fools enough to venture on to the Heath at night, and in that peculiar honour among thieves, respected him for it. Still, this one was a beauty . . .

'How do I know she's your old woman and not just a skirt you found on the way in? She might be too scared to say anything.'

Without hesitation Jason swung Blanche hard against him and kissed her full on the mouth, one hand crudely fondling her breast, then, at Black Jack's snort of approval, released her. 'There! Don't see her objecting, do you?' he asked—the instant before Blanche's fist cracked against his jaw, sending him reeling backwards.

''Ow dare you!' she cried, rounding on him, grey

eyes flashing. 'I might be your old woman, Jayce 'Unter, but that don't give you no right ter 'umiliate me in front of this 'ere cove.'

Black Jack's guffaw echoed from the grimy walls. 'She's your missis, all right, Jayce, and a right hell-cat she is, too! I can't see no other skirt doin' that to you and gettin' away with it. Still an' all, if she ever gets too much for you, I'll be around.'

'I'll bear that in mind,' acknowledged Jason, rubbing his jaw. 'Well, we won't hold you. I know your time's precious. Gotta go on your collections, eh?'

'Yeah.' And there was a note of deep menace in the rumble of the voice that boded ill for any girl who had not earned enough to satisfy him.

Jason stepped aside, pulling Blanche with him, allowing the giant to shuffle past, and his eyes were twinkling as he turned to her, still rubbing ruefully at his jaw. 'That certainly wasn't the reaction of Lady Davenport,' he chuckled.

'No,' Blanche admitted with an answering grin. 'But Trixie Devine would have been proud of a roundhouse like that and you did deserve it, you must admit.'

'Forgive me, but it seemed a time for desperate measures, and your reaction certainly turned the trick.' His eyes were on her mouth, feeling again the full lips crushed beneath his, remembering the perfection of the curves that had filled his hand, and his voice was a little husky as he said, 'I'd go through far more for a repeat performance.'

Blanche flushed, turning away. She, too, had been shaken to her very core by that fierce, passionless kiss that had branded her as his property, as had the power of the fingers that had moulded her flesh, bringing an overwhelming sensation that shot through her body like liquid fire. Characteristically, she found attack her best defence. 'You're no gentleman, Lord Hunterton! And what's this about a gentleman of the road?'

He accepted the change of atmosphere with a philosophical shrug. 'How else should I explain my not inconsiderable fortune? As Lord Hunterton I'd not last a day down here, but as Jayce Hunter, highwayman, I even earn grudging respect.'

'If you continue the way you're going for another year, it will be a sadly depleted fortune!'

He smile gently. 'Of course I may go through my fortune; it's not a bottomless well. But I've made a few friends and lost a lot of aquaintances from all walks of life over the years, and I feel a man can only be counted by the friends he's made. If I lost everything tomorrow, I doubt that I'd starve.'

They walked on, talking little, until finally he stopped at a dark doorway, turning to Blanche with a sad smile. 'The woman you're about to meet is the one exception to the rule down here and knows my true identity, though her children don't. She was a comtesse, now just Annemarie, or Annie Baines. She fell in love with a young English student on the Grand Tour, whose vows of undying love lasted only as long as there was no danger of an alliance. When it became increasingly obvious that the young Countess, married at that time to a man old enough to be her grandfather, was, as the French say, *enceinte*, her student lover panicked and decided to return home. The Count threw her out, swearing dire consequences if she ever showed her face in France again. She came to England to plead with her lover to acknowledge the child, but the French were far from popular in those years after 1816. So many *émigrés* were fleeing from the ire of Louis XVIII, pretending that they were aristocrats from the old families. Annemarie never did find her student, who had safeguarded himself by giving the trusting child a false name. She went from bad to worse. The child, a boy, Jean-Luc, was born crippled, and to keep him she slipped into debt and finally turned to crime, ending in Newgate. When she was released, she met and married Joe Baines, a big, handsome sailor who swept her off her feet, and they were happy enough for a while. They had a girl, Fleur, but then an accident on board cost Joe his right hand. He couldn't find work and turned to drink, and here's where they've ended. I wanted you to know all this because I'm afraid I'm the bearer of bad news—or good, depending on your outlook, for Joe would beat them all unmercifully when he was drunk, yet he was all they had as a provider with his begging and the occasional odd job on the docks.'

Jason knocked on the door and then again, but it was several minutes before the sound of a slow step approached. The door opened a crack. An eye appeared, half a face, then the door was pulled wide as something seemed to light up behind those eyes, those resigned, dead eyes. 'My Lord Hunterton!' the lady exclaimed softly. 'Oh, please come in, and your companion, too.' Blanche could hardly repress a cry at the sight of the bruised and beaten wraith-like creature that confronted them.

As they moved into the single downstairs room, the solitary candle that barely lit it guttered from the draught and there was a tiny, sharp cry from the shadows of one corner. 'It's all right, Fleur,' the woman quickly soothed. 'It's not papa; it's Mr Hunter and a friend.' She turned to Blanche with an apologetic smile. 'My husband has been known to drink upon occasion, and is inclined towards violence. He broke Fleur's arm a month ago and it still gives her a little pain.' The tones were those of an educated gentlewoman, and totally at odds with the double-patched cloth dress she wore, its demi-gigot sleeves and wide collar, its ruching from knee to hem, indicating a hand-me-down at least six years out of date.

The candle had settled again, and in the dim light was revealed a child of about three and beside her an older boy who had moved in silence to put a protective arm around her. Blanche felt her heart go out to him, this illegitimate child of such a rich union, now forced into grinding poverty. Children did not normally interest her in the least, and certainly the thought of having her own filled her with dismay, but there was something about this one, with his dark Byronic looks, that found a chord in her. 'You're Jean-Luc? My name is . . . Trixie Devine.' For an instant she had almost given herself away, but quickly turned from that silent, wary regard and held out her hand to his mother. 'Mrs Baines, Jayce has told me of you.'

The woman nodded in understanding of a secret shared. 'I'm glad you came. I wasn't expecting—Mr Hunter—until the end of the month. Please be seated. I fear I have little to offer you . . . Some tea, perhaps?'

'That would be most welcome,' Jason said before Blanche's instinctive refusal. She caught the warning shake of his head and understood. Whereas she had not wanted to take even a spoonful of tea from their precious hoard, Jason, with deeper understanding, accepted the widow's mite, and allowed them their battered pride.

Only when Annemarie had gone to put the kettle on did the children relax. The girl took a toy from the chair they had been sharing and brought it to Blanche with a tentative smile. 'My brother made it,' she explained proudly.

Blanche took it. 'May I see?'—and felt the wonder within her. The object was a wooden horse, not just a wooden horse, but a creature so lifelike that even its haunch muscles bulged as it reared and the mane positively rippled with life. 'But this is beautiful!' she exclaimed, then, eyes shining, turned to the boy. 'Do you have any more?'

He nodded and, dragging his left foot as he walked, took from a far corner a small cardboard box. 'I've only four left. I had more, but my father broke them up.' It was said with carefully-controlled neutrality, but handling the exquisitely carved works of art,

Blanche felt all of the pain and anger that must have tortured the boy.

Annemarie had returned with a tray of tea and handed a cup to her. 'I'm sorry we have no cake to offer you. Had I known you were coming . . .' But they both knew that cake was an unknown luxury in that house, and again it was left to Jason to bridge the awkward gap.

'The tea is fine, Annemarie. Please sit down. There's something I need to tell you.'

The brown eyes lit up. 'You've found him!'

But with a strangely urgent chopping gesture Jason cut her off, then shook his head and said quietly, 'No . . . No, I haven't found the boy. More than that.'

At the seriousness in his voice she tensed, then asked, 'Is it Joe? He hasn't been home for three days.' She indicated the deep cut on her cheek, which had barely begun to heal, and her left arm that was undoubtedly covered with bruises beneath the full sleeve. 'He had been drinking more than usual. Jean-Luc had some of his animals on the floor. Joe came home early and trod on one of them. Jean-Luc lost his temper, and Joe began to use his belt . . . he used to pick on Jean-Luc's bad leg. I stopped him, so he beat me, and that was when Jean-Luc took a kitchen knife and threatened to kill him. Joe must have been out of his mind. He began breaking everything within sight. I took a chance, seized Jean-Luc's arm, took up Fleur, and we ran.' The woman gave a resigned shrug. 'I knew he would be sorry and probably be asleep when we returned, but we haven't seen him since.'

'I hope he's gone for good!' muttered the boy, his eyes on the carving in Blanche's hands.

Jason hesitated, then holding Annemarie's eyes, said. 'He'll not be back, Jean-Luc . . . ever.' To the woman, 'I heard last night. He was involved in a brawl in one of the taverns.'

For a brief moment her eyes closed, but her voice

was quite calm as she said, 'It had to happen sooner or later. He—he *was* a good man, before . . .'

The boy came to put a strong arm about his mother's shoulders. 'I'm glad he's dead! I'll take care of you, ma. I can read and write and figure a bit. I've got work before.' He regarded Jason levelly. 'I'll even come with *you*, Mr Hunter. I might be a cripple, but on a horse I reckon I could be as fast as anyone. I'll be a highwayman like you; I'm not scared!'

'Then you should be, you young pup! I'll do what I can to get you a clerk's job—though heaven knows they're in short enough supply—but I'll not help to get you hanged, and that's the end for you if you take up highway robbery. Let me hear no more of it.'

'I'd be eternally grateful if there was anything you could do,' Annemarie said, laying skeletal fingers on Jason's arm. 'Though you've done so much already.' She smiled at Blanche. 'The very first time I met—Mr Hunter—it was in a store at which Jean-Luc got a job after Newgate. He came in to order some material, a sky-blue silk for a . . . friend, and because they were busy and I was . . . well . . . available to help, I took the order and offered to deliver it.'

Blanche nodded in understanding. 'It must have been quite a surprise when you saw him next, then? I received a similar . . . surprise.'

'And for similar reasons I received the self-same response from both of you.' He gave a deep theatrical sigh. 'I fear it is my lot to be misunderstood!'

'Rubbish!' Blanche snorted. 'If you spend half your life in an attempt to deny the other half, who could deny that you deserve the confusion you create . . . and get all you deserve!' But the grey eyes were twinkling, and she received an answering smile from the woman opposite. Then she turned to the boy by her side, noting that he had lost much of

his tension during the repartee, and returned the
horse she had been holding.

'You're wasted in a clerk's job amid dusty ledgers,
but I fear it's all Mr Hunter will find for you at
present. However, you've a talent in your hands—
no, a gift—that can be put to better use. Will you
sell me this horse so that I may show it to some
people I know? There is a group . . . a club . . .
called the Four-in-Hand Club. They are quite
eccentric about horses. Could you carve others like
this? Trotters? Racers?'

The boy seemed to grow taller, and a light shone
behind the dark eyes. 'Of course I can!'

Blanche turned to Jason and saw a slight frown,
caught a barely perceptible shake of the head, and
wanted to cry, 'But I *am* involved!' Instead, she
asked, 'Will you lend me five shillings, Jayce? Call
it a wager if you like, for I'll bet I can double it
with this toy alone, and bring in orders for more.'

Before he could speak, however, Jean-Luc had
put the horse into her hands. 'You can have this
one, Miss Devine. If you want to show it to some
toff . . . well, that's up to you, but no friend of Mr
Hunter's has to give *me* money.' He gave a
disarming grin, 'Especially a friend as pretty as you,
Miss!'

'Enough of that!' Jason retorted. 'Back to
business. Annemarie . . . I can't make any promises,
but I'll do my best, as you well know. Now there
are arrangements to be made, a place for you to
go.'

The woman lowered her eyes. 'We'll manage.'

'They can't stay here!' Blanche stated, her accent
forgotten in her emotion. She could stand by and
see those who were born to the slum living there,
helping where, or if, she could, but this too frail
French aristocrat whose only fault through all of
her life was to love, not wisely but too well . . .
'No! There is a place . . .' Then, catching Jason's
steady gaze, dropped her autocratic tone a fraction

but still the determination came through. 'There is room at my . . . with me. The children will be no trouble, and with Jean-Luc at work Mrs Baines may wish to help a little, though we must build up her strength first.' The Frenchwoman's protest was echoed by Jason's involuntary gesture, but Blanche was adamant, so it was left that Jason would collect them the following day. 'We'll work things out,' Blanche promised the woman, embarrassed by the tears of gratitude, but once in the street she rounded on Jason angrily. 'You would have left them there, given her a few coins, and seen her go to the workhouse!'

'No, not the workhouse, but a home of sorts. Jean-Luc can earn enough so that they'd not starve, but you can see that Annemarie would be useless as a kitchen-maid or anything else for that matter. She could no more lift a hod of coal or a bucket of water than fly.'

'She can polish silver and move the dust around! I've only the cook and Mrs Armitage, and the tweeny who helps both. Mrs A. has been on her last legs for the past decade and would no doubt enjoy being put out to pasture with a small pension.'

'You can't adopt all the strays who happen to be aristos!' Then something in his expression changed, and a strange bleakness flickered across those fine features. 'Nor find all those who are.'

'The boy you mentioned earlier?' Blanche asked, but found a bright smile covering the emotion of a moment before, and he gave a philosophical shrug. 'As I said, a never-ending quest . . . Now, I promised you an ale at the Prospect, I believe.' And she knew that he would reveal no more, yet the identity of the boy nagged at her female curiosity for the rest of the day.

They walked along to Wapping Wall to the Prospect of Whitby, where Jason's broad shoulders and rough good humour soon found them a place by the massive stone fireplace. The weather was not conducive to going out on the gallery overlooking the river, though still one or two roughly-garbed sailors stood staring into the fog, gazing with crinkled eyes upstream toward Execution Dock.

'Do you think they're thinking of a pirate ancestor?' Blanche whispered. 'Hung in chains at low tide and left until three tides had made sure that justice was done?' She gave a shudder. 'Change of subject is, I believe, in order. Do you think they'll ever finish Brunel's tunnel under the river? They must have started it at least eight years ago. The number of times it's been flooded, and the number of poor wretches who've lost their lives on it make one wonder whether Captain Kidd put a curse on the place!'

They argued amicably over their ale and pie for an hour and more while she watched the way those strange eyes changed from jade to sage green, and he watched the copper glints that the firelight caught in the honey of her hair. Blanche fought the warmth that his nearness brought, uncomfortably aware that her present guise would have brought far more than the occasional coarse comment her way but for her companion's muscular frame and the gleam of the knife observed once or twice beneath the cloak. 'You know, I find a certain comfort in your being here,' she admitted as the crowd milled and surged about them. 'However, I don't think the situation warrants your sitting quite so close!'

His eyes rested on her mouth a bare foot away, and one winged brow crept forward. 'Nervous? *You*, my lady?'

Blanche objected to being laughed at. 'Of course not! I simply find it uncomfortably warm here, and am quite sure that much of the unpleasant odour about us emanates from that unwashed object you're wearing.'

'Watch your words, woman, and your slipping accent, or I'll abandon you forthwith.' As if to lend weight to his words, he rose and took two paces away, then, seeing her stricken look, repented and with a laugh came to put an arm about her. 'Come, it's time we left anyway.'

'Would you have left me alone back there?' She had to ask as they returned to where a patient John nodded inside the carriage.

'You'd not have been alone for long, I'll warrant!'

'You brute! You unfeeling, callous brute!' Storming ahead of him, she ignored his laughter until lean fingers closed over her arm, arresting her flight.

'Slow down, firebrand! I'd not have left you. I don't allow anything that belongs to me to go unprotected.'

'And tell me, pray, whatever gave you the ridiculous idea that I belong to you? Why, if every man that I spent a few hours with took it into his head to claim ownership, you'd have to contest half the young bucks in London!'

They had come within sight of the carriage in a quiet lane near the Great Synagogue in Fournier Street, and again Jason turned her to face him, smiling a little at those stormy eyes. 'I believe I've already put in a higher claim than most.'

'High-*handed* more like, if you're alluding to that incident with Black Jack, and you know my opinion of that!'

He nodded, the smile dying, and a dangerous gleam appeared in his eyes. 'Your opinion, my lady . . . or a theatrical gesture for Black Jack's benefit?'

'Why, you arrogant . . .' But her tirade was cut off as once again she was swept into his arms. This time the mouth that descended on hers did not crush her lips in passionless possession but moved over them with sensual expertise, testing, tasting, teasing them apart until Blanche felt her senses reeling. Then, just as suddenly, she was released, her wondering eyes opening slowly to that smiling regard. 'Why, you . . .' But her voice was only a murmur of protest.

'Be still, my lady. I gave you only something to

think on. Now I'll get John to take you home. I've still work to do here.' His hand came to rest along her cheek, and his voice was slightly husky. 'Think of us,' he ordered softly. 'For I've thought of little else since we met.'

'I'll not think of you at all, Jason Hunterton,' she lied, and ran for the carriage, refusing the shocked groom's help, and uttering not a word all the way back.

CHAPTER FIVE

NOT THINKING OF those broad shoulders, muscular arms and possessive lips was far easier said than done, Blanche realised over the next fortnight, even though she assiduously avoided any gathering where she knew he might be. Her main problem was Annemarie Baines, who had arrived the afternoon following their meeting. After her initial shock at seeing Trixie Devine as Lady Davenport, the fragile Frenchwoman had emerged as a marvel of diplomacy, a connoisseur of culinary creations, and with a penchant for haggling over the freshest egg or the last inch of cloth that left the local tradesmen speechless. The cook adored her, and the ageing housekeeper found a gentle, self-effacing helpmate that never once gave her a moment's doubt that she was still sole custodian of the keys.

'She's a real lady, and that's a fact,' Mrs Armitage advised Blanche confidentially at the end of the first week. 'And those children are little angels. As you well know, m'lady, I'm not a one for children rampaging about the place, but I don't see hide nor hair of those two. That little lass just follows her mother around with nary a word, but still a little bob and a smile if you talk to her, and that John-Luke, why he just sits in a corner of the kitchen with a piece of wood and a couple of odd-shaped knives. He'd sit there all day—and all night too, if you let him.'

Blanche admitted that the arrival of the Baineses had considerably eased the running of the house, and quite understood their gratitude to both herself and

Jason for saving them from the workhouse, but privately wished his name was not on their lips quite so often, when all she wanted was to forget him! To this end she attended even more soirées and balls than she normally would and even encouraged the company of young Jeremy, whom she knew to be in love with her.

'I do feel quite guilty about it,' she confided to Alexandra Fitz-Hugh. 'But I've known him for simply ages and he's the one man I know with whom I can safely trust both myself and my reputation. I don't even have to listen to him, for I know exactly what he's going to say next!'

'You know, he has improved a great deal since his trip to Paris, Blanche my dear. Perhaps you should listen to him. I don't know whom Lord Hunterton wrote his letters of introduction to, and I suspect that as a happily married woman I really shouldn't know, but our young Viscount Carlysle is quite the thing now. Several young ladies have professed an interest who previously noticed only the weight of his purse!'

Blanche laughed, her grey eyes scanning the throng about them, alighting on a rose waistcoat here, a violet jacket there, visually supping from each floral display. 'If you're trying to make me jealous, Lexie, you really should know me better. I think the best thing that could happen to Jeremy would be to fall out of love with me, but he is so serious that he actually took me to meet his mother.'

'No! Tell me, is she as awful as they say?'

'Not at all, but then I don't judge at all by appearances, or gossip. I of all people can't afford to! No, I found her a rather sweet-natured and unbelievably naïve woman whose opulent bosom was always covered with as many ruches and roses as could be piled upon it, and who had a preference for expensive wrapping and cheap contents . . . A little like the men she married! She is, in her mid-forties, putting her seventh husband through his paces.'

'But at least thanks to the first Viscount's fortune

they all left far richer than they came! If Jeremy
marries, of course, there is a considerable trust for
him, too . . .'

'Lexie!' Blanche warned.

'But, my dear, I know your father left you only the
villa and a pittance to run it on, while your brother is
able to live like a princeling.'

'Alex is a dear boy, and was always the only one
father wanted. His guilt alone prompted papa to buy
me the villa, and the other money has been well
invested. For the rest, my rare talent for telling a
good horse or a run of cards has enabled me to live
well enough. But, Lexie, please don't spoil this
evening by suggesting I marry Jeremy—or anyone
else, for that matter. Look! There! That's Count
Verenska's son, isn't it? Come, you can introduce
me: I need new faces. You know how I love strangers.
No more of Jeremy now. I'm meeting him tomorrow
for a nice sedate ride through the park, so I see no
reason to think of him tonight.'

Alexandra shook her head, smiling. 'Blanche!
Blanche! What will I do with you! Poor Jeremy.
Hasn't he learned by now not to ride with you?'

Jeremy was himself having similar thoughts as he
watched with something akin to awe Blanche's
approach, soaring effortlessly over a four-bar gate
that she could easily have stopped to open and reining
in, turning her bay on a sixpence to come alongside
him. Her cheeks were flushed from the frosty air and
the grey eyes sparkled beneath the forward-tilted
brim of her white silk top hat. He wanted to tell her
that she was incomparable, adorable, terrifying . . .
and that he loved her, but not even his exposure to
the ladies—or the ladies of the night—in Paris had
prepared him for Blanche Davenport. All he could
think of to say was, 'Devil take it, Blanche, you
handle the ribbons like a man!'

'Thank you, Jeremy. Shall we ride?'

They rode on, she controlling the restive bay with

unthinking ease, he pulling at the roan which had caught the mare's mood and wanted nothing more than to hear the frost crackle on the grass beneath flying hooves. She led him to talk of Paris and the lessons he was taking in the art of self-defence at Gentleman Jackson's Rooms in Bond Street. 'Even your favourite poet Lord Byron was coached there.'

Finally, however, he could contain himself no longer and, reining in beneath a low-spreading oak, blurted, 'Blanche . . . There's something that won't keep any longer.'

'Jeremy . . . Please!'

'No, I'll not be put off! I—I had meant it to be at my mother's, and then at Vauxhall Gardens . . . but the fireworks interrupted me. Please don't be a firework, Blanche. Don't interrupt, I beg of you.'

Blanche bit her lip to keep from smiling, so intense was his expression. She had been likened to many things in her life, but never to a firework!

'You know how I have come to regard you, and must know my intentions. Oh, I know we've been acquainted for simply ages and it's said that friends can never be lovers . . . I mean husbands . . . I . . . Oh you must marry me, Blanche! You really must! I can offer you so very much.'

Blanche stemmed the flow by urging her mount sideways and laying a firm hand on his arm. 'Of course you can, dear Jeremy, but in truth you can offer me nothing in marriage that I can't have, should I so choose, out of it? And what would you want of me? Obedience? Loyalty? Children?'

'Yes, of course, but more—your beauty, your wit, and that infectious gaiety that draws people to you. You'd be all women in one.'

Blanche smiled gently. 'Do you really want me as a wife, I wonder, or as a paramour? You're two years younger than I . . .'

'I'm a man, I'll have you know, and an experienced one!'

Blanche felt her patience slipping. 'Quite possibly,

but I would rather imagine you more experienced at card play than love play!'

'Well, really!' he expostulated, crimson-faced. 'Your bold tongue quite undermines a fellow.'

'Forgive me, I meant no harm, but I fear that my errant tongue is all a part of me, and you must confess you'd secretly prefer a sweet and gentle child of . . . say seventeen who'd adore you. I need a bold lover, Jeremy, who doesn't give a fig for my bold tongue, and if ever I find him, a ring of gold won't be a necessary part of our union.' She knew that she had shocked him, but was unprepared for his next action as he turned, grasping her by the arm, and she knew that there would be bruises the next day.

'If it's boldness you want, then I'll tell you that I learned things in Paris that I could never have learned here, thanks to certain addresses given me by Lord Hunterton.'

'Ah, yes! Lord Hunterton. He spends so much of his life rescuing and educating children—of all classes—that I wonder he has any time for his own pursuits.'

'You'll not change the subject as easily as that,' Jeremy stated, his jaw tightening, and without warning kneed his mount close and dragged her into his arms, kissing her full on the mouth.

Blanche allowed the rough, inexpert kiss to bruise her lips, knowing that with no reaction on her part it would be over in seconds, and feeling a little sorry for the slightly shame-faced young man that finally released her.

'I . . . I . . .'

'No, don't say anything, Jeremy. I should be furious with you, but I'm not.' She allowed the bay mare to regain her composure, the creature being less accustomed than her owner to such cavalier behaviour, and patted her hair into place. 'I don't know quite what you were attempting to prove, but it couldn't possibly have been your maturity . . . or experience.' Irritably, Jeremy dug his heel in sharply; the roan let

out a snort of objection and began to caracole, but
Blanche sat back, smiling a little, feeling sorry for
both of them as the animal was brought under
control. 'I know the creature's no sluggard, Jeremy. I
need no proof,' she reprimanded gently.

He had the grace to look abashed. 'Deuce take it,
Blanche! You'd drive a man to bargain with the
devil! What must I do to make you marry me? I've
offered you a title, wealth . . . Why, when I'm twenty-
five, I'll come into ten thousand a year, which will
undoubtedly make me one of the richest young men
in England. I've offered you my undying devotion.
What more?'

'My freedom, Jeremy.' Then, reaching out, she laid
a softly persuasive hand over his. 'Find that sweet
and gentle child, my dear. I'm not the woman for
you.'

'I don't want a child; I want a woman! Oh, I know
marriage to you would be like trying to harness
Phaethon's sun horses—no, not even that, more like
attempting to capture and hold a butterfly—but I'd
not bind you with chains, you know.'

'Oh, Jeremy! Jeremy! Your chains of love would
weigh twice as much as shackles of iron. Come, now.
Please let's not spoil such a perfect day. I'll race you
to that elm. What do you say? It's a clear run, and it
will do both you and your roan the world of good.'

Jeremy's lip drooped petulantly. 'Oh, very well;
but I'll not always give in so easily. You can't expect
a fellow to wait for ever, you know, or always dance
to your tune. I'll wager Lord Hunterton wouldn't
give in to you.'

Blanche stiffened. 'Why that particular peacock? I
hardly know the man.'

'Oh, I hear things,' he said airily.

'Jeremy?'

He ignored the dangerous note. 'I have it on
excellent authority that he considers you quite unlike
any other woman he has met, and I didn't gain the

impression that it was meant in a complimentary way.'

'What authority would that be? Kitchen gossip or tavern tattle?' When he assumed an offended expression, she knew that she had hit the metaphorical nail on the head—and wished it were Lord Hunterton's! 'Well, then, now that you've begun, pray continue. How do you think his lordship could possibly have gained such an unfavourable view, when we are virtual strangers?' She was certain that the groom, John, would not have betrayed their secret excursion, and assumed it was no more than kitchen speculation.

Jeremy read the gleam of battle in those grey eyes, now the colour of the Atlantic rather than the soft morning mists. 'Oh, I'm sure it was nothing meant seriously,' he prevaricated, knowing that their ride was already over before it had begun, and cursing himself for his bluster. She simply looked at him, waiting. 'Well, it has been noticed that you and he have been avoiding each other, your even refusing an invitation to the Countess Vandaneuve's which simply everyone accepted—even Hunterton, who admits scant liking for the woman.'

'I had a prior engagement.'

'Oh, I know, but really, Blanche, to take your new housekeeper and her children to Astley's!'

'It was an amusing play, with the knight rescuing the right damsel, and the circus had an excellent horseback rider in the ring. They had never been, and I gained a great deal from watching them rather than the show. At La Vandaneuve's I would have gained nothing but local gossip . . . But what has this to do with Lord Hunterton?'

Jeremy looked awkward. 'Well, I'd gone over to St James's for a quick game of whist and Vanstone was there—you remember he was seated opposite you at the Fitz-Hughs' dinner. Of course we all noticed the regard Hunterton had for you there, but Vanstone said that he'd overheard that Hunterton was not quite so enamoured now.'

'Oh, get on with it, do!'

'Well, Vanstone was at this game, where one broad cove had quoted Byron by saying, "All a woman needs to be content is a box of sweets and a looking-glass", and his lordship laughed and said that there was one woman he could think of whom that missed by a mile. This fellow observed that his lordship should know women if anyone did, and was surprised that you had not been seen more often together. Hunterton said that you weren't like any woman he'd known. Since his usual . . . er . . . companions are more like those represented by Byron's quotation, well . . . you see what must be imagined, my dear.'

'So . . .' Blanche mused, her tone deceptively sweet. 'My Lord Hunterton prefers syrup to spice. It is thought that he is avoiding me!' She raised smiling eyes to the young man beside her, and it would have taken more observation and experience than he possessed to read the slivers of ice that cracked along her soft words. 'Jeremy, my dear, I'm grateful, truly I am, that you should confide in me, and I'm deeply honoured that you should think someone as forthright, as shocking, as—out of the desired pattern—as I deserve to be your wife. Generally speaking, I don't give a fig what society thinks of me, but I do object to being thought beneath *his* attention. He is going to that *après-théâtre* supper in Hampstead, is he not?'

'Not your kind of gathering, Blanche. They are a little . . . well . . . *risqué* at times. Many of the young bloods go there, and the supper is simply a line of platters along the wall of the salon. There are cards, and the play sometimes gets quite deep. Even the ladies play . . . though they are hardly of the first water, you understand. They have another type of game, too!' He looked uncomfortable, but this time found no pity in that disconcertingly direct gaze.

'Will you take me, Jeremy, or should I go alone?'

'Good grief, no! I mean . . . Well of course I'll

take you if you insist; I'd not have you walking in there unchaperoned.'

Blanche accorded him a sweet smile. 'I didn't think you would. Now, shall we continue our ride?' He made to protest further, but already she had dug in her heels and the bay mare leaped ahead, eagerly followed by the gelding.

Jeremy had been correct in his assessment of the late supper, but not of Blanche's reaction to it. She found the company stimulating, the men far more relaxed since their wives were abed or settled in a tiny salon where they could be kept fed and watered and placated with small change for their piquet or whist games. The women that did mingle in the main salon, eyes sparkling as brilliantly as the diamonds the covered creamy breasts with even less modesty than the dresses they wore, were courtesans or companions, kept women, or women who kept the men they were with. There was no talk of babies and budgets, but of blood-lines at Epsom and bets at St James's.

Blanche knew many of the young bucks and a fair number of their companions, and was accepted as 'something of an eccentric, but a dazzler nevertheless'. 'So what are they playing, Jeremy? That table where I see Lord Hunterton deep in play.'

'It's a fairly new game to these rooms, brought over from America, I believe, and a little like Brag. It's called Poker, and I think the variation they're playing is known as Five Card Stud, more complicated than ordinary Draw Poker, but equally conducive to heavy losses.'

They drifted over to the table, and Blanche took up a position directly facing the finely chiselled features that had not been out of her mind once since their last meeting. He glanced up, and those strangely hued eyes widened a fraction and then he gave a brief nod of acknowledgment before returning his total attention to his play.

In spite of his apparent concentration, Jason was

aware of the very moment she moved to stand behind
him. In his mind's eye he could see every line of the
white crêpe dress lavishly embroidered with silks, the
large beret sleeves topped by the huge *pélérine en
ailes d'oiseau* which stood out from her shoulders like
the 'wings of the bird' it was named for. He saw the
long pendant, whose single pearl led the eye inexorably
downward. He called and raised ten guineas—it was
too early in the evening for deep play—and finished
the game with an acceptable profit before turning to
acknowledge her formally.

'Lady Davenport. It's been a long time.'

'Far too long, Lord Hunterton. Why, if I didn't
know better, I'd say you were avoiding me.'

His eyes had sharpened a little at that ingenuous
gaze and slightly breathless tone, but then he made a
faultless leg, bending over her extended fingers, his
warm lips lingering a little too long for convention
against her flesh. 'Avoiding you, my lady? Never by
design. A man would have to be blind or a fool to do
that.'

Blanche remembered those lips all too well and her
colour rose slightly, but she firmly withdrew her hand,
turning to give Jeremy a beaming smile. 'You see,
Jeremy? I told you my Lord Hunterton wasn't
deliberately ignoring me. Could you possibly find us
all some champagne, while I allow his lordship, by
his very presence, to correct some of the erroneous
impressions that have been flying so fast they're
positively bouncing off the walls.' She turned again to
Jason. 'Unless, of course, you find a greater interest
in this new card game . . . What is it? Poker?'

Jason smiled easily. 'There are two great challenges
in my life at present, the lesser one being cards.'

It took some time for Jeremy to find one of the
liveried flunkeys and request his tray of champagne,
and when he returned, Blanche and Jason were deep
in discussion. Much to his relief, they had been
joined by several others, mostly older men and their
companions, mutual acquaintances, and the talk,

rather than being intimate, concerned carriage designs and blood-lines. There was talk of a race, and Jeremy joined in eagerly. 'The new cabriolet and the chestnut I bought last week don't even bother with roads; they float above the ground!'

'So does a balloon, but it won't win races,' laughed Blanche, taking the proffered glass of champagne.

'If that's Earl Dunlevin's animal, you've a fair chance,' Jason conceded graciously. 'He's certainly big enough with well-sloped shoulders, so should take good long, low strides to cover the ground well, and a deep girth for lung expansion. Yes, he should give you a chance.'

Encouraged, Jeremy asked, 'Even against your blacks, Jason?' and received a long look. 'Well? I mean . . . the blacks aren't unbeatable by Divine Decree!'

Jason sensed that there was more than a friendly interest behind the challenge and he noted the glance Jeremy had thrown toward Blanche, seeking her approbation. 'Not at all, Jeremy. In fact, I believe that over a timed five miles, Lady Davenport's own greys made faster time than my own—but of course I wasn't there myself.'

Blanche bit back the sharp retort that if he had been, they would not have needed a timepiece; the sight of him eating her dust would have been sufficient! 'I regret that, too,' she said, turning to him with a wistful little smile. 'Though I don't suppose it could ever come to a real race between us. I mean, it would be simply awful if you were beaten by a mere woman!'

Jeremy choked on his champagne, and there ran ripples of expectancy through the group.

'That'd be a bet worth taking,' laughed a middle-aged *roué*. 'The White Ladies against the Black Devils. I'd put a pony on it.'

'I, too,' cried another, but Jason held up restraining hand.

'Gentlemen! Gentlemen! Is this fair? One timed

run is hardly fair to Lady Davenport. Why, the blacks are built for both speed and endurance; a quick ride to the Heath would barely get them into their stride.'

'I'd put my chestnut against them over any run,' Jeremy challenged rashly. 'And Blanche's greys are stayers, too.'

'So's my pair of bays,' put in another voice, and Blanche saw Jason's smile. It was almost feral.

'Very well then, gentlemen, ladies. What do you say to an open race, any vehicle, any combination in harness, and a good clear run? Say from The Swan With Two Necks off Cheapside to The Greyhound for breakfast in Croydon. It is very approximately fifteen miles.'

There was an instant of silence, then a babble broke out, eager wagers, friendly badinage, then Blanche asked sweetly, 'And if I do arrive before you, Lord Hunterton, what should I order for your breakfast?' Another silence fell, an uneasy, stirring silence.

'Should I not be asking you that?' he queried, his light tone belying the glint of battle in his eyes. 'For there is surely no question about the outcome of such a race. Why, I'd even make a small wager myself.'

'A donation to my charity fund? How nice. And if I do win? . . . If on the remotest possibility that my greys can beat the famous Hunterton blacks?'

His eyes gleamed. 'Not a chance!'

Blanche felt like slapping that arrogant face, but vowed to hit him instead where it would hurt. 'Are you certain enough to put say a monkey on it?'

'I'm certain enough to put two.' He smiled at the murmur that ran round the table. 'And you, my lady. What will you put up to cover my bet should you lose? . . . No, not money, for whereas you could undoubtedly put my money to excellent use, I have little need for yours . . . with respect. What else can you offer that might be worth a thousand?'

Blanche stiffened, feeling all eyes on her, knowing that whatever was said in the next few minutes would be reported throughout the whole circle of their acquaintances, friend and foe alike. This had gone beyond a friendly game, and she had to choose her words carefully. But he had chosen them for her.

'A kiss, my lady. A kiss freely . . . nay, for a thousand, gladly given. What do you say?'

There was a roar of approval, and as her eyes flew to his he read the relief that covered the instant of fear flickering there. For her ears alone he asked, 'Did you doubt my honour? Trixie Devine wouldn't have!' Then louder, 'Well? Is it a deal?'

'Why, you . . . Yes, I agree.'

'Louder!'

'Yes, Lord Hunterton. Should I lose to you, a kiss gladly given . . . though I'll be even more glad when I relieve you of your . . . donation.' There was general laughter, and she pursued, 'But when is this jaunt to take place? Won't you need a day or two to rest after all this excitement—not to mention the excellent champagne?'

Jeremy saw Jason's lips tighten a fraction and, reading his mind, interpolated, 'Well I certainly do, and I'm sure I speak for a few others too. Shall we say the day after tomorrow . . . no, tomorrow, for it's already past midnight?'

'Agreed.' Jason nodded. 'The Swan at seven. That will put us in Croydon in good time for breakfast.'

'But it will still be dark,' objected the ageing *roué*, who made it a habit to lie abed until at least ten.

'Any later,' pointed out Jason reasonably, 'and the place will be positively crawling with coaches, passengers, drivers, ostlers and every other form of inconvenience. The darkness will also add a little spice to the race.'

This appealed to Blanche, but she allowed the others to express their views for her, and plans were enthusiastically finalised. 'Jeremy, I think I'm ready to leave now. I must plan how best to use his lordship's largesse.'

Jeremy allowed the slightest of frowns to mar his

handsome brow. 'I don't suppose it has occurred to either of you that a third party might win the race?'

'Frankly, no,' Jason stated, then fairly, 'though your chestnut has an excellent chance of beating the rest of the field. Lady Davenport, win or lose, I look forward to our race.'

'I, too, Lord Hunterton.' She hesitated, then echoed softly, 'Win or lose.'

Then she sped away on the glowering Jeremy's arm before her errant thoughts showed in the sparkling grey eyes.

CHAPTER SIX

'I THINK THE man made a fool of both himself and you,' Jeremy stated, the moment Blanche appeared.

'Good morning, Jeremy.'

'A kiss worth a thousand pounds, indeed! I don't care what he said; we all know what he meant, and it isn't a *kiss* he expects. I know Hunterton, and so does everyone else. Why, it has gone about half of London!'

They were gathered in the courtyard of the coaching inn with several others who had appeared early, and Jeremy had pulled Blanche aside the moment she had alighted from the elegant Parisian phaeton. Releasing her leather-gloved hand from his bruising grip, Blanche retained her smile with difficulty. 'Surely not half of London. Really?'

'It's no jesting matter. I'm in love with you. Hunterton's a devil with the women and doesn't take any one of his *amours* seriously.'

'Neither do I, and I haven't the slightest intention of becoming one of his conquests. You say you know him—though I doubt that you've seen more than his society face or heard more than gossip—but you should also know something of me by now, too . . . which is why you of all people shouldn't echo the asinine assumptions of others.'

'I don't want you even to kiss him.'

'You assume I'll lose?'

His anguished eyes looked over to where a groom was holding the delicate heads of the restless Thoroughbreds, murmuring to them soothingly while their pawing hooves struck sparks from the cobbles.

'They're magnificent animals. I'll give you that, but they're not the blacks. No.' His jaw tightened. 'He's not going to have you. You're mine!'

The grey eyes turned glacial. 'Listen to me, Jeremy, and listen carefully because I'm going to say it only once. I belong to no one but myself. I'm not going to marry you, or Jason, or anyone else just now, and until I do, I shall behave as I please and speak as I please. Now, I'm going to do all I can to win this race, and if I do I know that Jason Hunterton will be the first to pay his dues, as I shall if I lose. Is that understood? Heavens, man, he's not the first I've kissed!'

Jeremy would have said more, but at that moment the subject of their discussion came careering into the yard, his infamous Troika Curricle drawn by the magnificent matched blacks, three abreast, broad chests heaving, nostrils flaring, manes tossing as they were brought to a sliding halt alongside Blanche's greys. Instantly his tiger leapt down; not John, but a strange, Moorish-looking creature, hair as black as the animals he controlled, whistling and clucking to them, talking in a strange dialect and using an old Romany trick of blowing into their nostrils. Almost instantly they quietened, and Jason came striding over to where Blanche stood. 'Jeremy. Blanche . . . Or would you prefer Lady Davenport?'

'We're not in company now, so Blanche is quite acceptable. I'm grateful to see that you've decided to lengthen my odds by running your animals into the ground before the race begins.'

He laughed, flashing even white teeth. 'Not a chance! They just needed a little warming up.' He appraised Jeremy's rig and gave an approving nod. 'Big brute, isn't he? Must be almost seventeen hands, and I see you've pared your carriage down to the barest essentials even to removing the hood and apron. You're really determined to give me a race, aren't you?'

'I'll give you a better race than you bargained for,

unless you insist on us clocking in at the stage stops. My animal will go straight through and not even feel it over that distance.'

'Then by all means let him, dear boy. We've no rules imposed except to arrive at The Greyhound with both carriage and horse reasonably intact, so forge ahead. I hear their pigeon pie is second to none, and I'd hate you to miss it all.'

'Don't worry . . . dear boy . . . I shan't,' answered Jeremy through gritted teeth.

'Ah, here are the stragglers!' put in Blanche, not at all happy about the new antagonism Jeremy was showing toward the totally immune Jason. 'There's Gerald Pelham-Carter. Ye gods! What is he doing in that Stanhope gig? The thing will take off if those nags are pushed above a canter!'

As she crossed to where the young man was already in the midst of a laughing group, Jeremy turned to Jason with a frown. 'Look here, Jason, I don't want you to win this race.'

Jason's brow quirked upward. 'Of course you don't, nor do any of the others. That's why we're all here.'

'You know what I mean. I want you to let Blanche beat you.'

The green eyes sharpened a fraction. 'Why? Does she need the money so badly?'

'Yes . . . No . . . Oh, I don't know what she does with her dratted slum children, nor do I care! I don't want her to lose, and be forced to accept your unwanted attentions.'

Jason looked at him with new eyes and gave a slight nod of understanding, but could not resist a little taunting. 'Are you so sure they would be so unacceptable?'

'Of course!' Jeremy exploded, reddening. 'Devil take it, we're almost affianced!' and was mortified by Jason's bark of laughter.

'My dear Carlysle, that's like being almost pregnant! Believe me, there's a great deal between the word and the deed. Has she accepted you?'

Jeremy remembered Blanche's words exactly, but this only made him more angry with the smug expression of the man he had once called friend. 'She will,' he stated confidently; then, with less conviction, 'She will if you stay away from her.'

The green eyes changed to the deepest sage. 'And if I don't?'

Jeremy felt an icy trickle down his spine, but he had already passed the point where discretion was the better part of valour. 'You know St James's as well as I; the clubs where true gentlemen don't go, the little secret corners . . . like Pickering Place.'

Jason's eyes narrowed. He had not realised that the young man was so serious. 'Don't be an ass, Jeremy!'

'Do you know it?' There was a whiteness about the mouth and a tautness about the jaw that could not be ignored or diverted by either jest or insult.

Wearily, 'Yes, I know it. A tiny square of old houses, almost impossible to find unless you know the narrow timbered passage next to number three St James's Street. Used, quite illegally I must remind you, by young idiots who think a duel can solve anything. I'm twelve years older than you, Jeremy, and have long outgrown such idiocy, so I've no intention of spilling your blood, or of giving you the slightest chance of spilling mine.'

'You'll not meet me? Are you a coward, man, or is it that you don't think Blanche is worth fighting over?'

'Don't try my patience!' And there was a crack like a pistol-shot in the command that sent Jeremy back apace. 'For the friendship we once had, I'll not teach you what it means to call me a coward, and as for Blanche Davenport . . . What I think of her is my affair entirely. Stop behaving like a jackass. Everyone's here, and our good host is ready to start us. We've a race to run, Jeremy, and I suggest you allow this icy air to blow some of those cobwebs from your brain. I'll see you in Croydon.'

'You'll see me before then,' muttered Jeremy vengefully as the other strode off. 'By fair means or foul I'll stop you winning this race. Blanche is mine. It just needs time to convince her, and if I win this race she'll look up to me as a victor, and we all know that to the victor goes the spoils.'

The proprietor of The Swan With Two Necks had been on the scene since the first arrivals and was taking a vicarious pleasure from the excitement about him. Portentously he announced, 'This will be a race to remember. To your carriages, then, lady and gentlemen.' At once all social chatter ceased. Lips tightened. Eyes hardened. Muscles tensed as they hurried to their conveyances. The purse was two thousand guineas made up by wagers and sponsors' money, and the highest known for years. The personal bet between the White Lady and the sable-haired Hercules—called only half jokingly the 'Black Devil' for the carriage and the stallions he drove and his racing habit of unrelieved black—added an extra fillip to the event, increasing the punters' interest. 'Very well, then,' the inn-keeper called, his stentorian tones echoing from the walls. 'May the greatest heart of the finest horse, the firmest hand and the best whip win.' His eyes flew the length and breath of the yard. 'Go!' he cried, bringing down the large white kerchief he carried.

Whips cracked. Cries rang out. High-strung horses whinnied as iron-shod hooves struck sparks from the stone. Each carriage raced for the narrow exit archway, creating a suicidal bottleneck where whip and rein were used indiscriminately in order to gain the road . . . All except two.

'After you, my lady.'

'Thank you, but I've a feeling to pace my horses, my lord.'

'Faint hearted, Blanche?'

'You know better, Jason.'

He smiled—and in that instant, her way clear, she

had cracked the whip above those silver-grey necks, and the animals—sisters from the same dam—bunched powerful hindquarters and leaped ahead. He heard her laugh ring out as the phaeton almost left the ground, forcing her to brace her feet and lean against the taut reins, shortening them expertly while still giving the horses enough of their heads to send them into a flat gallop through the still-dark streets.

Jason manoeuvred his team with more circumspection, only calling to them once on the road when, as one, the trio turned and raced for Southwark Bridge. Some preferred the recently opened and much wider London Bridge, but he had absolute faith in his team and they in him . . . and could also pass the toll-gate with a wave rather than a coin, since the keeper preferred the occasional ale rather than putting every penny into his master's pocket; Lord Hunterton was never above a touch of bribery in a good cause.

He passed Pelham-Carter and his gig before they reached the main Brighton road. As Blanche had prophesied, the light gig had taken a corner too fast and its reckless driver, whose aspirations were far healthier than his corpulent frame, had been thrown into a high-piled vegetable cart from the near-by market at Kennington and was now apologising profusely to an extremely large and extremely irate trader.

Blanche, too, had swerved round the unfortunate Gerald, one glance assuring her that he was not hurt, and swept on. For two miles she raced neck and neck with another phaeton, but outmanoeuvred the young driver on a narrow bridge. Others had dropped out or pulled aside good-naturedly to allow the flying hooves of the greys to overtake. She saw Jeremy way ahead, standing like a Roman charioteer urging the chestnut on as if his very life depended on it. He was almost a mile in front but, knowing the road, Blanche knew that she could still pass him in a final spurt, and allowed the greys to set their own pace. They were enjoying the run as much as she, and kept up the

smooth, long stride with only the increased sway of
their heads betraying their tiredness.

There was a sudden thunder of hooves behind her,
and, without turning, she knew the team. The man
must have driven like the devil himself to have
overtaken the whole field, when she knew she had
left him standing at the inn!

Jason saw her suddenly tense and then lean to flick
the reins over the horses' backs. Gamely the greys
found a reserve of strength and inched ahead, but
they were no match for the blacks, and he drew
abreast. 'I'll see you in Croydon,' he called.

'You're not there yet,' she answered breathlessly,
her cheeks flushed with the icy wind, her hair escaped
from her bonnet and flying behind her, her will to
win showing in every taut muscle of that slender
frame.

With an admiring shake of the head, Jason called
to the blacks and they pulled inexorably ahead, then
were past and clean away. He saw Jeremy in first
place, and knew that they had only four miles to go.
He was determined to beat him, with no doubts at all
who was the winner. The animals laid back their ears
and surged forward. Closer and still closer, until the
two carriages were running neck and neck, the foam
from the chestnut's mouth flecking the nearest black's
shining neck. Jason frowned as he saw the signs of
Jeremy's heavy-handedness, and when the younger
man brought his whip into play, it drew blood from
the russet hide. 'Damn you, ease off!' he commanded.
'Your fight's with me, not the horse!'

'You'll not win, Hunterton,' came the answer, and
the veins stood out on Jeremy's forehead. 'You won't
take the race, and you won't take Blanche!' Wrenching
at the reins, he pulled the great horse over to crowd
the nearest black. Angrily the black turned to nip at
the offending neck, but it was enough to break the
team's stride and Jeremy moved ahead again, but not
content with that, he swung his whip and cracked it

hard across the black's back. The black screamed, and a thin trickle of blood showed on the satiny coat.

'No one beats my animals!' Jason cried, enraged, all ties of friendship severed by that one cruel blow. With a high whistling call learned from his Romany groom, he sent the horses, necks outstretched, to career in a mad race alongside Jeremy and then, in spite of the other sawing at his reins, ahead. Jeremy turned, eyes wild, raised his arm and sent the whip to crack against Jason's own back, but at the last instant Jason turned, grasped defensively at the lash and felt it cut into his hand.

With a cry of rage and fear, Jeremy was pulled off balance, and he flung out his hands to seize the side of the carriage, losing both whip and reins in the process. Uncontrolled, the chestnut veered defensively, and the inner wheel of the carriage caught the side of the road.

When Jason looked back, he saw the shafts snap as the cabriolet and rider were overturned and the chestnut went down in a tangle of thrashing hooves and reins. Instinctively he hauled his team to a rearing halt, and before even the curricle had stopped swaying, was down and running back to the fallen Jeremy. 'You damned fool! I should leave you to rot. What kind of man are you to treat animals so, and what in God's name possessed you to attack me?' He took in the young man's ashen features, and how, when he tried to sit up, he clutched at his left arm with a gasp, but such was his anger that he turned his back and went to the chestnut, who had risen shakily and was now standing trembling, magnificent head lowered.

'I think my arm's broken,' came a plaintive cry from behind him, but he refused to turn.

'It should have been your neck!' he declared, his fury abating a little as he ran expert fingers over the abused animal and found no sign of damage other than the weals on his heaving flanks. He talked to the horse soothingly until the head came up, and with a snort the chestnut looked about him.

There was a clatter of hooves and a whinny as Blanche pulled her greys to a slithering halt, leaping down with a cry. 'Jeremy! What has happened? Oh my dear, you're hurt!' Her eyes took in the scene, the overturned carriage, Jason attending the horse while ignoring the injured Jeremy, and Jason's team standing patiently a few yards down the road, unharmed. She rounded on him, eyes flashing fire. 'Did you run him off the road? Oh, Jason, how could you! He was winning, and you couldn't bear that, could you? You couldn't just pass him, so you had to teach him a lesson . . . prove your superiority. I can see it all!'

'Enough!' Jason's harsh command cut off her angry flow. 'It's not the first time you've judged by appearances, and been just as wrong.' He turned to the man, who was kneeling now and nursing his broken arm. 'If there's a shred of decency left in you, Carlysle, you'll tell her ladyship exactly what did happen, and how it is that both your horse and mine bear the marks of your lash! Since you've obviously no need of my services, I'm going to rest up my team at a near-by tavern I know—not the Greyhound, for I've no desire for your company or anyone else's at the moment—and then I'll return home. I trust you'll make my excuses to the others, and convey my congratulations to whomever does win the race. As for me, I've no further interest in it.' He looked directly at Blanche then, finishing, 'Any of it!'

There was a long silence as they watched him put the blacks into a gentle trot toward Croydon, then Blanche turned that speculative gaze on Jeremy, assisting him to his feet then stepping back, adopting a waiting regard. He held those cool eyes for as long as he could, then blurted, 'I only did it for you . . . for love of you.'

Still she waited, feeling the chill inside as hesitantly, with excuses and entreaties for understanding, he told

her the whole sordid story from his conversation with
Jason at The Swan and Jason's refusal to meet him to
the present time. Finally he ground to a halt before
the contempt and, what was worse, pity in her eyes.
Neither had heeded the others passing with shouts
and offers of help, and now Blanche ran her fingers
through her wind-blown hair, turning aside tiredly.
She was confused and angry, hurt by Jeremy's
stupidity and yet in her woman's heart flattered by
the intensity of his feelings, blaming herself in part
for not discouraging him more firmly.

'Blanche? What will you do?'

'I think . . . I think I'll take the next stage home.
Once having reached The Greyhound, the others will
be back soon enough with help and medical attention
for your arm. You'll tell them you lost concentration
and ran off the road. I've a feeling that Lord
Hunterton . . . Jason . . . won't deny it, and neither
shall I.'

'But you . . . I mean . . . Why leave?'

The grey eyes looked into his very soul. 'You
might possibly have won, Jeremy, with honour.
There's really no other way. For what you did, for
what you thought of doing, for what you are . . . I
don't want to see you again.' She turned to stroke
the velvety noses of the greys.

'Wait, Blanche! You can't! I mean . . . You must
see me again!'

'Yes, I can't see a way of avoiding it, since we
have so many mutual friends. What I said was that I
didn't want to see you again, and I trust that there is
enough of a gentleman left in you to accede to my
wishes. Please see that my horses are rested and
stabled with your own. I'll send my groom for them
this afternoon. Goodbye, Jeremy.' Then, mourning
the end of their friendship, 'You really are an utter
ass, you know! No woman's worth losing your honour
for.'

He watched her walk away toward the stage stop,
realising for the first time how damnably his arm

hurt, so it was not entirely due to self-pity that the
tears came to his eyes. 'You are . . . my White Lady!'
he choked, and sank to the pavement, burying his
head until the first clatter of hooves heralded the
approach of friends.

Jason closed his front door, shutting the world out,
and leaned against it for a moment. He had given the
servants the morning off, as he had not expected to
be back himself much before mid-afternoon. There
was a flickering light in the study, and he smiled.
Considerate of his man to see that there was a
banked fire in his favourite room just on the off-
chance he should return early. Throwing aside his
riding-coat, he made for the slightly open door,
picking up his mail from the silver salver on the hall
table as he went, and pushed the door wide. He
stopped dead.

'I can't stay.' She had not changed, but her hair
was brushed and fell in honey-gold waves about her
shoulders. She did not move from her place by the
fire, even as he crossed the room to stand before her,
lifting her eyes to his, dark in the firelight. 'I came to
pay a debt . . . and to apologise.'

His voice was husky, almost angry. 'There's no
need. I told you. I'm not interested in who won the
race . . . or who might have.'

'You lie.' Softly. The eyes were direct and unafraid,
neither evading the issue nor denying what was
between them. 'You would have won, Jason.'

'I told you. I don't care.'

'Then tell me to leave.' But he could not do that
either, and as her hands slipped up that broad chest
to his shoulders, he gave a low groan and swept her
into his arms, his mouth descending, then stopping, a
breath away from her lips.

'Gladly given?' he murmured, and for answer felt
her fingers on the back of his neck drawing him
downward as her body moulded itself to his. Slowly
he cherished her mouth, savouring the incredible

softness of lips that clung and parted and moved beneath his with a leashed passion of which even she was not wholly aware. The kiss deepened, tongue meeting tongue, tasting inner sweetness, breath drawing breath, until the earth spun about them.

Suddenly she went limp, and as he raised his mouth from hers, easing his grip, her head fell back against his arm. 'Blanche? Blanche!' Sweeping the unconscious girl into his arms, he carried her to the chaise-longue, worriedly chafing her hands, kissing her temple, cheeks, lips, looking round for water . . . But at that moment the long lashes fluttered, and the grey eyes looked into his.

'Damned corsets!' murmured Blanche Davenport. 'I couldn't breathe!' She blinked at his sudden shout of mirth.

'My love, you're priceless!'

A little hesitantly she smiled, then a giggle escaped, and unashamedly she joined in his laughter.

Still chuckling, he lifted her to her feet, holding her close for a moment before reluctantly releasing her. 'Promise me one thing, Blanche? If ever you break into my home again, please, please don't wear that infernal contraption.'

'I didn't break in.' Then, as that eyebrow quirked upward, 'When your tiger took me home from Wapping, he tactfully suggested that I might wish to avail myself of your quarters to wash and change before returning to respectable society. I refused, of course, but when I arrived and he had helped me to alight—rather clumsily so that I dropped my purse—I found that he had slipped a key into it. Incidentally, what was the man before he came to you?'

'You wouldn't want to know.'

'That's what I thought! So here I had your key, with absolutely no intention of using it, and, since I was ignoring you, little chance of returning it.'

'Ah, so you were avoiding me!'

Blanche felt the colour rise to her cheeks. 'Well . .

be that as it may . . . I had your key, now on the desk there.'

'Won't you keep it?'

'Of course not! I came only to . . . to pay my debt.'

'And you'll never come again.'

'Of course not.' But she knew he was laughing at her, and the warmth she felt at being so near him fought with the annoyance that he should think himself so irresistible that she would be unable to stay away. 'I must leave.'

'I'll call a carriage. It may take a while. Can I offer you some tea . . . or anything . . . while you wait?'

He was close, too close. She felt the magnetism of the man drawing her to him, felt the warmth of his body moving like a heat wave across the inches between them and caught the tangy male scent of him in her nostrils. With a conscious effort she stepped back apace, looking up at him with eyes in which a hundred conflicting emotions mingled. And he read them. Every one.

'Come, I'll walk you home through the Park. It will do us both good.'

'Jason . . .' He turned. 'Thank you.'

'For you, my lady, anything.'

CHAPTER SEVEN

'I WOULD DO anything for you, madame, anything but please don't ask me to go with you this evening.'

Blanche stared at Annemarie in surprise. 'But it will be perfectly safe, my dear. We shall have a quite adequate bodyguard, I assure you. It's Christmas Eve, and I always distribute these little gifts to my friends after I've left the soup kitchen.'

'How can you call those people friends? Women of the streets, thieves, little animals that bear no resemblance at all to children.'

Blanche gave a gentle smile, regarding the woman who sat opposite her with deep pleasure. Annemarie Baines had lost that skeletal appearance, and was transformed into a slender beauty with deep russet hair and clear brown eyes, eyes that until this moment had lost the haunted look of their first meeting. 'My dear, a friend is simply a person with whom you share a mutual liking and trust, and enough in common to keep up an interesting conversation all the while you're together. It is someone whom you think of with affection when apart and look forward to meeting again. Those one or two . . . women of the streets as you call them, have taken up the world's oldest profession either to keep their family from the workhouse and near starvation or, in one case, to keep a young and extremely talented opera star touring Europe without even knowing who her benefactor is and believing her mother dead. Thieves? Yes, one of my friends was sent to Botany Bay for stealing two loaves of bread and a string of sausages. He had eight children under fifteen, and his wife had died giving birth to twins. I have found work for the two eldest, and make sure they have more than sausages for Christmas dinner. The children, the little animals . . . No, there is really no excuse for making friends with them, and absolutely no reason to feel affection . . . except it is the one thing they've never experienced.'

'I can't go!' It was whispered, and Blanche's scrutiny sharpened; then she gave a nod of acceptance.

'Very well. You have your reasons. Perhaps you'll help me put these little gifts into a couple of baskets.'

The Frenchwoman eagerly bent to gather the assorted packages from the floor and a busy silence fell, then suddenly she said, 'I . . . lived there, you see.' Blanche's hands never faltered in their task, but she glanced up with an encouraging smile. 'There was a time before Mr Baines . . . A bad time.'

'Lord Hunterton told me you had committed some crime which sent you to Newgate.' Her tone held no judgement, and encouraged Annemarie began, bitterly, 'I read once that a goddess Circe turned men into swine. It's a wonder she saw the need to!' Once the flood-gates were opened she unfolded a story of humiliation and degradation, rape, abuse and cruelty such as Blanche had never heard, made somehow all the more terrible because it had happened to this willowy French aristocrat who had become closer even than her own family. When it was finished, Annemarie raised those deep brown eyes, disdaining the tears that dampened her cheeks, and said simply, 'You'll wish me to leave now, of course . . . Now you know what I am.'

Blanche felt the other's agony of soul, and for a moment could not speak. Eventually she reached out to cover the tightly-clenched fingers with her own, giving a little cough to clear the choking feeling in her throat. 'Mrs Baines . . . Annemarie . . . I know what you are. What you were has never mattered to me or ever will, even less so now than before.' She gave a shaky smile. 'You've no need at all to return

to an area that holds such horrendous memories, but
one thing I do ask of you. From now on, there must
be truth between us. It's a two-edged sword—truth
between two women—but I've come to the conclusion
that you are quite indispensable to me and, apart
from Alexandra Fitz-Hugh, I can't think of another
person I've said that to.'

The velvet eyes had widened endlessly at Blanche's
speech, and now there was a suspension of all
movement, a waiting time, when for an instant Fate
rolled her dice. Then, with a sob, Annemarie flung
herself into Blanche's arms. 'God, you don't know
how lonely I've been! So many long, long years!'

It was this picture, this chaos of parcels and the
two woman clutching each other, beyond tears,
beyond all feeling but the moment, on which Jason
Hunterton walked in.

The announcement of his arrival had gone unheard,
and it was only his carefully polite cough, covering a
multitude of emotions, that sprang them apart. As a
man of the world, essentially a ladies' man, he could
find some small amusement in the way their hands
flew to their hair in a totally feminine gesture. As a
human being with a deep respect for the all too few
fine qualities of his fellow men, he was moved by the
genuine emotion on the lovely faces turned toward
him. 'Should I retire and announce myself again?'

Blanche, the first to recover, gave a wave of her
hand toward the sideboard. 'Since you are here, you
may pour us some sherry, and I'm sure you can find
something there to accommodate your own taste.
Annemarie and I have made what is for the average
woman a momentous decision—that is, to extend the
hand of friendship to one of our own sex. It calls for
a celebration. And what, may I ask, are you doing
here so near luncheon on Christmas Eve? Did I
invite you? I have the most appalling memory.'

Jason poured the drinks, handed them to the two
ladies still kneeling on the floor, and took his seat in
a deeply sprung armchair. 'Your memory is as sharp

and as appropriate to the occasion, as your wit. No, you did not invite me for luncheon—a quite unacceptable oversight—so I decided to request the pleasure of your company on a ride out to the Heath, with a short stop at the Spaniards Inn for a touch of pigeon pie and turkey, perhaps a sliver from a saddle of mutton or a bite of rare beef.'

Blanche rose—with surprising grace, considering her position—and pondered the matter while crossing to replace her barely touched glass on the tray. 'Annemarie, what do we have for lunch?'

'Why . . . a little ham . . . some eggs . . . I could concoct something, madame . . .'

'Blanche.'

'Er . . . Madame Blanche.'

Laughing. 'Oh, Annemarie . . . just Blanche. We've come beyond titles, surely . . . Which relieves me of a great strain, for I can call you an ass of an aristo when you put on the airs and graces you've suddenly become afflicted with since Jason's arrival, and you may call me a fool, which I am—more often than you may so call me! Very well, we have nothing for lunch, so I shall be delighted to accompany you, my Lord Hunterton—so long as you have me back by five, for I must take an early dinner and be in Soho by seven.'

'I, too, have a similar schedule; a man I must meet over in Essex.'

'Any news?' Annemarie interjected, then caught Jason's frown, made an awkward excuse and left the room, murmuring something about the children's lunch.

'Now what was all that about?' Blanche laughed. 'You've scared the poor woman half out of her wits.'

Jason echoed her laugh, though to Blanche it seemed to have a false ring. 'It's nothing of importance. This boy I may have mentioned. I received news that he may be with a family in Romford, and I was going over to talk to them. Probably only another in a long line of red herrings.

Come, now, let us forget the unfortunates and lost boys and concentrate on the Spaniards' platter and the clean fresh wind on the Heath guaranteed to bring your cheeks to the colour of ripe apricots.'

It was only much later that she wondered at his choice of phrase, referring to the journey to Essex as a red herring—intimating a deliberately false trail—rather than calling it a wild-goose chase.

It was clean and fresh on the Heath, with the lightest sprinkling of snow swirling down to settle in secret corners and causing Blanche to pull her ermine-trimmed hood tight about her face.

'I must be quite, quite mad!' she called to him, above the crack of ice in the branches and the thud of hooves, the creak of polished leather and crunch of wheels on the icy road.

'I wonder if we'll see Turpin's ghost with his black coat and three-cornered hat?' he called back, having noticed a vehicle ahead long before she had shielded her eyes to make out the fast approaching driver.

'I'll not share my lunch,' she answered. 'I'm ravenous!'

'Most ladies are supposed to eat like birds.'

'Only those who've had a good meal before the event. Just look at that fool!'

The driver of the hooded cabriolet had veered off and raced past a tiny uninhabited cottage near the toll-gate. Even over the wind Blanche heard the horse whinny in fear and, almost imagined, a tiny, high-pitched animal cry. Already Jason had turned the horses and within seconds they arrived at the scene of the tragedy, a very insignificant little tragedy in the course of the universe, but a real one nevertheless.

'Oh, Jason, the poor thing!'

The dog's back was broken, its eyes glazed with its final agony as it tried to drag itself towards the undergrowth at the side of the road. It was mostly mastiff, and the scars on its hide represented a long history of ring-fighting, a still thriving blood-bath at the Westminster Dog Pit in Tothill Fields.

Jason moved to the bitch's head and feebly she snapped at his hand. 'There's nothing we can do to save her, Blanche.' Without waiting for her reply, he suddenly brought his hand down in a chopping motion, and the taut body went limp. 'I'm sorry, my dear.'

Then, from the hedge, a faint growling sound, not quite formed.

Instantly Blanche ran to pull back the branches to reveal three pups, golden skinned, fat as butter and with the floppy disjointedness of the very young. The largest had its nose buried in a rabbit, fresh killed, and was dragging it to and fro, preventing the other two from feeding. 'Oh, Jason!'

He gave a deep sigh, yet there was a strange warmth in his eyes as he watched her gather the pups into her arms. 'Do I take it that lunch is postponed?' She threw him an eloquent look, and he bowed to the inevitable. 'Why in heaven's name did I get mixed up with a woman who can't resist strays and lost causes!' Then he noticed the tears, star-bright yet unshed, in her eyes, and his eyebrow arched upwards. 'Not tears. Not you!' And they were blinked back.

'I never cry! It's this damned cold. Let's get this bunch home before they wipe rabbits' blood all over me and chew through my muff, not having the sense to tell mink from coney.'

Inwardly Jason smiled. Any other woman would have obligingly collapsed sobbing into his arms at such a gibe, but not Blanche Davenport: beneath the velvet and silk there was pure steel . . . or was there?

They reached the house in record time, his blacks skittish from the scent of the blood and not run enough to gain satisfaction from the exercise. The moment he had helped her down, her arms full of wriggling mischief, Blanche turned with a quick dismissive smile.

'I'm sorry about the lunch, Jason. Another time, perhaps.' No date. Not even encouragement.

'What about supper?

'It's Christmas Eve, and we've both a lot of walking between dinner and midnight; in fact I doubt that I'll bother with supper at all.'

He nodded in acceptance, not offended, realising that he would have to come to terms with this independence in her or be aligned with her other suitors. Blanche had a great capacity for love, of that he was certain, but as yet no man had tapped her capacity for passion. She saw men as collectable items; handsome, amusing, rich, gay, sympathetic, flattering . . . but never as real people. She used them quite unknowingly, as diversions from the pain and loneliness, as an escape from the dark corners of her real life . . . and trusted not one of them. To gain her love he first had to gain her trust . . . a new feeling for the Lord Hunterton—half saint, half satyr—into whose arms women had so far fallen like a tower of cards at a single breath. He gave a short bow.

'I'll always be there when you least expect me! You'll have to get used to that, my Lady Davenport.'

The cool grey eyes kindled a little. 'And if I choose not to?'

He extended a finger to the largest of the pups, the one who had savaged the rabbit carcass and kept it from his weaker brothers. Instantly the milky fangs sank in, drawing blood. Jason never flinched, but smiled a slow, wolfish smile, not attempting to withdraw his finger until, realising that no threat had been intended, the pup loosed hold. Jason, still smiling, surveyed his hand. 'I'll be there anyway, Blanche.' Turning on his heel, he leaped into the carriage. A crack of the whip. Simultaneous bunching of powerful ebony haunches. The wheels almost left the ground, and he disappeared in a flurry of snow.

'Damn you either way, Jayce Hunter!' But he had veered round the corner as if the hounds of hell were

behind him. When he had gone, Blanche gave a slow
smile and bunched the largest pup closer under her
arm. 'Good for you, mutt,' she chuckled. 'yet—in all
honesty—I can't stay angry with him for long either.'

Anger . . . Yes, pure unadulterated anger was what
kept her walking those icy streets, she realised. Anger
at a government who would not release funds to pay
rubbish collectors for the rookeries but kept their
own cesspits emptied weekly. Anger against the
vagrant herd of rooting swine who found a filthy,
disease-ridden repast on the rotting vegetables and
meat in the City of Westminster itself, and against
those who would not drive them off. Anger against
the gin-soddened mothers of wizened children fishing,
playing, sailing paper boats in contaminated gutters.
Anger against the stench of refuse . . . But most of
all against the stench of corruption, the uncaring
class . . . not an upper class, but a class who did not
accept that anyone was superior—and did not even
see those inferior, and was therefore beyond salvation.
In the recesses of her brain, as she ladled soup into
wooden bowls held by icy, bloodless hands, came
something she had heard from an aristocratic
old French exile—the battle-cry of the French
Revolutionaries as they marched to de Lisle's 'Song
of War for the Army of the Rhine'—the Song of the
Marseillaise in that summer of 1792.

> *Aux armes, citoyens!*
> *Formez vos bataillons!*
> *Marchons, marchons . . .*

Oh, you fools! she remonstrated with the formless,
faceless officialdom. Can't you look down as well as
upward? Do *we* need a revolution before you realise
that these people form the majority? God help you if
they learn to speak out! But still she smiled and said,
'Merry Christmas', and put a shred of meat in with
the weak soup and a slice of plum-pudding in an

accompanying napkin, until . . . 'Hello, Liza . . .
How are you, my dear? And your brother Billy?
How's he getting on with the Parkers? And you are
keeping warm, aren't you?'

The ten-year-old looked at her with cool eyes.
'Thank you, yes, milady', and made to pass on, but
Blanche felt the hairs prickle at the nape of her neck.

'Liza? Tell me. I know something's wrong.'

Something moved—and was gone. 'I'm well,
milady—thank you.'

Immediately Blanche signalled to Alexandra to take
her place and came round the table to take the child
by the arm, giving her a little shake. 'Not me, Liza.
You don't put *me* off so easily.'

Without warning the child crumpled, folding into
Blanche's arms, letting her bowl drop to the table.
''E's dead, miss! Billy's dead!' There were no tears,
but a grief too deep for tears that shook her frame.

Blanche felt the chill deep inside. 'Tell me.' And a
tale was unfolded that again brought into sharp relief
the chasm between the classes. The family who had
accepted Billy had thought to convert him into a
model of propriety, but Billy was a creature of the
streets, a victim of violence, abuse and multiple small
cruelties. He had hoarded food in his room, yet could
not trust them enough to tell them that it was for the
time he was certain they would evict him. He took a
quantity of small change, and a lace handkerchief for
his mother. The family had called in a constable to
give him a warning, and as a result the child had run
away in terror. Hunted down and brought back, he
had been sent to Maidstone prison after having
attacked the constable with a shard of glass . . . and
there was no one to tell the prison authorities that
Billy was petrified of the dark! Screaming, he had
been locked in a tiny black cell—a routine punishment
that could last up to three days. Early the following
morning his hysterical screams had ceased. When
they came with his lunch, he was dead—the cell door
gouged—the child's fingers torn to the quick—in his

eyes a terror that made even the toughened warder cringe.

Blanche gathered the girl into her arms. 'Come on, Liza. Let's get you home.'

'Me dad'll kill me if I don't bring in some grub! He swore to cripple Billy if ever he came back, and he will cripple me.'

'Not this time, my dear!' Lady Davenport's fury iced her words. 'Never again will he give any of you trouble, I promise you.'

And he did not. Forging through those narrow mean streets, heedless of the icy chill or the scarecrows who watched her pass with speculative, avaricious, fearful, hate-filled, respectful, knowing and occasionally loving eyes, Blanche felt only rising fury within that was colder even than the frost about her. She banged on that door, Liza behind her, the ever-present giant bodyguard close, and as the bull-necked brute opened it—swaying, reeking of whisky and sweat and the stench of unwashed rags—she commanded, 'Get out here, you filth, you pig-swill, you ordure of vermin! I've a bone to pick, and you're it!'

In all fairness, it was undoubtedly the presence of the man behind her that kept her alive while she told Liza's stepfather exactly what she thought of him and what would be done to him—'by my friend here and several more like him'—if he ever touched Liza or her mother again. However, even Liza—that gutter brat, that creature of the streets—marvelled at the diversity of language that was delivered in aristocratic tones by that rosebud mouth.

Later Blanche turned to the ape-like creature by her side and gave him a brilliant smile. 'You know . . . I truly enjoyed that!'

He shadowed her, saying nothing, his presence a comfort nevertheless, for the next three hours and more as she went from cellar to attic, distributing her gifts. She had remembered those with special needs, so that the mother with a new baby was given a warm shawl as well as an address at which she would

receive a little milk each day and a bowl of thick
stew.

There were shoes, scarves and mittens for the
children who had none, all second-hand but more
precious than gold in the icy wind that cut through
alleys and thrust frost-tipped fingers into bare rooms.
Finally it was done, and exhausted though content,
Blanche turned back to the soup kitchen, where her
bodyguard would melt back into the shadows. This
time, however, she stopped him with a gesture. 'You
know, you and your friends—you in particular—have
cared for me for over a year, and I don't even know
your name.'

He shuffled his feet awkwardly and touched a non-
existent cap. 'It's Jem, m'lady. Just Jem.'

Blanche smiled. 'Well, Just Jem, I'll never be able
to thank you adequately for enabling me to carry out
my work here. It was probably today that I realised
how I've come to rely on you when I confronted
Liza's stepfather with no doubt at all of your support.'
The giant reddened to the roots of his hair, and
Blanche took pity on him. 'I won't detain you, Jem,
but I'd like you to take this with my heartfelt thanks.'

He accepted the heavy purse reluctantly, not
opening it but aware by its weight that possibly it
held more than he could earn in a year. 'I—I don't
want this . . .'

'Of course you do. Put it to good use, and I hope
to see you after Christmas. Go on! You may do your
vanishing act now.' With a warm smile she turned
into the chill hall where Alexandra was clearing away
the débris. Tired as she was, she set to with a will
until all was again clean and bare, the tables washed
over, the floor swept.

'Will you come back with me for some supper?
Just the family.'

'That's sweet of you, Lexie, especially since it's
Christmas Eve and I know you've enough to do, but
I think I really need to go home and sink into a deep
tub before sinking into a deeper pillow. I promise a

visit after the festivities are over. I'll bring a basket, and we'll have a pic-nic.'

They parted, and Blanche drove wearily home, allowing the horse to find its own pace. Only when she turned into the narrow street and saw the black carriage and pair outside her house did all trace of tiredness disappear and a tiny smile touch her mouth. Allowing her elderly groom, who had hurried from the house, to set her down and take the horse, she approached the door of Jason's hooded curricle.

'I suppose you are looking for consolation, my Lord Hunterton?'

His face appeared, as drawn as hers but with the dark eyes alight with laughter. 'I thought to give it. It appears that we have both experienced a wearing day, so can we not pool our limited reserves and share a glass of claret?'

Blanche pretended to give his suggestion some consideration. 'I doubt that there will be much more, but I'm sure Annemarie won't mind the small inconvenience of a surprise visitor.'

'You could have it sent out to the carriage—in which case I suggest a stout ale and hot poker, lest I freeze to death and inconvenience you even more!'

'Put so . . . how can I refuse?' Once inside, she noticed that he had already changed, and when the delighted Annemarie had taken his greatcoat to reveal an exquisitely cut black kerseymere suit and white satin waistcoat, Blanche pursed her lips.

'Your dress puts me at a disadvantage, sir. Will you excuse me while I, too, take time to remove a little of the streets?' Without awaiting a reply, she left him to the attentions of Annemarie and went to wash and change. In her room she pulled out a simple white merino, but then with a sudden twitch of the lips exchanged it with a gown of heavy satin, a *robe de chambre*, a compromise between the casual and the wanton. It covered—yet clung, intimated and almost revealed with its wrapped neckline—yet was totally modest.

'Madame!' came Annemarie's shocked voice from the doorway. 'You can't!'

Blanche could not help teasing her. 'I thought it entirely appropriate for an evening by the fire.'

'But . . . you have company!'

'No, I have Lord Hunterton.'

'You are *en déshabillé*!'

'I'm far more covered than usual! This falls to below my ankles and has no neckline worth speaking of, whereas my ball-gowns reveal more of me, considering my figure, than even I approve of, yet I wear them because it's the fashion.'

Annemarie pursed her lips and went in disapproving silence to a drawer, returning with a froth of white lace shawl which she settled firmly over Blanche's shoulders. 'To each its occasion, madame. You do not wear your ball-gown for shopping, or your night-wear when entertaining a gentleman—even such as Lord Hunterton! If you are determined to do so, then, with all respect, I shall sit very quietly at the window behind you.'

Blanche gave a gurgle of laughter. 'A chaperon? Annemarie, you're priceless—especially when you're so disapproving as to forget my given name! Come, then, let's join the company.'

Jason's green eyes kindled at her appearance, but as the Frenchwoman settled herself firmly on the window seat, staring determinedly out at the darkness, he too saw the humour in the situation. Determinedly he ignored the full breasts that rose and fell, unconfined by anything but the lightest chemise beneath the satin, and the length of leg that made the folds fall just so as she seated herself on the opposite end of the couch. Putting down the huskiness in his throat he asked politely about her day, the children and the affairs of the house—while wondering what she would do if he seized her in his arms and buried his lips in the tantalising fold of that precarious neckline.

'I expected the house to be full of mastiffs—three

pups can create quite a bit of mayhem over an amazingly large area.'

'They are too boisterous, and need far more exercise than we can give them. Of course the children adore them, but Jean-Luc can't walk them so it's left to the groom, and they're a little too much even for him. He's not as young as he used to be.'

'You need a man about the place,' he agreed, then stopped at her expression and laughed. 'Have no fear! I wasn't applying—not for your groom's position, at least.'

'And what position did you have in mind? Then, at a cough from Annemarie, 'Don't answer that!'

There was a moment of silence as their eyes met, and his smile died. 'You're the only woman I know,' he stated softly, 'who can walk for miles through icy streets, wear herself to a shade by helping filthy, lice-ridden paupers whose existence no one else will even acknowledge, and emerge at the end of the day, utterly beautiful.'

Blanche felt the deep warmth inside as his eyes caressed her as surely as if he had reached across that small space and touched her. She gave a small cough. 'The . . . the pups . . . will have to go to a good home.'

'There is one waiting.' Then he did reach out to take her hand. 'Blanche, you need a rest from London, from all that you went through today. My brother Hector and his wife have an ancient house just outside Brighton in the middle of the Downs, modestly named Hunterton Hall. They have an assortment of dogs from every breed imaginable, and the pups would simply join the pack. There's a New Year's Ball each year, quite an affair with a dozen of their closest friends and a hundred or so . . . what you would call butterflies . . . all intent on meeting as many beautiful strangers as possible. Why not come with me? We can take the dogs down next week—or even before—the day after tomorrow.'

He smiled persuasively, noting the softness of the

hand still resting in his. 'Why not? Fresh air, quiet
evenings, early mornings with a gallop on the Downs.
They have a fine hunter that would prove even your
mettle.' He knew by the gleam in her eyes that he
had said the very words that would stimulate her
interest, for there was only one interest in Blanche's
life greater than her love of meeting strangers, and
that was her love of horses.

She felt those warm strong hands cradling her own,
his thumb moving almost absentmindedly across her
palm, sending rivulets of fire up her arm. Carefully
she withdrew her hand and straightened her gown,
even though it had not moved. 'I . . . don't
know . . .'

'You accompany me into the devil's own play-
ground without hesitation, and now you're afraid of a
few days with my family! They won't attack you, and
neither shall I . . . Unless you wish it so.'

'I'm not afraid!' she shot back. 'I was simply
thinking of all there was to do here.' But they both
knew she was lying.

'I think it's an excellent idea,' put in Annemarie.
'The house will run itself, and Those People will not
starve for a few days without you. I'll tell the others.
Cook, at least, will be glad to lose the dogs, she can't
leave a thing out, edible or otherwise.' She rose
animatedly, then hesitated, suddenly remembering
her self-imposed duty as chaperon.

'Oh, go!' smiled Blanche. 'Very well, Jason. I'll
come with you, and leave you to make all the
arrangements. However, you'll have to leave now, or
Annemarie's diplomacy will be sorely tried.'

He rose with an answering smile of acceptance
and, relieved, the Frenchwoman left to break the
news.

'I gained the distinct impression' said Blanche, 'that
I was being given little choice,'

'For your own good!'

She, too, had risen and turned to face him, causing
the gown to swirl out around slender thighs. 'Now,

just a minute . . .' One hand came up in protest, then connected with that broad chest and the rippling muscles beneath.

His eyes had turned to the green of the deepest forests, and just as mysterious. 'One day, Blanche Davenport,' he promised feeling those slender fingers tremble just a little, their touch burning through the fine linen shirt. One day, he vowed, I'll teach you the meaning of the passion that's in you. His eyes moved to the taunting line of the wrap-over bodice and the tempting swell beneath it, the desire was a volcano within him, a volcano that in a minute more . . . 'I must go!' His voice was thick with the effort it took him to leave her there.

Blanche watched him stride out to his carriage, and found herself trembling. She had seen men look at her like that before, controlling the naked lust in their eyes, but not until tonight had it affected her in the least, not until tonight had something leaped within her to meet the fire in a man's eyes. For the briefest instant there had come the thought that if he had torn that gown from her . . .

'No! I'll not think of it!' she stated aloud determinedly, and closed the door on him, and on her forbidden thoughts.

CHAPTER EIGHT

JASON ARRIVED EARLY on Boxing Day, so early that Blanche was still at breakfast. Unperturbed, she waved a hand toward the table before her on which were arranged soft crabs on toast, pancakes filled with crab and mushrooms and topped with cream sauce, and pears with brandy and cream. 'You could not possibly have eaten to have arrived at such an unholy hour! I hate to hurry food, so I suggest you help yourself.'

He unfastened the loops and frogs on his long Polish greatcoat, and approached the table. 'Do you always breakfast as well as this?'

Blanche poured out coffee for both of them. 'Always. I frequently find myself too busy to stop at midday, and have taken to dining at any totally uncivilised hour from six onward. Did you enjoy your Christmas?'

He helped himself to one of the savoury pancakes and took an appreciative bite before answering slowly. 'I don't know . . . I had much to think about. A hard gallop on the Heath cleared my head, but the horse undoubtedly gained more from it than I. Still, more of that later. And you?'

Blanche gave a smiling shake of the head. 'I'm as uncertain as you. I'm accustomed to spending Christmas Day alone, not wishing to intrude on my friends for what is essentially a family affair; though I have gone to the Fitz-Hughs' for an hour after supper when the children are abed. This year, however, I seem to have acquired some sort of family of my own . . . one mother, two children, three dogs . . .

and four servants who, until this year, I had thought to be quite sane!' She finished her coffee, and rose, patting the stiff folds of the pelisse-robe into place. 'Do you know any reason at all to rise at five-thirty on a day when one needn't rise at all?'

Jason gave a sympathetic smile. 'Put it down to experience. I have never, fortunately, been blessed with the chatter of children, but I understand it's something that grows on one.'

Blanche gave him a glare. 'So do measles! Are you ready, or would you like that last, lost lonely crab?'

'Well . . . put like that . . .'

Already she was ringing for Annemarie, who appeared as if she had been waiting outside the door with her mantle and white leather gloves from the stand. 'I've packed for all events, so I do hope you've not brought the curricle.'

'I have a fairer knowledge of women than that! Since we're going for a week, I assumed you would pack for a month. Riall will exercise the blacks while we're away and cut quite a dash in the Park, no doubt; he's almost as black as they are.'

'Your gypsy-looking friend?'

'Neither gypsy nor friend. I found him in a back alley in Marseilles when he attempted to plant a stiletto in my ribs. I convinced him that I could be of more use to him alive and with purse intact. He still prefers the blacks to me!'

Blanche gave him a long look, not doubting his story in the least. There was a lethal quality beneath the suave exterior that could not be brushed aside, as she was accustomed to brushing aside any men who might present the slightest impediment to her independence. 'There has been the odd moment or two when I might have appreciated his point of view! However, just now—and after yesterday—I'm willing to call a truce and accept . . . gladly accept . . . a few days of late mornings and early nights, but I never did ask whether your brother and sister-in-law would welcome a strange female in their midst. It is one thing to find the extra body—or ten—at a ball, but quite another to entertain a stranger for the preceding week.'

'And you wouldn't wish them to think there was an ulterior motive in my introducing you?'

'Neither them, nor you.' She hesitated at the door, and the cool grey eyes regarded him levelly, but then as she searched that ruggedly handsome face which had disturbed too many of her nights and most of her days, her expression changed. The coolness vanished, and a certain questioning brought a flicker of a frown to her brow. 'I wonder if I should have accepted your invitation at all—for whatever reason,' she mused.

Jason gave a nod, unsmiling. 'I've wondered about that, too. I asked you without motive, that I promise you. Since then . . . I'd be a fool or a liar or both if I didn't confess to a certain amount of soul-searching.'

'The ride on the Heath?'

'And others like it.' He took her hand in both of his, upturned it and studied the palm. Quietly, so quietly that she had to lean forward to hear, he stated, 'Any man who fell in love with you, Blanche Davenport, would be a fool!' Her breath stopped as he gave a crooked smile, raising those strange multi-hued green eyes to hers, holding her gaze for several seconds before releasing her hand and stepping away, physically putting a space between them, and then he smiled—that flashing smile that had caused more than one female heart to pound. 'I'll take my chances, if you will. Shall we see what a week in each other's company achieves? Shall we tempt the Fates, and defy them to do their worst?'

Blanche brought her erratic pulse under control with some difficulty. 'It'll be no more than I've always done. Shall we go?'

They said brief goodbyes to Annemarie, certain that the house would be run equally as smoothly whether Blanche were there or not, and went out to where John waited. The two horses were sturdy bays of just over fifteen hands with powerful haunches and broad chests that would undoubtedly pull the heavy travelling carriage as if it were a gig. Carefully Jason settled Blanche into her seat, arranging the voluminous mantle so that she was totally covered from the neck downward.

'It will take us over three hours to reach Hector's, and this icy wind won't be kept out entirely by the hood.'

'Oh, I think we'll be warm enough.' Blanche smiled, curling her fingers into the unfashionably large fur-lined muff. 'It's poor John I feel sorry for.'

'He'll be thoroughly spoiled when he arrives, so doesn't mind so very much. The journey will pass remarkably quickly, you'll see.'

He was right, of course, and Blanche, with her custom of flitting from one party to the next, held him enthralled with her knowledge of political and social gossip, and amused with her anecdotes. He watched the lovely animated features change and change again with the content of the story, the grey eyes sparkling, her lips moistened with tongue-tip, and white teeth flashing as she laughed aloud at her own mimicry of pedantic statesmen and pompous peers. They stopped briefly to rest the horses at a coaching inn, and her frank appreciation of the large wedge of cheese with hot fresh bread and tankard of mulled ale brought a blush of pleasure to the innkeeper's swarthy features.

'You can't help it, can you?' remarked Jason. 'You have to capture hearts wherever you go.'

Blanche regarded him in surprise, searching for the humour that was not to be found in his tone. 'Does that bother you? I am what I am, and can't see any reason at all for not making people feel an inch taller than they are: it takes so little effort!'

'Perhaps that is what bothers me. When so little effort is involved, I can't help but wonder at the sincerity behind it. Your ability to flatter without thought or concern for the consequences nearly ended

Jeremy's life—or mine . . .' But he stopped in mid-flow as he saw the shock in her eyes—eyes that a moment ago had been so alive with laughter. 'Blanche, I'm sorry! I didn't mean . . .'

'Yes, you did!' Agitatedly she rose, her food only half eaten. 'I think we should go now . . . lest the innkeeper call you out for sitting too close to me!' Her words were cutting, but there was deep hurt mingled with the anger in her eyes and he could only follow her out to the waiting carriage. John helped her inside, and when Jason would have settled her mantle about her, she pulled it aside. 'I can manage well enough, thank you.'

There was a heavy silence for several miles, Blanche too upset by his accusation and Jason at a loss as to how best to repair their friendship. Then the carriage hit a deep rut in the road, and she was thrown hard against him. Instinctively his arms went round her in protection, and just as instinctively, as her head was thrown back, he kissed her. It was a hard, almost savage, kiss that shook them both. 'I'm not going to fall in love with you!' he growled and kissed her again, taking her breath away, punishing her for her beauty, her charm, her easy laughter, and the way she had of making everyone fall in love with her.

Even then she surprised him, for instead of anger, tears, recriminations when released, she simply sat back against the upholstery and regarded him for several seconds, only her heightened colour betraying her emotion; then those mist-grey eyes softened, and the tiniest smile touched her mouth. 'I'm glad of that, for it means we can work at being friends again. Love is such a time-consuming emotion, don't you think?'

He could not help laughing, and shook his head in disbelief. 'You're like no other woman I've met. I insult you, hurt you, almost ravish you, and you still talk of being friends!'

'An almost is a long way from the final deed, and as for insulting me . . . It's true I wasn't expecting such an accusation and you were wrong, of course, for I had spoken to Jeremy only ever as a friend. When I realised that he was so jealously infatuated, I told him quite clearly that I couldn't countenance that kind of a relationship with anyone. I swear to you, Jason, that I've never deliberately hurt anyone, and my flirtations have always been started with both thought and concern for the consequences. I've never broken up a marriage that did not already have a crack in it, or encroached on another's territory. I regret the incident at the race, but I can't feel that it was entirely my fault.'

'And the way I hurt you? Am I forgiven that, too?'

'If I didn't . . .' she hesitated, fighting commitment, 'care for you . . . just a little . . . as a friend . . . I couldn't have been hurt.'

'As a friend?'

She did not attempt to evade his eyes, but with great deliberation said, 'I think you should tell me about your family.'

Jason took a deep breath, and capitulated. 'My mother, as you may have heard, was French, and extremely aristocratic.' He laughed at her startled glance, repeating, 'Extremely.'

'I . . . see . . .'

'No, you don't! She was an actress at the Comédie Française, and what an actress! My father was a rake, but an exceedingly rich rake, attending the Comédie while on holiday in Paris, and after the performance he went backstage and bought her.'

'Jason, you're trying to shock me!'

'Very well. Allow me to rephrase it. He admired the barely-clad body and fell in love with the quite brilliant mind—apparently instantly, for he took her from there that very night and brought her to England, paying her a quite exorbitant sum to convince his father, my grandfather, that she was the Duchesse de Gevereau—and his intended.' Deliberately he turned to look out of the window, a slight smile intimating the laughter within as he awaited her response.

'Jason, you can't leave me there!' Then, as those laughing jade eyes swung to her face, 'Tell me!'

'Well, from what I understand, my grandfather fell in love with her equally as precipitously, and she and my father were married in a quite embarrassingly short time. Society accepted the beautiful, extremely aristocratic duchess—I mean . . . one can tell blue blood, can't one?—and I was born eight months later . . . obviously due to her riding so enthusiastically! Hector was far more decent . . . he is three years younger than I!'

Over-riding her burst of laughter, he told her with an insight born of love of his quieter brother who openly adored his tiny dark-haired wife Rebecca, who, in spite of her Lilliputian size, ruled Hunterton Hall and its army of servants with a rod of iron. 'Becky is a real martinet,' he smiled. 'And it's not the first time assorted crockery has been hurled at some lazy servant's head. On the other hand, she travels all over Sussex on charity-raising sorties, and woe betide any affluent landowner who doesn't give generously!' He gave Blanche a considering look. 'You and she will undoubtedly get along famously.'

Blanche chose to ignore that. 'Children?'

'Unfortunately, no. I say "unfortunately" only because it is the one thing they both want more than anything else in the world. Becky is nearly thirty now, so I doubt that there is much hope . . .' Then he smiled. 'For heaven's sake don't tell her I revealed her age, or she'll take a hairbrush to my head! Now, as for the house . . .'

Blanche loved Hunterton Hall on first sight, even though her true taste was more oriented to the simplicity of the Greeks. The creeper-covered manor house bore no resemblance at all to its original medieval structure, for a series of owners had added a Gothic tower at each end, a huge glass conservatory that reached to the second floor at the back, and a wide porch supported by clematis-covered columns. The house was a mongrel, and bore no air of apology for the fact.

Almost before the carriage had stopped, a man who could have been none other than Jason's brother appeared at the front door and with a shout ran down the wide steps and across the shingled drive. 'Jay! You're early! I hardly expected you before mid-afternoon!'

His hair was as black as Jason's, but the eyes that appraised Blanche with unfeigned appreciation were a rich dark brown. If anything, Blanche assessed, he was more handsome than his brother, but as introductions were made she found that Hector's hands were soft, and the face that she smiled up into had not been lived in. Jason had experienced all facets of life, the good and the bad, but the man before her had always been loved and pampered and rich after the death of his 'extremely aristocratic' mother ten years before, following her husband by less than a year—a husband she had loved so completely that her life had virtually ended with his. Yet there was an open candour and warmth about Hector that Blanche found endearing, so that when he offered his arm, she took it unhesitatingly.

Jason heard his brother's laugh ring out as he led this lovely stranger into the great hall of the house, and he smiled. 'Just can't help it, can you?' he murmured, but there was no recrimination there.

In the large square hall they were met by Rebecca, and Blanche knew that even if Jason had not told her of the woman's character, she would have made the same instant assessment. The very way that tiny bundle of dynamite moved, positively marching across the hall, hand extended, the way she carried her head, tilted to one side, a little like a bright-eyed robin, and the voice!

'How do. You must be Jason's White Lady. Prettier than I imagined. Positively beautiful.' She took

Blanche's hand in a strong grip, and gave a wide grin. 'Still . . . that's not your fault! You're the first Jason's brought home, so that makes you all right.' Then, when Blanche found herself at a loss for words, she continued with a laugh, 'You're shocked. Good! May as well accept that we're all mad here, even the servants.'

'Leave her some sense of reality,' came Jason's deep voice behind her.

Blanche turned laughing eyes to his. 'You said I'd like her!' Then, to the tiny woman, 'I wasn't at all sure about coming this morning, but now I'm very very glad I did.'

A plump and beaming housekeeper had appeared as they spoke, and two servants with the luggage. 'This is our Mrs Benson. She'll show you to your room. I'd do it myself, but I like to make her feel important.'

'Really, my lady!' the woman protested, yet Blanche had seen the grins they exchanged, and gave a laughing shake of the head. This was definitely her kind of 'family'! At the top of the wide, curving staircase, Mrs Benson turned to the right and opened a door in the west tower, preceding Blanche into a large airy room in which a log fire cast a warm glow. 'Your baggage will arrive in the shake of a lamb's tail, my lady,' she announced cheerfully. 'I'll send up your maid right away. Will you be taking a bath, or just a wash? For the one you'll wait for ever, and for the other you'll either have to break the ice on the water they'll bring, or you'll scald yourself.' There was no disrespect in her tone, and her advice was delivered with a sure knowledge of below-stairs staff.

'I'll just wash for now, but perhaps you'd be good enough to arrange for a bath before dinner? Does that give you enough time?'

'You're a real diamond, my lady. We'll do very well together, I can tell.' With a nod and a smile, but no bobbed curtsy or request to leave, she vanished, and Blanche gave a low chuckle. She hated false obsequiousness in servants, but had never been in a house, apart from her own, where they were so outspoken. Still smiling as she removed her bonnet and mantle, she looked about her.

The room, being in one of the towers, was a spacious, hexagonal chamber with all walls at odd angles, three of them containing tall windows that revealed breathtaking views of the rolling South Downs. Blanche went to kneel on one of the window seats and threw open the window to let in the crisp air, drawing a satisfied breath. For the first time she allowed the peace and quietude seep into her.

'Just for a few days,' she murmured, realising just how much the continuous round of parties had taken out of her, not to mention the stress of playing the White Lady—with bright smile and breaking heart!

A light tap at the door admitted two large and ruddy-faced boys who could have been brothers, and a plump young woman carrying a water jug. The brothers set down her trunk, hat-box and valise, and the woman put the jug beside a matching washbasin on the marble topped stand before asking, 'Is there anything you'd like me to unpack first, your ladyship?' Then, 'Well, don't just stand there gawking!' without pausing for breath, so that for one incredulous second Blanche thought it was her the maid had addressed rather than the two boys, who promptly disappeared. Containing a giggle, Blanche coughed and shook her head. 'No. No, I'll decide what to wear later.'

While she washed, the maid bustled to and fro, hanging dresses and carefully folding underthings into drawers, exclaiming softly over lace-trimmed chemises and pantalets.

'That one. Yes, that's the one I'll wear,' Blanche instructed, as the girl lifted out a full-skirted day dress with full hanging sleeves caught up at the elbow. 'The one with the large sleeves, and those slippers with the rosettes.'

She allowed the girl to help her to dress, but insisted on doing her own hair, and when the maid had gone, she gave herself a few minutes to explore the room and the adjoining boudoir, a fantasy of blue and gold, the blue matching that of the bedroom, the curtains at the long window edged with gold, a delicate gilt escritoire set out with paper and envelopes holding the Hunterton crest. 'Modesty, modesty!' smiled Blanche, and turned to make her way downstairs.

As she approached the slightly open door of the drawing-room, she heard Rebecca ask, 'So you don't trust her, then?' Jason replied, 'I trust her with my life, but I'll not endanger hers.'

Blanche gave a frown as she pushed open the door, not at all happy at his tone, but the moment she entered, Rebecca crossed to meet her with outstretched hands.

'My dear Lady Davenport!' She took Blanche's hands in a warm clasp that was quite impossible to resist.

'Won't you call me Blanche, since everyone else is on first-name terms?' But it was to Jason that her eyes had turned, and she felt the tiniest leap of her heart as he left his brother by the roaring fire to cross to her side with a deceptively languid stride.

'Forgive my state of undress,' he said, gesturing back to where the velvet trimmed petersham frock-coat lay across the back of an armchair. He wore strapped pantaloons and a shawl-type waistcoat in cashmere, the 'mail-coach' neckcloth almost hiding the frilled shirt. It was not, however, the casual elegance of the outfit that caused her heart to skip a beat but the breadth of the chest and shoulders beneath it and the look in the jade green eyes as they moved over her face. 'So . . . once again you venture on to my territory, Blanche!' he smiled as he led her to the fire.

'At no little danger to life and limb, apparently,' she said with forced lightness. 'Forgive me, but I overheard such a statement the instant before I came in, since the door was ajar.' She caught their exchanged glances, and felt a little prickle at the nape of her neck. 'Won't you enlighten me, Jason?'

He looked uncomfortable, but then cleared his throat and began obliquely, 'On the sixteenth of October 1793, Marie-Antoinette of France went to the guillotine, leaving a fifteen-year-old daughter, Marie-Thérèse, and an eight-year-old son. Madame Royale remained in prison throughout the Revolution, and was released in December 1795 in exchange for some French prisoners held by the Austrians. She married the eldest son of the Comte d'Artois, who renounced his right to the throne three years ago when his father abdicated. The Dauphin, it was said, contracted tuberculosis during his incarceration in the Temple, and died at the age of ten.'

Jason hesitated, and Rebecca put in, 'If the Dauphin had lived, he would be forty-eight now.' There was a note of subdued excitement in her tone, which caused Blanche's heart to quicken its beat. 'There have been a number of Pretenders over the years, each claiming to be the Dauphin, and almost to a man they've been destroyed by either force or fact. We know that, thanks to a calculated regime of terror and cruelty, the young child was turned into a depraved slanderer of his mother and sister, a blasphemer, and taught moral values worse than those of the lowest peasant.'

Blanche ventured, 'But you don't believe he's dead?' Then, incredulously, 'Why . . . You actually believe that the Dauphin of France is still alive . . . a contender for the throne of France! That can't be possible! Not after so long . . .'

Jason turned to look into the flames. 'No. A child did die on the eighth of June, though not the Dauphin, that I'm certain. I'm equally certain that the Dauphin is now dead; that he died in a hospital for paupers in Paris, declared insane, decried as one of the many who laid claim to the title of Dauphin.' He gave a deep sigh. 'I was there on a mission of mercy—five years ago, you understand. This old, old man, broken by the life he had led, white-haired at only forty-three, convinced me that he spoke the truth. He also begged me to find his son . . . the grandson of Marie-Antoinette and Louis XVI of France. He had fallen in love with a gypsy girl during his life of enforced poverty, and married her four years before we spoke. She bore him a child, but vanished a year later, returning to her own people and taking the child with her. I gave him my word that I'd do all in my power to trace the only true king of France.'

'An unknown gypsy child?' Blanche asked in amazement. 'Somewhere—perhaps in France—perhaps alive?'

'The baby, a boy of almost ten now, had a birthmark, a large red circle on the back of his left hand.'

'But what makes you so certain that this man was the Dauphin?' she asked, still unable to believe in so fantastic a story.

The jade eyes went to that terrible place, to the bedside of that strangely lucid old man. 'He remembered things—small, apparently unimportant things—being given a box of dominoes made from de Launcey's marble mantelpiece when the mob tore down the Bastille, picking flowers in the Tuileries garden . . . Happy memories . . . and others not so happy . . . memories too terrible to repeat here.' Then she saw a muscle leap in his jaw, as grimly he finished, 'And then within six months of my making enquiries, there was an attempt on my life. In the years since, there have been others . . . which is why I wish you hadn't heard my ill-timed remark from outside the door, and why you must forget everything I've said.'

Ignoring his last command, Blanche asked, 'Yet you work around the docks, when I should have expected you to be searching among the itinerant gypsy bands that come over from Europe and roam all over England?'

Jason gave a mirthless smile. 'I can attempt that in

France because all the tribes eventually find their way to Paris, but to come to England they first have to make the crossing, do they not?'

'And pass through the docks, where you have friends, like Annemarie, who are your eyes and ears!'

Rebecca put a hand over hers. 'Please forget it now, Blanche. You are our guest, and I won't have you taking our worries on to your shoulders.'

'That's right,' Jason agreed. 'We are here for a well-earned rest, and I for one intend to treat it as such.' Deliberately he turned the conversation into safer channels until it was time to change for dinner.

They ate simply, the table set *à la Russe* with the various dishes set around a central arrangement of flowers and vines, for everyone to help themselves. Being so near the coast, there was a variety of fresh fish as the first course, the rich oxtail soup being removed by fillet of sole, with a choice of shoulder of cod and stewed eels. The second course consisted of ham with a mustard and orange sauce, with tongue and roast chicken as alternatives, and finally plum pudding and mince pies, cream and jelly, with a bowl of fruit and a selection of cheese.

'What is the programme for tomorrow, Jay?' asked Hector. 'Will you take the gig out and show Blanche the countryside?'

Jason caught Blanche's eye. 'No, I think I'll introduce her to Saladin.'

'Saladin? Are you sure? He's a bit of a handful at this time of the year: doesn't get half enough exercise over the winter.'

Blanche had felt a small surge of excitement, but kept her voice level as she suggested, 'Then perhaps I could rectify that.'

Jason nodded agreement. 'Don't worry, Hector! My lady's equestrian skills are legend . . . though I must confess I've only heard the legend!' He winced as Blanche's square-toed shoes clipped his shin, but then laughed and continued the conversation on the subject of the Hunterton blood-stock until late in the evening.

'I can't remember a more entertaining dinner,' Hector enthused when at last Blanche announced her desire for her bed. 'You really do know your horses, Blanche. You must come down when we go to the auction.' Then he hesitated, as if unsure whether he should have invited her without first consulting his brother.

But immediately Blanche accepted. 'I'd love to, Hector!' Then, with a sideways glance at the smiling man to her left, 'Perhaps I'll even bring Jason!'

'Don't need to,' stated Rebecca with an affectionate punch at her brother-in-law's shoulder. 'All that interests him in a filly is performance,' then, realising her *double-entendre*, blushed, causing general laughter.

Blanche took pity on her. 'Well at least this Saladin of yours will give him some competition tomorrow. What shall you be riding, Jason, that can keep up with me?'

'You'll see,' he promised, but would say no more.

That night, as Blanche snuggled deep into the thick blankets, feeling the tease of the lace-edged pillow against her cheek, she turned to look past the rich velvet curtains to the deeper velvet of the night sky outside the window, and gave a sigh of content. For the first time in many weeks there was no sound, no clip-clop of horses' hooves on the street outside, no restless chatter of servants, or the fretful whimper of young Fleur who still had not fully accepted that her father would not return to beat her. Blanche allowed her thoughts to drift. Dark eyes of a strange jade green and sage, a mobile mouth that could laugh so easily . . . No . . . mustn't concentrate on the mouth . . . hands? Strong, lean, brown hands, totally in contrast to the limp-wristed, fashionably pale appendages of the day. Hands that could control a team of horses without chafing their delicate mouths, kill a lion-necked mastiff . . . and yet . . . No, not the hands, either. 'Damn you, Jason!' she murmured, as she drifted into sleep.

The house was awake early, yet still not as early as Blanche, who had slept very little. She donned a habit of bleached waterproof zephyr cloth with a many-buttoned corsage and huge gigot sleeves. Her tight pantaloons, revealed by the looped-up skirt, were tucked into shining black boots, their spurs glinting.

'What kept you?' queried Jason as she came into breakfast, and she made a pretty grimace at him before helping herself to a generous portion of ham and eggs, a sausage, kidneys and bacon.

Rebecca arrived within minutes, revealing a bird-like appetite totally at odds with her pleasingly plump proportions.

'She sneaks food into her room like a child,' Jason whispered with a conspiratorial wink. 'Well?' as they finished their meal. 'Shall we earn our keep and go to exercise these two rocking-horses?'

Anything, Blanche realised with a surge of deep pleasure, anything less like rocking-horses than the two descendants of Bucephalus led out for them could not have been imagined. Saladin, as black as the highly polished ladies' saddle he carried, sported a diamond-shaped white blaze on the broad forehead, and was slightly shorter than his stable companion, though still a fraction over sixteen hands. Powerful quarters would make him a good jumper, and the deep girth with well-arched ribs would give plenty of lung expansion for endurance, with the added advantage of wide-open nostrils to suck in the last ounce of rarefied air. 'He's a beauty!' whispered Blanche. 'A blue-white diamond!'

But her eyes were already assessing the larger animal, standing all of seventeen hands with a deep chest that would enable him to run for days and barely feel winded, sloping, laid-back shoulders that would lengthen the stride to eat up the miles, and a

proudly arched neck, denoting Arab blood. Too
heavy for a true Thoroughbred, he yet exuded power
and a certain aristocracy in his structure that would
make any other horse pale into insignificance. He was
a strawberry-roan, and in the rising sun he gleamed
red as fire.

'I raised Firebird from a foal,' Jason stated with
quiet pride, offering the expected chunk of apple to
the questing lips. 'It's to him I return after months
abroad or to escape the poverty and pestilence of the
London slums.' Then, as if afraid of revealing too
much of himself he gave her a disarming smile. 'Very
well, my lady. Let's ride!'

And ride they did, the horses almost matched,
eating up the miles, occasionally taking a low hedge
or gate in their stride and once racing flat out for a
distant windmill. Finally, regretfully, he called, 'We
should be getting back, or we'll miss lucheon, and
Becky will never forgive me. She's taken quite a
liking to you . . . It's unusual for her to find a kindred
spirit.'

They turned their mounts and headed back, holding
the animals to a gentle canter, a decision which
pleased the black not at all and he fought the bit
restlessly. 'Saladin's tireless,' Blanche laughed, holding
him easily. 'He's as eager to run as he was this
morning. I think he'd go all day, given the chance!'

'I know the feeling: when I get out here, it takes a
considerable effort of will to turn back.'

'One more run, then. I can see the towers of the
Hall from here. What is it? A mile and a half . . .
two miles . . . with nought but a few insignificant
hedges in the way? I'll race you to the stables.'

His eyes gleamed. 'The same stakes as before? The
same prize I won from you last time?'

Her colour was high, and only partly due to the
crisp breeze. 'This time, I'll win,' was all she said,
and without warning dug in her spurs. The black gave
a snort and from a standing start plunged ahead into

a flat gallop, those powerful hindquarters thrusting up and out into a great leap that left the roan standing.

'She-devil!' Jason laughed, and kicked his mount into pursuit, almost . . . almost loving her for her spirit.

He knew that the black was built for speed and the roan for endurance, but he could still admire the courage—the almost suicidal courage—of the woman who put her mount at hedges without slowing his pace and rode at an equally breakneck speed uphill or down. Her hat flew off, and her hair was torn free of its pins by the playful wind, streaming out behind her as she bent low over the black's neck, and he knew that she was calling to the animal, urging him on, even though he could not see her face.

They were in sight of the stables and the black was tiring, yet Blanche knew that they would win. The thunder of hooves behind her was close, but not close enough. There was the drive, the avenue of elms, the open doors . . . and with the tiniest smile Blanche pulled hard at the left rein.

Jason saw the black break stride, saw her lean in and tug at the rein, and then he was past and had reached the stable forecourt. He swung down, and had reached for her as she pulled to a halt in a slither of stones. 'Why, you little . . .' And then she was in his arms, laughing, mischievous, breathless, and he kissed her long and hard. When finally he released her, they were both quieter, each searching the other's eyes. 'What shall I do with you, woman?' he asked, only half jokingly, but she flushed.

'Take me into luncheon?' she suggested, feeling warmed by his low chuckle, glad that he had not pursued the matter. Oh, Blanche! she whispered, soul to soul. Don't care! Please don't care too much!

CHAPTER NINE

OVER THE NEXT few days it seemed that the Fates conspired against her, for however hard she tried to avoid being alone with Jason it invariably ended that way. If she sought Rebecca's company, there was always a servants' squabble to resolve, and Hector seemed determined to gain a sister-in-law!

'It seems incredible,' he had begun, 'that one as lovely and vibrant as yourself has never married. It can't be for the want of proposals! I've heard that several young blades have declared they'd gladly die for you.'

Blanche had given him a sidelong glance and a tiny smile. 'I'd be far more complimented if they'd said they'd live for me.' Then, in her usual forthright manner, 'Of course I've had offers, Hector, but no one has offered me any more than I have now. I've a minor inherited title and adequate funds. I have the companionship of good friends, and gifts from admirers who will take me anywhere I wish to go. I have a house of my own—admittedly bought by a father who acquired a sense of guilt a little too late for it to earn him forgiveness—and I can be of service to those who need me. Tell me, if you can, what more a husband can provide . . . and please don't mention children! I'm not in the least interested in providing the world with a poor replica of either myself or anyone else I've so far met, and if I wish to hear squalling, I can go to Scotland and hear the pipes!'

Hector had chewed on his own pipe and not

pursued the subject further, but since then had done all in his power to promote the institution of marriage.

'It's all right for him,' thought Blanche, half-angrily. 'Rebecca wants nothing more from life than to spend the rest of it at Hunterton Hall and, apart from this annual ball, cares for no entertainment but what the family and a few close friends provide. I'm as different as chalk from cheese. I'd die in one place without outings, the theatre, and balls at least once a month, and I'm sure even Jason would pall if I had to look at him across the same table day after day.'

Regarding him now, however, she accepted that it might take a great number of days before she tired of drinking in those ruggedly handsome features. Hector was relating an amusing anecdote about their twin younger cousins who had met Jason for the first time. 'They were very much young men about town,' he laughed. 'Real broad coves who had no intention of losing face. They approached Jay with dignity and respect—though not obsequiousness, you understand.'

Blanche nodded. 'What you mean is they were petrified.'

'They were petrified!' Amid general laughter he went on with his tale, but Blanche was watching the way Jason's eyes changed colour and how the dark hair gleamed in the firelight. 'I think family ties are so important, don't you?' Hector was finishing. 'Even the most obnoxious members can furnish us with something—even if only a deeper pleasure in the others! What do you think, Blanche? I hear you have a younger brother. Do you never see him?'

'Never,' she stated flatly, not wishing to discuss the pain and emptiness of her childhood—ostracised by a father who wanted only a male heir, punished for her unfeminine intelligence and forthright manner, and eventually, in her mid-teens, sent to live with an aunt and uncle who never had nor wanted children of their own. It had been no comfort at the time that Alex, the Davenport heir, was a gay, lovable extrovert who openly adored her and even now found time to write at least once a month—even knowing it might be five or six months before she would reply.

Tactfully Jason changed the subject, and she threw him a grateful glance. One day, he reflected, she might trust him enough to tell him the whole story, but until then there were dark corners of the soul that they both felt the need to conceal. 'I have decided to write my memoirs,' he said with a grandiose gesture, 'dwelling especially on my innumerable conquests!'

'Ah,' Blanche nodded seriously. 'A work of fiction!'

'She has your measure,' grinned Rebecca, and the mood lightened again.

The days passed all too quickly, for Blanche had determined to return home the day after the ball, not from any desire to continue her crusade through St Giles, but simply because she found it difficult to concentrate on anything without a thought of Jason slipping in. It was against her character to play with anything she could not control—whether horses or emotions. It was time to stop the game . . . and yet . . .

That night before the ball she tossed and turned restlessly, aware that midnight had long struck and that she would have to take a nap after lunch if she was to look her best. With a sigh she rose and drew a white silk *peignoir* over her nightdress. Perhaps an hour with Byron—she had seen his work in the library—but not poor Childe Harold—too unhappy— too much of a fool. She had taken several steps into the library before she realised she was not alone.

'Another nocturnal wanderer,' he said softly, turning from the low embers of the fire.

She hesitated, realising that she was hardly dressed for company, and if any disturbed servants saw them so . . . 'I came only to borrow a book, not to stay.'

'Your character would undoubtedly be the subject of speculation should anyone else appear, even my matchmaking brother.' Although his tone was quite serious, the twitch at the corner of his mouth gave it the lie, and Blanche felt a delicious tingle down her spine.

'My character has always been the subject of speculation!' She smiled, coming to stand before the fire and spreading her fingers to the lingering warmth.

'You can't always fight society's rules.'

'I don't. I make my own!'

'And what does society have to say about that?'

'Strangely, it seems to enjoy it. At the very least I provide small talk at almost every party I leave. However,' she turned to look up at him, suddenly serious, 'I have a very great respect and more than a little affection for Hector and Rebecca, so their opinion means a great deal to me. For the others, I don't give a fig.'

'You know they have a future already planned for us.'

'I shall be sorry to disappoint them.'

'Would a future with me be so very impossible?'

Blanche felt her heart begin to pound. 'I . . . must go.' His fingers curled over her shoulder as she turned aside.

'Would it, Blanche?'

'Yes!' She faced him squarely, fighting both his magnetism and her own heart. 'A future belonging to any one man is impossible.'

'You lie, my lady!' He swung her to face him, and brought both hands to close over her arms. 'You're mine, and you know it,' he growled, the vice-like grip drawing her close. 'Whether you admit it or not, you can't lie to yourself.'

Blanche struggled half-heartedly, the splayed fingers that pushed against his chest wanting only to curl about the broad shoulders. 'No!' she reiterated. 'I belong to no one, nor ever shall! Let . . . me . . . go!'

Ignoring the flashing grey eyes, he read only the message in the voluptuous curves that moulded to his and the parted lips that ached to be kissed, and he swooped to capture them. For a moment out of time

he felt her respond eagerly, melt against him . . .
then:

'No!' She tore free, eyes brimming. 'Damn you,
no!' and spinning, ran to her room. 'I won't give in!'
she vowed, hurling the *peignoir* into the far corner,
following it with slippers and, in a final fit of self-
disgust at her own weakness, the pillow off the bed.
'I'll teach him! No man owns me. Nor ever shall!'

The following evening Blanche surpassed herself. She
wore her hair in a fantasy of basketwork on top of
her head that had taken an hour to create, with tiny
curling ringlets escaping from it to caress her ears and
neck, and adorned with seed-pearls. Her gown of
white brocade bespoke Paris, its low scooped neckline
dripping with rich Valenciennes lace that reached
almost to her elbows. A deep ruffle of lace also
bordered the wide skirt and was drawn up by bows of
silver ribbon, each with a pearl at its centre. Unlike
the other female guests weighed down with diamonds,
rubies and sapphires, she wore no jewellery at all,
and her ivory skin gleamed in the candlelight as she
made her way slowly downstairs. It would have been
noticed by only one that her head was possibly held a
little too high, her smile a fraction too bright, but he
was not in sight at her entrance, so it was achieved
with its usual *éclat*.

The great hall was ablaze with light, the twenty
long mirrors catching the brilliance of the candelabras
and reflecting them over and over on to the five
crystal chandeliers. The walls were festooned with
holly boughs and trailing ivy, as was the adjoining
salon, where several inscrutable gentlemen in claret
livery circulated with trays of champagne.

Rebecca saw her and hurried forward, reminding
Blanche of Alexandra Fitz-Hugh with her natural and
undemanding friendship. 'I've invited at least twenty
of the most handsome men in the county,' she
confided with a grin. 'Jason tells me you aren't in the
marriage market, so these are strictly for amusement.

adjourn to the small salon and have some champagne . . . and perhaps a touch of caviar . . . brought to us? We'll talk of Byron and Beethoven and other revolutionaries, and then we'll dance, and I'll realise a lifelong ambition to hold a moonbeam in my arms.'

Deliberately Blanche put her hand onto Edward's extended arm. 'I'd like that, Mr Courtney. I'd like that very much.'

Jason saw that gesture and his throat tightened, all thought of any other woman driven from his mind, but then his lips curved into a smile of its own volition. That ridiculous basketwork of hair would take an hour or more to untangle—interspersed with kisses as it would have to be—but, he reflected, the result would probably be worth every minute of it. Then he recognised her companion, and the smile died. Surely Becky would have told her who—and what—Teddy Courtney was? The boy's reputation as a highly paid gigolo was known throughout their society. It was also said that he had never harmed a lady physically or mentally and had always left them the richer—in all but money! Nevertheless, Blanche should be warned, and with a regretful adieu to the lady at his side he made his way across the room. Realising that they were heading for the small salon, he moved to intercept them as they reached the door.

Blanche had seen the manoeuvre—how could she not, when he was a head taller than most of the men there?—and kept her tone cool as she said, 'Good evening, Jason, I'm sure you know Edward Courtney . . . He has just offered to go to France to bring me back some vintage champagne.'

Jason could not resist asking, 'What kept him?'

'Why, I did! He obviously knows all the gossip about everyone here. Don't you, Mr Courtney?'

'At least about most of the ladies present,' Jason agreed, then saw the warning glint in her eyes.

With deceptive sweetness, she enquired, 'Was there more, Jason, or may we proceed?'

Not wishing a confrontation at this juncture, he

could do little but make a short bow and step aside,
and Edward Courtney drew a relieved breath. He
had already caught the white-hot lightning that had
flashed between these two, and was man-of-the-world
enough to recognise when two people were in love
and denying it with their entire beings! He therefore
spent the following hour keeping his beautiful
companion amused, enthralled . . . and at a distance.
There was much about Lord Hunterton that he knew
he should fear, a coldly feral quality behind that
smile that could be ignored only at his cost.

It was therefore almost expected that a soft voice
behind them should state, 'Enough, dear boy. Lady
Davenport has promised me this dance, though I'm
sure your company has driven it quite out of her
head.'

Blanche's eyes opened wide. 'A quadrille, sir? You
surprise me.'

'I assure you I can point a toe with the best.'

She turned to her watchful companion, feeling a
little guilty in accepting Jason's game. 'Forgive me,
Mr Courtney? Apparently I promised to watch Lord
Hunterton point a toe! I do hope we may continue
this fascinating conversation later.'

With murmured regrets Edward relinquished his
hold on her attention, watching the tell-tale stiffening
of her spine as she rose, adjusted the full skirts and
laid rigid fingers on the muscular arm, throwing a
sidelong glance at the man by her side, at the same
time questioning and challenging.

Wordlessly Jason led her into the hall, where
couples were forming into squares, laughing and
chattering like a flock of brilliantly-hued parakeets.
'Jason?' No word; and when her fingers would have
left his arm, an iron hand closed over them as he led
her, smiling and nodding into their midst and across
into the hall. 'Jason!'

'Be quiet, Blanche!' Only when he had thrown
open the door of the library, silent and empty, did he

turn, moving her to face him. 'Do you know what kind of a man Courtney is?'

Blanche bristled at his tone. 'An amusing, entertaining and extremely handsome one.'

'Don't be deliberately obtuse! He practises those skills well, and gets paid well for them.'

'Not by me!' she flashed back. 'Your own sister-in-law introduced us, and obviously had more faith in my level-headedness than you do. If I were in the market for either a husband or a lover I'd not choose Edward Courtney, but if I were, I should not seek your approval, either. Just who do you think you are?'

His eyes darkened, and a muscle leapt in the chiselled jaw. 'The fool that's in love with you—in spite of you, and certainly against my better judgment! No!' as she made to speak. 'Don't say anything . . . not a word! I don't need one of your *bons mots* just now. Hold your tongue for once, and come dance with me where everyone can see us.'

Blanche stared at him in amazement, reading the truth in his angry eyes, then swiftly lowered her gaze, concealing the sudden rush of emotion that swept through her, the flash-fire of a bursting volcano that began deep in her loins and shot upward to her heart. Yet, was it love? Her limbs felt weak, her heart pounded, she was aware of every muscular inch of him that was pressed against her. She knew that if he had said he desired her, if he had attempted to take her then and there, drawing her down on the rug, there might have been a chance that her own desires would have matched—even exceeded his . . . But love? Carefully she drew a deep, ragged breath. 'Jason?'

With equal care he set her gently away from him, forcing a brightness into his tone that cost him dear. 'I seem to have joined the throng, my lady. Should I now threaten to kill myself if you leave . . .' Only then did he take in the brimming, star-washed eyes raised to his.

'Don't . . . please don't! Jayce, I don't know my feelings. I've always been afraid of love, always avoided accepting or giving it with every instinct for self-preservation I have. If I love, I lose part of myself, and if I accept love, I take a responsibility I'm not sure I can cope with. Jason, I want you . . . You know that with all that devilish instinct you have for a woman's feelings . . . Yet even I don't know whether that is love.' She gave a choked laugh. 'You see, for all my reputation, I'm a very archaic woman. For me love is for ever . . . and even I know that love only lasts between the last hello and the first goodbye. I know that most women leave their husbands eventually . . . a few take their bodies with them . . . few take their whole mind. I don't know what I can afford to lose, Jason. It took too much of my childhood finding each tiny scrap of myself. I don't know whether I'm ready to let even one of those pieces go.'

Jason, in those few seconds, realised more of the kind of woman he held than he had ever realised before. Gently he cupped her face in his hands. 'Enough, my dear.' Light as a butterfly's touch, his lips brushed hers. 'You've learned a lot about Lord Hunterton and a little of Jayce Hunter. There is another you must become acquainted with, but not just now. They have started a waltz, which I'm told even the young Victoria disapproves of, so it should suit this gathering quite well. Apart from which it's only a short while to midnight, when masks will be removed and the New Year may officially take charge of all our insignificant dreams and hopes and plans. Take a breath . . . and hold it!'

In a strange floating kind of fantasy, Blanche accompanied Jason on to the dance floor. She heard no music, no laughter about them. In this suspension of feeling, where the reds seemed more red than ever before, the chandeliers purest blue-white diamonds, and voices drifted in from a great way off, she followed his every step, swayed at his lightest touch, dipped and spun, yet saw only his eyes . . . the deepest, most mysterious, jade.

Without warning, midnight struck, and the relieved drummer sounded a great tympanic roll. Amid laughter and cries of 'Happy New Year!', masks were removed and kisses exchanged.

Softly, 'Happy New Year, Blanche.'

'Happy New Year, Jason. May it bring you all you desire.'

'It already has, in some measure.' Then he kissed her, drawing her slowly, surely into his arms, moulding her body to his as his lips descended, gently exploring at first, then as the kiss deepened and he felt her response, sweeping aside all restraint and plundering with a passion that took her breath away. And it went on—and on. While other couples drew apart and the chatter and music recommenced they remained locked in that embrace oblivious to all about them, her fingers entwined about his neck, his arms crushing her against the hard length of him.

Blanche felt that she would surely faint as the world spun about her. Her lips parted and clung and returned kiss for kiss as that expert, sensual mouth plundered the inner recesses of hers, until a faint sound of clapping broke in upon them, and she felt him raise his head.

To her embarrassment, Blanche found Jason and herself the centre of attention. Only he appeared unperturbed—and only she had felt the shudder that ran through him—as with a laugh he begged, 'Bear with me, friends; after all, it's the first this year!' The crowd broke up with good-natured ribaldry and the band began playing again.

'Blanche, we must talk.'

By the time they reached the sanctuary of the library again, however, she had regained a little of her equilibrium. Before he could speak, she turned to lay a slender yet firm finger across his lips, not deigning to hide the tears that refused to fall. 'I think a long holiday is in order,' she whispered huskily.

'So do I,' he agreed, reading her eyes better than her mind. 'Where shall we go?'

'No . . . Not "we" . . . I. I need a time of re-assessment, an uninterrupted reviewal of my life.' Before he could put the disbelief, the instinctive stiffening of his frame, into words, she hurried on, 'I think the sooner the better. I need to get away. Oh, Jayce, please understand. Try! You've spoken of Paris, of searching for this boy king. I could help you, while still ensuring that our paths don't cross. There's an old friend of my mother, a Comtesse de Chauvenay, with whom she went to the same seminary, having been brought here as a baby with her mother, spirited over during the Terror. Brought up in London, the countess returned to marry and have a son of her own. She and my mother kept in constant touch, and occasionally she would request the pleasure of my company. Twice, I believe, she sent her son André, who is a little older than I, to holiday with my parents and my brother Alex. Alexander in turn visited them, of course.' Her tone changed, lowered, was not of the present. 'Of course! Yes . . . of course . . . And my father deemed my character past redemption at the time and would not consider the effect of it on Parisian high society. However,' and her chin came up, 'since my late father can voice no objection, I think I shall take up one of the countess's many invitations.'

Jason's jaw tightened. 'And those of the son, no doubt?'

'I know nothing of the young man, but as far as I'm concerned, I'm visiting a friend of my mother, an aristocrat and, therefore, surely, an ardent royalist. I shall have time away from your disruptive influence on my thoughts, and if this André can divert me for a while then, frankly, I shall welcome it.' She read again the hurt that cut as deep as a knife, begging, 'Jason, help me!'

He stiffened. 'Blanche, I thought I was the fool! I was wrong. When will you leave?'

'I'll return to London tomorrow, then take the steamer to France at the end of the week, having written to the countess. Will you see me home?'

'No.'

'Then when . . .?'

He took her hard by the arms. 'I won't let you free for long, I promise you.' She heard the diminishing murmur of departing guests and knew they should have been there. His hard fingers bruised her, but then he thrust her away. 'I shall come for you, Blanche. When you have this idiocy out of your mind and stop trying to run away from yourself, I'll come for you.' Abruptly he turned and walked from the room, not looking back.

'Jason?' But he was gone. A log fell into the dying embers, and a sliver of burning wood fell on the rug, which she tossed back on the instant. 'It's a good thing I was here,' she said aloud. Why was it then that her heart called it a lie?

CHAPTER TEN

As THE DAYS passed, the bitter-sweet leavetaking from Jason faded a little, though Blanche had kept herself in a state of perpetual motion and permanent exhaustion to achieve that end. At last there was a rough trip across the Channel by steamer which confined her in her bunk for the entire four hours, bending weakly over a basin and apologising to Ellen, the genial giantess she had hired as a maid and chaperon. Finally the bumpy, icy-cold journey in a hired berlin to Paris, so that by the time they reached their destination, Blanche wished she had not chosen such a totally uncivilised time of the year in which to travel.

The carriage drew up before a grey-walled house in the fashionable Faubourg St-Germain district, set well back from the road and almost hidden behind a tree-lined courtyard. At the driver's ring the front door was flung open—as if the occupants had been waiting behind it, and a plump little woman bustled out followed by two young men, both darkly handsome and obviously brothers. 'Welcome, Lady Davenport. I am Josette. Madame la Comtesse is expecting you in the salon.'

Thanking their driver, Blanche followed the housekeeper into a long, dark hall that appeared to bisect the house. The exterior of the house had appeared much like its neighbours', inside, however, there was an air of what Blanche could only call 'genteel poverty'; not dirt, for the rug-scattered wooden floor gleamed and the portraits of ancestors that hung on the panelled walls showed no trace of dust, yet the gilding, worn off the frames over the years, had not been replaced and the rugs showed signs of patching and re-patching. She was prepared, therefore, for her first sight of the grand salon as she was announced.

At a glance she took in the walls hung with tapestries, faded now, their emerald greens turned to sage, their crimsons to dusk rose, but exquisitely worked and vibrant in their portrayal of medieval battles and processions. It was, Blanche thought, more than a little uncharitable of her to wonder what cracks and holes they concealed.

Then, rising from an armchair by the great marble fireplace, a woman who could be none other than the Comtesse Marie-Josephine Victoire de Chauvenay, and Blanche knew that the reputation the French aristocracy had for indulgence bordering on gluttony was in dire need of re-assessment. The countess was tall, and as slender as a reed in spite of her years. The ebony hair was liberally streaked with grey and drawn off her high forehead into a plaited coronet, and her finely-arched eyebrows accentuated eyes of the deepest velvet brown and the slightly Roman nose. She would have looked the epitome of Parisian aristocracy—but for the full-lipped, too wide mouth that seemed permanently to hover on a secret little smile, as if she had seen the world for what it was and found it slightly comical.

'Lady Davenport! Welcome! I'm afraid your letter only arrived yesterday. It was, of course, time enough to prepare your rooms, but not, I regret, to arrange a welcome party of all the people you simply must meet. I have put your maid in the room adjoining yours rather than in the servants' quarters, so that she may be at your instant bidding.' Her voice was almost accentless, because of her English education, Blanche guessed, and had a slightly throaty quality. 'You will need a bath . . . Those terrible roads . . . Such a journey . . . and the weather! You are fortunate to arrive before the storm that is brewing.'

She took Blanche's hands, and smiled into her eyes. 'So at last we meet. I do hope we shall be friends.'

Her gaiety was infectious and Blanche felt the exhaustion drop away. 'I'm sure we shall, but only if you forget that I'm Lady Davenport. My friends call me Blanche.'

' "The White One." Ah, yes, I see. Then I must be Marie to you. Please, I will personally show you to your room. André will be here shortly. He is visiting friends, but will be back for supper. Your letter could not give a time of arrival, or he would have been here to welcome you.'

Still talking, she led Blanche to a room overlooking the small back garden, a large square room whose walls were almost covered by tapestries, more recently woven than those in the salon and mostly of animals, one in particular drawing Blanche's attention. 'Yes, that is my favourite, too,' Marie said. 'You'll meet the direct descendants of those dogs later. Now I shall leave you. Please take your time. Relax. I fully believe in living for today. There is simply no tomorrow.'

She left with a smile. However long or short Blanche's stay was to be, the countess had proved a warm and welcoming hostess, and she knew that the villa would give her the ideal retreat for the soul-searching she needed. 'I'll begin tomorrow,' she said aloud, then smiled as she remembered the countess's words.

By the time she descended to the grand salon it was almost nine o'clock. As she entered the room, Marie hurried to welcome her. 'Blanche, you are a picture worthy of Botticelli!' Turning, 'Isn't she, André? *Ma chère*, come and meet my handsome son.'

'Oh, treacherous butterfly!' thought Blanche as her heart skipped a beat.

He had been standing with one arm along the mantelshelf, whip thin, and everything that was opposite to Jason Hunterton! Crossing swiftly to meet her, André bent low over her hand as introductions were made, then slowly he raised thickly-lashed brown eyes to her face. 'My home is yours, Mademoiselle Blanche . . . and everything that is in it.'

'I'm very grateful, sir.'

At that moment supper was announced, and André extended an arm, first to Blanche and then to his mother. 'There is not a man in France . . . in the whole of Europe, I'd change places with now,' he smiled.

Blanche refused to be swept off her feet; she would have to come to terms with these fulsome compliments, she realised. French men were quite . . . different . . . if André was a true representative of his race, and she contented herself by returning his smile.

The smaller dining-room—'We keep the main hall for banquets'—was warmly panelled and glowed in the candlelight. The dark oak refectory-style table and matching chairs gleamed with a rich patina only achieved by years of loving care and attention. The house might be old and sadly in need of repair, Blanche reflected, but it showed no sign of neglect in any other way. The silver shone, the linen was white as snow and the furnishings, though faded, held not a speck of dirt. Why, then? Are they unaware of their surroundings? Marie's necklace alone would surely repair much of the crumbling walls?

It was a problem, however, that she gladly put aside as the light though mouth-watering meal was served, and the countess went into a detailed description of regional cooking that Blanche found utterly fascinating, enjoying food as she did. Her hostess appeared not to share her enthusiasm, moving her morsel of salmon quiche round her plate and taking minuscule nibbles until the table was cleared for the second course. As she talked away gaily, she finished only half her glass of dry white wine.

Blanche hid an internal groan of despair, realising how it was that Marie kept that superb greyhound figure. 'I'll never achieve such self-control!' Then she relinquished all hope, and allowed the maid to pour thick cream over the dessert of baked peaches stuffed with crushed almonds and cheese.

'I'll need a whole new wardrobe!' she cried to her maid that night. 'Oh, Ellen, however can I resist?'

The woman gave a chuckle, unlacing her mistress and sympathising only a little with the marks on the firm flesh. 'You shouldn't have had me lace you so tightly, milady. I've no use for the things at all.'

'How did you fare? Did you eat well?'

There was a moment's hesitation, then the woman said, 'Yes . . . I can't say there wasn't more than enough,'

'I detect a "but" there. Come on, Ellen! We've become more than maid and lady since leaving London, and you know I appreciate honest speech.'

'Well . . . I've worked in one or two houses in my time, for real toffs too. Most of them neither know nor care what goes on below stairs and, in the kitchen especially, there's usually so much wasted from the top table that they feed the beggars that come to the back door.'

'But not here.'

'No, milady. The kitchen is told just how much is needed, no more nor less. They're fed well, make no mistake, and each one thinks the world of the countess, but there's no waste in any part of the house.'

'But what of the banquets she mentioned in the great hall?'

'Oh, no, milady! There hasn't been a banquet since before the old count died in the Revolution three years ago, nor much company either, they say, just a few friends dropping in.'

'All right, Ellen,' Blanche said thoughtfully. 'That will be all for now. I'll be able to think more clearly tomorrow.'

Yet, the following day, it was not the question of the de Chauvenays' financial problems that absorbed her, but her own more urgent quest. She had waited until the afternoon, when André was taking a carriage ride and Marie was alone reading in the library.

At Blanche's entrance she looked up with a smile, yet the frown that had marred that smooth brow a moment before still darkened her eyes. 'Come in, Blanche, and take my mind off these troubled times.'

'Something worrying you? Can I help?'

'No, it's just that my poor France seems to go from one revolution to another with no one learning and no one forgetting. I remember nothing of the Terror, of course, since I was only a child in England, but the last one three years ago seems to continue in the papers even though that bourgeois Louis-Philippe has been accepted . . . at least by some.'

Carefully Blanche asked, 'But what if there were a legitimate king of France? Would there not be an even more terrible revolution?'

The dark eyes look faintly amused. 'You are thinking of those rumours of the Dauphin being still alive? *Ma chère*, there have been more Pretenders than I can count. Don't tell me you know of yet another! In England?'

'No, not the Dauphin. But what if the Dauphin died years later than they said . . . say five years ago, and had married and left a son . . . a son . . . just as a hypothetical case . . . who had been spirited away by the boy's mother . . . say a gypsy woman, for example?'

'Blanche, you have heard something! Ah, but you must say nothing.' For an instant there was fear in the woman's eyes. 'No, not even to me. I don't wish to know of any more kings.'

'Then what of a small lost boy with absolutely no chance of influencing anyone? A young aristocrat condemned to live among peasants—as his father was?'

With a sigh, Marie surrendered. 'I'll talk to André. He has far more friends among the *haute bourgeoisie* than I. Their contacts are that much more . . . cosmopolitan, shall we say? Leave it to me.'

But it seemed that over the next few socially hectic days the opportunity never arose, and all too quickly a fortnight had passed. André appeared determined to make her forget every care that had beset her. He became mentor, guide, historian, confidante and friend. He still paid her compliments but now they seemed more sincere, and she revelled in his company. Almost every day he would accompany Blanche around Paris or they would drive for miles in the surrounding countryside. They spent a complete day at the Louvre, André pointing out with a chuckle the ambiguous monogram left by Henry II on the south-west wing of the courtyard. 'The "H" for Henry surmounts two crescents which could refer to either his queen, Catherine de Medici, or his mistress, Diane de Poitiers. I choose to believe it is the latter.' The dark eyes turned to her face. 'We French have always revered our mistresses!'

'It says little for the insitution of marriage, but then since most men prefer to marry witless ornaments, one can quite understand their seeking stimulation elsewhere.' With a wicked glance upward, 'I should probably do the same myself if I married for ought but love, for should not a woman also be allowed a degree of . . . stimulation?'

She had expected the same shocked reaction that she would have received from Jeremy and many other of her peers with their double standard, but instead found her hand seized and brought swiftly to his lips. '*Ma belle* Blanche! To hear you say that is joy to my heart. Since the first moment I saw you . . .'

'Stop that!' Blanche laughed, made uneasy by the intensity of his gaze. 'I was only jesting!' She withdrew her hand firmly. 'I'm going to have to treat you Frenchmen with the utmost care. Between creating or evading revolutions and mistresses, it's a wonder you have time to eat!'

His eyes widened. 'Dinner! I had quite forgotten!' His expression was so comic that Blanche had to laugh.

'Your mother won't beat you, but the cook may take reprisals.'

'You don't know my mother!' He smiled, but somehow the smile never reached his eyes, and she wondered at the volatile relationship she had encountered once or twice before over the past few days.

The air was distinctly chill over an excellent meal, at which they had arrived a bare ten minutes late. Blanche apologised, saying that she had kept André overlong at the Louvre, but the countess would have none of it. 'My son has little sense of time at best, and none at all of *la belle cuisine*. Tell him that a perfect soufflé is a dish of delicately held bubbles fit for the gods, and a collapsed soufflé is a mess of egg-white, and he will show you that polite smile he is wearing now and say *"Oui, maman"*, all the while thinking of his gambling friends and the reactionary students that are fully set for another revolution.'

'Surely your collapsed France is more important than a collapsed soufflé,' put in André, his mild tone belying the spark in his eyes. 'Or are you saying that any king is better than none, even one who attempts to placate the bourgeoisie by sending his sons to their schools and still shuffles the cards of power with a marked deck? France can no longer afford kings, *maman*.'

Blanche felt a chill at his words, but already Marie had risen, obviously distressed. 'Your father died to preserve the monarchy you would destroy. He died leaving us with nothing but debts and the necessity of dealing with people whom we would not formerly have acknowledged. Forgive me, Blanche. I speak this way only because of what you have told me, but you see how impossible it is when there are revolutionaries even within our own family.' With a shake of her head and another apology, she left.

'I'm sorry.' André said, echoing his mother. 'I did not mean to belittle her royalist views. There is much in Louis-Philippe that is good, but still the working classes become poorer and instead of the aristocracy, who will never recover again, it is the business classes who are taking their place. The bankers and lawyers will rule France when Louis-Philippe is gone.' Then he smiled into Blanche's troubled eyes, his gaze sliding down to the full curves revealed by the extreme *décolletage* of the draped bodice of her dress. He gave a cough to clear the tightness in his throat. 'Shall we forget politics? Let me show you a room you haven't yet seen. It's our museum, and we keep it locked at all times. I think you'll find it interesting.'

Blanche had, in her wanderings, come to the locked door and found her curiosity piqued, but then had forgotten about it in the fullness of her days. They returned there now and, having ordered the housekeeper to use her keys, André urged Blanche inside while the servant lit candles, placing them strategically about the room.

It was a strange room, she thought. Family portraits covered the walls, and between them hung swords and pikes, spears and guns, axes and halberds of a bygone age, no less lethal for being decorative. One portrait in particular caught her eye. 'That dress!'

'That's la Comtess Angelique de Chauvenay in her favourite Court gown. What a vain woman she was!'

'With good reason, it seems. Those colours!'

He laughed. 'Yes, they are dramatic, are they not? The style was *à la polonaise*, but only she would dream of attaching gold tassels to those draperies that puff up under the panniers. Fragonard must have torn his hair attempting to capture that pink—not quite rose—beneath the royal purple draperies.'

'And the tiniest pink bows on the panniers scattered over that mass of lace on the sleeves. I've never seen anything so lovely.'

'I have,' he said huskily, his eyes on the creamy

shoulders and not in the least interested in old family portraits. But already she was moving on.

Suddenly she froze, staring at a glass case of rare butterflies, each carefully pinned and labelled. 'I hate it!' she cried. 'I hate all killing of helpless creatures, and to exhibit their corpses is just as barbaric as leaving the felons on Tyburn tree.' She spun, bright-eyed, and his arms went round her in comfort, but rather than collapsing against his chest as he had hoped—as any other woman would have done—she pulled free and strode to glare out of the window, gathering her stormy emotions with difficulty.

'Blanche,' the soft purr soothed from behind her. 'Don't let it upset you. I can't bear for you to be upset.' When she did not speak, he put his hands high on her shoulders, his thumbs moving gently, insistently on the back of her neck. She gave a sigh and bent her head fractionally so that he could ease the tense muscles. André felt his heart begin to pound. From this position he could see over her shoulder and down to where the full breasts were almost revealed beneath the silk. Bending, he kissed her neck, then, when she voiced no objection, moved his warm lips over to her shoulder, pushing the sleeves down even lower with the slow insinuation of his fingers.

'No, André,' Blanche murmured, her thoughts many miles away, wondering why these warm, gentle fingers did nothing to stir her, whereas the lightest touch of Jason's had set her afire. Where was he now? What was he doing? It had been almost a month. He had said that he would come for her. Had he run into difficulties? Was he in danger? There was so little she could do. She gave a deep sigh . . . and aided by the working of André's fingers, the movement was enough to reveal the barest fraction of deeper pink at the peak of one breast.

André could take no more. *'Ma perle! Mon coeur!'* He swung her sideways, bending her over his arm as his hand plunged in to cup that perfect globe. With a groan he rained kisses on her breast, her neck and lips—parted with surprise—while fondling boldly.

Blanche recovered from the shock of his onslaught almost as quickly as it had begun, and hauled him from her with a handful of hair, eyes blazing. 'How dare you! I'm not a kitchen-maid to be mauled!'

Immediately André dropped to his knees, burying his head in her skirt. 'Forgive me! Forgive me! I don't know what came over me!'

Blanche looked down at the curling hair and bent shoulders, and her quick anger died. 'No harm done,' she said gently. 'I should not have worn the dress without a fichu. I confess I had thought of you more as a brother than a lover. Come now. Get to your feet.' She bent to raise him, smiling forgivingly as he lifted his head, but as she did so the already loosened bodice gaped wide, exposing her bosom completely, only inches from his eyes.

'Blanche! *Chérie!*' He plunged forward, lips pillaging the soft flesh . . . until a fist crashing against his ear sent him sprawling.

Wordlessly Blanche stormed out, slamming the door violently behind her, striding to her room and summoning Ellen with an uncharacteristic shout. 'Get me out of this dress,' she ordered, when the startled woman hurried in. 'And then throw it out. I shan't wear it again. Ever!'

Ellen knew when to give advice and when to keep her peace, and, taking in her mistress's stormy eyes and the red marks on the lovely breasts, knew that this was a time for silence. Only later, when Blanche had washed and changed, asking for a cool cordial and apologising for her anger, did the maid venture, 'He's only a boy, milady; not used to a beauty like yourself. Quite turned his head, no doubt.' At Blanche's hint of a smile, she dared, 'Such a pretty boy, though. And one that loves you, I'll be bound.'

'That wasn't the word I'd have used for his feelings,' stated Blanche drily, 'though it begins with the same letter. Fools come in all sizes, Ellen, and age is no cure. Still, he went too far, and deserved a box round the ear.' Then suddenly she gave a choked giggle. 'Oh, but he did look a fool sprawled out on the floor, arms and legs flying, and mouth agape!' And it took only an answering chuckle from Ellen to set the two of them into paroxysms of laughter.

Blanche missed breakfast the following morning, not because she could not face André, for she had forgiven him even while laughing over the incident with Ellen, but because she did not want to embarrass him before his mother. Over the past month the countess had betrayed surprisingly tyrannical qualities on more than one occasion, and Blanche was in no doubt that should she hear of her son's assault on their guest, he would receive a tongue-lashing second to none.

She decided to take the carriage out alone for a change, and to cheer herself, went to the flower market, where even in February one could buy flowers brought up from the Mediterranean. This time her quest was even more pleasurable than purchasing a bunch of flowers for her room, for it was Sunday, and the flowers were supplanted by caged birds. André had bought her a linnet that first Sunday after her arrival, and told her of the tradition whereby the bird-sellers would line up at the entry of each king into Paris and release over ten thousand birds in welcome. 'May I?' she had enquired. 'You'll not think it a waste of money?'

With velvet eyes caressing her face, he had replied, 'I would buy every bird in the market if it would keep that wonder in your eyes!' Blanche had opened the cage to watch the joyful linnet surge skyward.

Each Sunday after that they had come to free one of the tiny prisoners, and so he had known she would be there. He watched her move between the cages, a slight frown as she deliberated over her choice, then the moment she pointed to a particular cage he moved swiftly to her side, paying for the bird before she could recover from his sudden appearance, saying, 'Blanche, forgive me.' Then he eloquently pleaded, 'I swear it will never happen again! I'll not touch your hand, even.'

Blanche moved away from him. 'I don't wish to speak of it, or even think of it. I came out to enjoy a drive alone, but the mood has gone.'

'It is all my fault. You wish never to see me again. It is understandable. How can I ask your forgiveness when what I did was unforgivable?'

Blanche felt her lips twitch, quite unable to remain angry with so handsome a supplicant. 'Oh, stop babbling, André! I've a high tolerance for fools and flatterers, and you appear to have excelled as both. Now I'm going to drive out to the Bois de Vincennes and release our feathered friend. You may either accompany me, or remain here looking like a kicked pup.' Cutting off his gratitude with a gesture, she turned back toward the carriage.

They drove eastward into the cool avenues of the park, and André tentatively put a supporting arm about her as the carriage bounced over a frost-filled rut. Blanche felt it, and gave a sigh, remembering the great fireplace in the Prospect at Wapping and another arm, muscular and sure, that had been thrown confidently across her shoulders as if it had every right to be there. Why did he not come? The waiting was intolerable. She could do nothing in France and without the countess's help had no chance of making contacts. 'I think I must go home.'

André's dark eyes gleamed. 'I'm so glad you can call it that, *ma chère*.' Blanche gave another sigh, not deigning to correct him, opening the cage to watch the tiny bird flutter into the nearest tree, where immediately it began to sing.

He was delighted. When his mother had questioned him on Blanche's absence from the breakfast table, not believing for one moment her guest's excuse of a slight headache, he had been forced to confess his lapse from grace. The countess had exploded—

quietly—which made it far more lethal than any
tirade he had so far received. She had also issued him
with an ultimatum—one which would have been
impossible to obey without Blanche's total forgiveness.

On their return, Marie was full of the fancy-dress
ball to be held at the Hôtel de Sully. 'Of course you
will come!' she enthused. 'We have many costumes in
an unused room at the back of the house. I shall go
as the huntress Diana, with toga and bow and
arrow'—with a wicked wink—'I have the legs for it,
don't you think? What shall you come as, Blanche?
You always wear white. Why not the virginal Juliet?'

'And I shall be Romeo!' André suggested.

Blanche smiled, but her thoughts were far away,
her normally healthy appetite for once absent.

'If only we could entertain on a grander scale,'
Marie sighed. 'The great hall would serve admirably,
and the musicians could take up that corner where
Tante Joséphine's portrait now resides.'

Blanche nodded. 'It is a beautiful house. With the
right care and attention . . .'

'And also a fair degree of wealth . . . Which, as
you by now appreciate, we do not have,' André
added.

'That, too. I wish I could help.' She gave a rueful
laugh and a shrug, all too conscious of the effort it
took to keep her own modest villa in a state of
repair.

He reached to cover her hand with his, smiling into
her eyes. 'Wisdom and wit, beauty and generosity
too.'

And the next day, André asked Blanche to be his
wife . . .

It was windy, and Blanche found an exhilaration in
the sudden flurries that caught at her on each corner
as she walked, plucking at her bonnet and sweeping
her skirts aside.

André marvelled at the laughter that came so easily
to her lips and the sparkle to her eyes. 'You give so
much of yourself,' he complimented.

'I love the wind! It clears the cobwebs from the corners of the mind.'

They rounded another corner and so strong was the sudden gust, funnelled between the narrow streets, that it caused her to stagger. André put a protective arm about her, and his breath caught as she raised laughing eyes.

Her laughter died as she read that dark regard. This was going too far. He was much too handsome to resist, yet she could not feel more than a transient physical attraction and a warm affection. She also knew that he was falling in love with her, and did not want to hurt him more than her decision to return to England would already achieve. 'Don't like me too much,' she ordered softly, but he shook his head.

'Too late.' Then, seeing the unhappiness in her eyes, he raised a finger to brush her cheek. 'But that is my problem, no? Let us continue our walk.' As they wandered into the winding back streets of the Latin Quarter, he said, 'Perhaps I should not have brought you this way. I want you only to see the most beautiful parts of my city. Yet it is here where the students come, here where they keep the cauldron of progress boiling.'

The wind had dropped considerably, and Blanche brushed a drop of rain from her cheek, looking up at the heavy clouds building overhead. 'I think perhaps we had better make all haste back to the carriage, and leave the students to their narrow streets and cold attics. For the moment I find it far more civilised to be a member of the aristocracy who can find a carriage awaiting her.' But in truth she did not mind that the warm rain was completing the demolition of her coiffure that the wind had begun. Vanity, she reasoned, was all very well in its place, but should never be allowed to spoil one's pleasure in the elements.

By the time they reached the house they were soaked, and they were met at the door by a concerned and clucking housekeeper who took their dripping cloaks. 'I have taken my bath already, it seems,' André told her, turning with a laugh—then stopped, riveted. The rain had wrought havoc with Blanche's hair, but it was to the once modest, high-necked muslin dress that his gaze was drawn, beneath which Blanche had worn only the flimsiest of chemises for comfort, all of which was now almost transparent. His hands clenched as he remembered his mother's warning, and yet the temptation was almost too much. He had felt that velvet flesh beneath his hands, knew what it was to mould those curves. 'Go!' he croaked. 'For heaven's sake, Blanche, go and change!'

Startled, Blanche followed his gaze, and felt the colour flood her cheeks. 'I think I must,' she agreed and ran for the sanctuary of her room. An hour later she emerged, bathed and changed, a little subdued but determined to tell the countess of her resolve to leave . . . preferably as quickly as possible. André might be a gentleman but, as she had found, he was first and foremost a man—and a Frenchman.

He was waiting in the grand salon. 'My mother left a message that she had to spend the night with an old friend,' he told her, coming forward to put her fingers to his lips before leading her to the fire. 'Dinner will be the quieter without her, but I'm sure we shall be able to manage. I've ordered it a little earlier than usual as I want us to have a long evening. There is much I wish to talk of.'

Blanche felt a warning prickle at the back of her neck at the seriousness of his tone. She wondered whether she should advise him now of her decision to return to England, but knew that her hostess should really be the first to know. Certainly it would do no harm to wait until the countess's return in the morning.

André seemed to wish to know every aspect of her life in England, and in her present mood, she was only too glad to talk of it. The only times he stopped or changed the direction of her flow were when she mentioned returning home. 'I must cajole cook into giving me this recipe,' she said, stirring a forkful of rice. 'It has grapes, and I can taste the garlic . . . a touch of parsley, is that? Some cheese?'

'Parmesan, and the grapes are from Malaga.'

'My cook would enjoy experimenting. Do you know she actually hated cooking when I first hired her, but once she'd discovered my preference for sauces and dishes more exotic than roast beef she blossomed, and of course under Annemarie's tuition . . . I can't wait to see how they have fared.'

'Some more wine? Tell me of those terrible slums you worked in. How hard your life must have been.'

Later the baked peaches topped with macaroons were served. 'The children will love this idea!'

She had told them of a little of the 'family' and now he nodded, smiling. 'You are very fond of children.'

'Not generally, though I can't admit to knowing a fair cross-section. Those of my acquaintance are either the starving waifs of the slums or the pampered pets of my friends. Still, I must confess to an affection for Jean-Luc and Fleur.'

'Just imagine, with all of your experience and compassion, what a perfect mother you will make.'

Blanche moved to leave the table, and he rose with her. 'Surely motherhood presupposes marriage, André? At the present time that is the furthest thing from my mind, so your observation must be purely speculative.'

He looked uncomfortable for a second or two, then took her hand, gazing down at it broodingly.

'Blanche, you know how I feel about you. You know too that my mother looks upon you with favour . . .'

'Please, André . . .' she stopped him. 'Please don't say any more!' and she put a soft hand to his lips.

'But you must see that a union between us would benefit all. I love you, and I know that you have a fondness for me which I am certain I could change to love in time. You would become a countess, and

your dowry—as well as the rest of your estate—
would refurnish the house, return it to its former
glory . . .' He broke off, for the grey eyes had
widened, but then turned as glacial as mountain peaks
in winter.

'I have a title, André, albeit a minor one. What I
do not have is a fortune.'

'But the Davenport name . . . the estates . . .'

'My father left me nothing, and my only estate is a
tiny villa in London, run by my own business acumen,
and an aptitude for telling a fast horse or a good card
hand.'

'But I thought . . . My mother said . . .'

He looked so stricken that her icy anger and feeling
of sick betrayal almost faltered. 'I'm sorry, André.
I'm afraid we've both been duped; unknowing players
in a farce written by others.'

Desperately he caught at her hand. 'It doesn't
matter. I can marry some other heiress for the sake
of the house. You and I can still have it all. When I
have the money, I will buy you a house on the Ile St-
Louis, one of the prettiest in the Quai de Béthune
with a balcony overlooking the river. You'll have
jewels, rich dresses of the finest lace and velvet . . .'

'You contemptible cur!' Blanche said so softly as to
be barely audible and with almost no feeling.

'Blanche! *Chérie!*'

'I'm leaving. *Now!* Please advise one of the servants
to escort me to a hotel. I'll send for my things
tomorrow. No!'—as he went to speak—'Not a
word . . . in any language!' She forced herself to
walk slowly to her room, calling for Ellen in a voice
that was only a shade higher than usual. She did not
shout, scream, curse or throw anything, but simply
said, 'Ellen, the holiday is over.'

Looking at the set, ashen features, the woman
moved silently to pack.

When they came downstairs, André was awaiting
them in the hall. Blanche looked through him but,
not daring to touch her, he could only block her way

with his body, and she caught the rich scent of him as she stepped aside. 'Blanche?' Softly, 'I won't detain you. I've arranged for you to go to a good hotel. I shall come tomorrow with your things. I'll do anything you want of me.'

'Send my things. I want nothing of you.' Then, as he continued to bar her way, her voice cracked out like a pistol-shot. 'Move, damn you!' Like many before him when faced with the ice-cold temper of Beatrice, Lady Davenport, he did as ordered.

It was only when shown into the hotel room, quietly elegant in white and gold with a huge chandelier, that Blanche's anger cooled a little. 'It's not the first time that I've been mistaken for a rich heiress, after all,' she confided to Ellen, her voice breaking only a little.

'But this one was different,' the woman sympathised.

'Not in retrospect. A little more handsome than most, with an appealing accent.'

'But you liked this one more than most, milady?'

'Yes, I liked this one; but more, I thought I could have brought him round to accepting that the old royalists were not entirely wrong, that a king of France . . .' She broke off, not wishing to make Ellen a part of her deception. 'We have a monarchy,' she finished, 'and it works well enough in England.' Then, mourning a lost friend, 'Why couldn't he simply have remained a fool?'

CHAPTER ELEVEN

'YOU FOOL!' the countess raged at her son, striding across the room like a caged tigress, dark eyes flashing, magnificent in her anger. 'She was lying to you. How can she have no money when Davenport is a name to be reckoned with all over England? The boy has done the Grand Tour and has several carriages of his own. They have a house that makes this resemble a peacock's hut; stables; an army of servants. No wonder Blanche is tired of suitors after her money—though in all honesty she has both a fine mind and beauty too—which was your undoing, *imbécile!* She reacted in fright to yet another, this time a man she was almost in love with, with a weak lie.' She took another turn about the room, her very energy causing his head to throb. 'There is still a chance. I'll go to her, apologise for your clumsy stupidity and, believe me, it will be no lie. I'll remind her of the ball. Yes . . . she was looking forward to that. I'll tell her I've sent you away, and persuade her to come back here to change. She and I are friends, are we not?' A nod, as she spoke her thought aloud. 'You'll be at the ball, of course. She is too much of a lady to create a scene. You will convince her that you love her with or without money.'

'She knows that,' he ventured, 'it was that which brought the house down about my ears.'

'I should think so! You don't tell an English lady that you're thinking of setting her down in some riverside villa on the income of some fictional future wife. An Englishwoman lacks our red blood; she needs to be brought to the boil slowly, with finesse, with comfortable surroundings, sweet perfume . . .'

'A little like a lobster,' André grinned, earning a glare

'I should wait for a day, perhaps two, sending flowers this morning and chocolates this afternoon, each with a note of sincere apology and requesting her permission to call. By this evening, she should have calmed a little, and by tomorrow she will begin to mellow,' advised the countess.

'And then an orchid—there must be one somewhere—or a crystal container of the finest perfume, something subtle but sensual.'

'You're learning!' Marie nodded approvingly.

The flowers went out of the window, off-season roses of pink and cream. Blanche watched an urchin grab them and run off, and hoped he would sell them at a good price, then resumed her contemplation of her letter to Annemarie telling her of her resolve to leave Paris. She heard the raised voice of the chambermaid, registered the bustle of Ellen moving about the room, and wished she could think of an errand on which she could send the woman, wishing to be alone.

'It's no use dwelling on the past, milady,' the woman chided her. 'Given enough time, you know, even stones can become diamonds.'

Blanche gave her a surprised look, then smiled. 'You're the diamond, Ellen! What shall I do without you when we get back? I told you at the beginning that I could afford your wages only for the duration of this visit. The best I can do now is to find you a good position and give you the best reference I can.'

'I never expected more, milady,' she smiled philosophically. 'It's more than I ever dreamed of, this opportunity to come abroad. Why, I've stories enough to keep me in free ale for a year and my grandchildren amused for life!'

When there was a knock at the door, Blanche told her not to answer it, but with a reproachful look

Ellen went over, returning with a huge and ornately wrapped box of chocolates. 'Another note, too! Same as before. You're surely not going to throw these at some poor passer-by's head?'

'Do as you please. If I touch even one of them it'll quite spoil my dinner, and I hear we are to have saddle of pork!'

'It isn't the chocolates,' Ellen muttered. 'It's who sent them!' Then, louder, 'You can't judge her, milady, when it was her son who insulted you.'

'It's not something that André would think up alone. She talked so much about her beloved Paris, her beloved home, and what it had come to, that it was enough to turn the head of any dutiful son.'

'Wasn't there some king of England who said in a temper that he wanted to be rid of his priest? I don't suppose he really wanted his friend to be killed. We none of us can help another's interpretation of our words.'

Blanche shook her head in amazement 'Don't ever let me underestimate you, Ellen! Very well, I may see Marie, but certainly not her son. Go on, now. I'll read for a while.'

The chocolates vanished, and so did Ellen. It was, therefore, no great surprise that by dinner-time she emerged from her room with a distinctly greenish pallor. 'A slight headache, milady, nothing more.'

Blanche restrained a smile. 'Perhaps you should go to bed with a little laudanum to make you sleep through until morning, and forgo that succulent roast pork, all crisp fat with garlic and rosemary . . .'

'Oh, milady!' and Ellen staggered back into her room.

In spite of having to dress herself and arrange her own hair, Blanche thoroughly enjoyed the meal. The elegance of her surroundings and the perfectly prepared food all helped to soothe her, so that by the time she returned to her room her previous anger had quite dissipated—until the manager delivered a small package, according it his personal attention.

Feeling the heat rising within her, she thanked him sweetly, closed the door and went to put it on the marble-topped chest. She studied it, chose to ignore it and changed into the comfortable white wrap-over. When, after a full half-hour, she opened it, from its bed of black velvet the ruby eyes of an exquisite gold filigree butterfly stared back at her unwinkingly. There was no card.

A light tap came at the door. 'Well timed,' she muttered, then, 'Go away!' A soft laugh, a male laugh, and the door began to open. 'Go away!' she repeated, 'I never want to see you again. Never!' And, snatching up the brooch she hurled it at the door.

'I believe you,' Jason Hunterton assured her, bending to retrieve the missile. 'But may we not discuss it?'

Blanche felt the room move beneath her feet and for a long moment was unable to speak, drowning in those rare jade eyes, taking in only on the edge of her vision the dark hair glistening with the rain, the smiling mouth and tanned, chiselled, features. How dared he find a sunny climate in March! 'Good evening, Jason.' Well done, Blanche! Wit personified! 'Come . . . in.'

'Are you sure?' He entered nevertheless, placed the brooch on a side-table and slid off the damp Petersham great-coat. 'I always seem to arrive in Paris when it is raining! I should have stayed in London, perhaps.' His jacket followed the coat, revealing a fine linen shirt and silver-grey watered waistcoat.

'London?' echoed Blanche, recovering slowly. 'I was going to return there myself . . .'

The searching gaze bored into her soul. 'I expected you, but undoubtedly you found something to keep you here. Are you, then, totally enamoured with Paris?'

'The city, yes.'

'Ahh!'

'What does that mean?'

He threw up a defensive hand in mock alarm. 'Don't attack me. I surrender!'

Blanche turned away, emotions in a turmoil, hating all men—especially too handsome ones with silver tongues and false friendship. 'I'm not dressed for company.'

'You had no such qualms last time I saw you in that very robe.' he reminded her. 'I said I'd come, and I didn't come to talk of social graces or the state of your wardrobe.'

Half angrily she shrugged him off, more angry with herself than with him, angry with the weakness in her limbs and the fire within her that his very touch induced. 'Much has happened since I left London.'

He grew very still. 'The son?'

'Of course the son!' Glaring at him, she read nothing in the darkening eyes that reassured her. 'Well, what did you expect? We've been living in the same house for over a month.'

A muscle leapt in his jaw. 'You're still wearing white; or have you had no time to shop?'

'Oh, you men!' Blanche cried, incensed, 'That's at the root of everything with you. If your all-too-obvious charms don't cause the lady to swoon into your embrace, you'll use every other trick in the book. Ye gods, it's like a magic show! Out of the hat comes a bunch of flowers, a pair of gloves, a piece of jewellery. If that doesn't work, the magician really excels himself—a fur coat, a diamond ring, an apartment in town—or a house overlooking the Seine! If all else fails, he comes out with those magic words "I love you", and, of course, his audience, already mesmerised, collapses completely.'

'Did you?' The voice was soft, tightly controlled, and she missed the stress that ran beneath it.

'I'm not a child!' she snapped. 'Do you think it's the first time I've had a man tell me he loved me? No . . . but this one I thought was a friend!' She did not see the total change in him, so preoccupied was

she with her own betrayal, did not notice the letting
go, the draining of the tight-coiled tension, the deep
steadying breath. 'He didn't even want me . . . Oh,
he wanted me all right, even after he tried to assault
me and I boxed his ears . . . But not in an honest
way.

'You did what?'

She pulled herself back to the present with difficulty.
'You know I don't like to be mauled. No, don't you
dare to smile! And all the time he was planning and
plotting underhand to marry me . . . or anyone else
who would repair that grey stone mausoleum! Don't
look so blank. The man wanted me only for my
money. How dared he!'

Jason's relief was so great that it erupted in a burst
of laughter. 'Oh, my poor girl!'

Blanche exploded. 'It's not funny! I was duped, led
on, betrayed, and you laugh. Get out! You're all the
same.'

'Blanche,' he murmured, coming forward.

'No! Out!' In a rage at his unfeeling, uncaring . . .
stupidity, she took a cushion from the brocaded settee
and flung it at his head.

He fended it off with ease. 'My dear . . .'

'I'm not your anything!' A heavy paperweight
crashed against the wall, missing him by inches.

'That's enough!' With a spring, he captured her
hands, bringing them behind her, lifting her off her
feet, holding her hard against him.

'Let me go!' A slippered foot cracked into his shin,
and he gave a soft curse.

'I said, that's enough!' He threw her on the bed,
holding her wrists captive, his hard body preventing
her struggles until the flashing eyes suddenly changed
as she realised her helplessness and felt her own
anger in him. Something almost akin to fear flickered
in the depths—and was seen and recognised. 'No, I
could never, ever, hurt you,' he said softly.

With deliberate slowness he lifted her, one arm
about her waist, lean fingers splayed over her back,

the other smoothing the tumbled hair from her face
and tracing a path of fire down her cheek. As his
fingers moved down over the curve of her throat,
Blanche began to tremble and as he covered one
breast, slipping inside the disarranged robe, she gave
a tiny gasp—and found his mouth covering hers, his
tongue taking advantage of her parted lips to probe
inward. He kissed her with a sensual expertise,
bringing her hard against the taut length of his body,
and a soft moan was torn from her throat as she felt
his need of her. His mouth had travelled down over
bare shoulder, then lower to the silken fullness of a
breast, and Blanche shuddered in exquisite torment
as his lips and tongue brought waves of sensation up
from her stomach, and lower.

'No!' she murmured, yet clung to him as if
drowning. 'Please, no!' But she knew she was lost as
she felt his husky laughter against her throat.

'I'm not going to rape you, woman. I'm going to
change your mind!'

With lingering sensuousness he brought his lips and
tongue into play over every curve and hollow of her,
shifting his weight so that at the same time he could
divest himself of his clothing, not leaving her for a
second, and even while she begged him to stop, her
writhing, helpless body gave her tongue the lie. She
began to weep, yet knew not why, as that muscular
body covered hers and for a second he tensed, then
moved slowly upward to kiss away the tears. She
searched the long-lashed eyes for . . . she knew not
what, but then his hands began that fiery torment
again, and her moment of fear passed as she
surrendered, clinging to the bronzed shoulders above
her, allowing him to bring her to that peak of ecstasy
so that even that small instant of pain, her gasp taken
into his mouth as it covered hers, seemed only a part
of that greater starburst that made her cry out his
name. Then slowly, so slowly, it died, and with a
shudder, she felt his weight leave her as he moved to

her side, cradling her as he could a child, searching the wondering eyes as she had searched his.

'Don't speak,' he whispered, smoothing back the silky hair from her forehead, sensing that she was on the edge of some precipice.

Tiny sobs still caught at Blanche's throat, the last of the storm that had shaken her, but very slowly she brought up one finger to trace his mouth. 'Is it over?'

He laughed then, a deep joyous sound. 'Oh, my lady . . . my White Lady . . . it's only just begun! You've tasted the wine . . . now the champagne!'

It was mid-morning when he awoke, immediately turning to her, then smiled and lay for a long moment to feast his eyes, as she slept bathed in a shaft of sunlight, glowing in the radiance of after-love. He had not realised any woman could appear so utterly perfect in the morning light. No other woman—and there had been many—had aroused such passion in him, yet a passion held in check by a deep desire to please her as much as himself, and no other had returned that pleasure so fully and unashamedly. Bending, he touched his tongue to the rose peak of her breast, and a quiver went through her. It was irresistible, and he repeated the procedure. Blanche made a sound between a moan and a purr, and awoke.

'Again.' Laughing, he drew out the kiss, then felt her tugging at his hair. 'No!' Instantly he raised his head, seeing with surprise the perspiration beading her forehead, the rapid rise and fall of her breathing. Then the fire in her eyes died, and she gave an unsteady laugh. 'You taught me too well.'

He was staggered. 'You mean if I just . . . touch you? Like . . . this . . . and this?' She gave a soft, ragged purr. 'You mean . . .?'

Blanche stretched—completely—the way a cat stretches, bringing her arms up to draw her fingers through her hair, spreading it out over the pillow, arching her body sinuously. The grey eyes held the deep mysterious changeability of the Irish mist. 'Jayce?'

'Yes?' Softly. Deeply. Knowing.

'Make love. No . . . Make . . . Jayce, I'm afraid I don't know the words . . .'

He smiled. 'Don't ever be afraid . . . I know the *words* as well!'

'I think we should take a carriage ride,' he suggested . . . much later.

'Why?' Lazily. Languidly stretching.

'Because, my insatiable darling, if we don't, we may never leave this room, and I may well starve to death!'

A wicked twinkle. 'Oh, I doubt that!'

Jason chuckled. 'Even I can't live by bed alone, my lady, and poor Ellen has been sent away three times already.'

'Was that very wicked of me?'

'You didn't have to open the adjoining door wearing nought but a smile, and tell her to take the rest of the week off!'

'Oh, very well.' She rose, and went to throw open the heavy brocade curtains. 'Somehow Paris seems more alive today, more . . . Oh, I don't know . . . Perhaps it's the sun after the rain that gives that shimmer to the air.'

Jason marvelled yet again at her total lack of false modesty. She had given herself to him, at first with an innocent passion, but then with a fire that matched his own, holding no part of herself from him, revelling in his worship of her body and openly satisfying her own too-long-subdued desires. He watched her now, slim-hipped, full-breasted, and a tiny handspan waist between, letting his eyes wander over the sun-bathed skin, down over slender thighs . . . She turned to face him, smiling, reading his thoughts, but . . . 'For sanity's sake, put something on!' he growled.

On the carriage ride, he spoke to her of his failure in London, the paths that had led nowhere, the

number of rumours—some bought dearly—that had
led to boys ranging from seven to seventeen, all with
disfigured hands but none with royal blood. 'I've
covered gypsy encampments from West Devon to the
Wash, and an assortment of farms, back rooms, huts
and ships' cabins that I never thought existed.' He
ran lean fingers through his hair, betraying his
frustration and tiredness, only giving a nod of
acceptance when Blanche confessed how little she
had even attempted. 'I never expected more. You are
somewhat limited in your connections, and would
have done far better to have stayed in London. Will
you return there now?'

She gave him a long look, then said quietly, 'I'd
like to stay with you . . . wherever that may be.'

At once his tiredness dropped away, and he swept
her into his arms, the mouth crushing down on hers
telling her far more than words could of his elation.
'Then . . . "Come live with me and be my love",' he
commanded softly, adding, 'now, Blanche!'

She watched the jade eyes darken with his desire,
and a quiver ran through her as their eyes met and
held. He did not even have to touch her, now. 'All of
my thoughts are horizontal,' she whispered helplessly.

A wide berlin pulled to a halt behind them, unable
to pass, and its driver let out a stream of invective
against love-lost aristos who blocked the road, holding
up the progress of one such as his master. Good-
humouredly Jason reined in to one side to allow the
coach to pass. Neither of them noticed the passenger—
his brown features suddenly pale, the long-lashed
eyes aglitter with tight-leashed emotion as his knuckles
whitened on the silver-topped cane.

'Let's go back to the hotel,' murmured Blanche,
conscious only of the strong hands that had captured
hers. Jason nodded, the hunger a white-hot furnace
within him, aware only of the lush curves hidden by
the all-enveloping mantle . . . And André, Comte de
Chauvenay, drove past—knowing only that the woman
he loved was in another man's arms . . . and that

love turned to a fanatical desire to take her from that
man at all costs.

Jason drove at a fast trot back to the hotel,
betraying his eagerness that was reflected in the
flushed, laughing face of the woman clutching at his
arm. As they entered the elegant salon, however,
with its huge gilded mirrors, the manager approached
them. 'A lady to see you, Lady Davenport.' He
gestured toward a low couch at the far of the room.
'Madame la Comtesse de Chauvenay.' His tone held
respect bordering on awe.

Marie rose to meet them. Her eyes took in the
faultless elegance of the man by Blanche's side, with
her woman's vision seeing the broad shoulders and
muscular thighs, the chiselled features and aristocratic
bearing—not to mention the proprietorial arm that
came to rest briefly about the slender shoulders as he
led Blanche forward. More than all of this, the
countess saw the undeniable aura about his companion,
and knew that her mission was already a lost cause.
However, Marie de Chauvenay was nothing if
not adaptable. With quiet dignity, therefore, she
approached the couple.

'Lady Davenport . . . I feel I've lost the right to
call you Blanche . . . I would consider it the greatest
favour if you would give me a few moments of your
time.' Before Blanche could deny her, she had turned,
extending carmine-tipped fingers to Jason. 'I am the
Comtesse de Chauvenay.' She gazed at him deeply.

'Jason, Lord Hunterton,' he responded, automatically bringing her fingers to his lips, thinking, 'Her
beauty is ageless. She has the sensuality of a leopard,
golden, fine-boned, sleek . . . and equally as lethal!'

Blanche saw that silent exchange and bristled,
surprising herself. 'You've called me "Blanche" for
too long to change now, Marie, so for those happier
times, a glass of wine, perhaps?' She indictated a
quiet corner of the salon, and Marie had to be
content with that, although it was a little more public
than she would have liked.

The trio made their way to an arrangement of brocaded chairs, and Jason seated the elder woman first as a matter of etiquette, noting how she appeared suddenly tired. She thanked him with her eyes, but there was none of the subtle invitation in them that he had received before, and he wondered whether he could have been mistaken.

'André has gone to the country,' she began. 'I sent him there for his unforgivable insult to you, his clumsiness and downright stupidity.'

Blanche raised an eyebrow. 'I had thought to hear you plead his case.'

'I do.' Suddenly, incredibly, there were tears in the fine dark eyes. 'None of it was his fault, Blanche. Oh, his attack on you was real enough; his love for you was real enough; but it was I who ordered him to marry you for your fortune. Only I am to blame . . . for loving my home too much, having nothing else to love . . .' She went on, twisting her glass between her fingers, not touching its contents, throwing eloquent glances at Jason, apologising for boring him with the story of a Breton peasant girl who had fallen in love with a nobleman. Then, before either of her audience had time to question her further, she rose. 'But I mustn't keep you, Blanche. I know you'll never be able to forgive me; I ask only that you don't shame me before my friends.'

'Shame you?' repeated Blanche, honestly puzzled and touched in spite of herself.

'The ball . . . Had you forgotten? At the Hôtel de Sully. I had sent out invitations for my friends to meet you. You were to come as Juliet.'

Blanche had forgotten, and a slight frown touched her brow. 'I . . . don't . . .'

'*Pour moi.*' Drawing it out into more than a simple 'for me', and again turning speaking eyes to the man who had risen with them. 'Lord Hunterton, can you not prevail upon Blanche? It will be such a grand affair, and she was so looking forward to it . . . before all this occurred. I have a whole room of

costumes and you, too, could come as my guest. I'm
certain we have something in the house to suit you,
though there weren't many of my ancestors as tall or
as broad in the shoulder, or slim of hip. Oh, forgive
my boldness . . .' She blushed delicately, but not
before the eyes that had moved over him, cutting
through his clothing as if it did not exist, had flickered
to catch his own amused gaze.

Jason had glanced at Blanche to see whether she
had caught that predatory look, but she was
preoccupied with her own thoughts, and when his
gaze swung back to the countess, it was to find her
eyelids demurely lowered. A smile touched his lips. 'I
see no harm in it,' he said, playing her game, thinking
what a great actress—or courtesan—she could be.
'But, of course, it is up to Blanche.'

'Will he be there?' asked Blanche, aware of the
charm of the countess, but wondering a little at
Jason's easy capitulation.

'It would seem strange if he were not.' Then, at
the other's stiffening, 'Oh, but so will hundreds of
others. You don't have to see or speak to him,
although . . .' she put out her hand in graceful
supplication—'he seeks only to apologise and explain.'

'No need for explanation. All of that was made
perfectly clear at our last meeting.'

'There is nothing that I can say, Blanche, that will
unsay what has been said. If you can find it in you to
question the reasons behind it . . . We live in such
different worlds, and in mine it is not so uncommon
to marry for money and pray that love, or even
liking, will follow.'

'Nor in mine,' Blanche admitted, knowing that
already she had lost her argument and, with a glance
at the handsome features beside her, knowing too
that André could not hurt her any more. 'Very well,
Marie. We'll stay to attend the ball.'

Marie was far too clever to push her advantage any
further by mentioning her son's presence again, but
contented herself with asking, 'And you'll allow me

to dress you? You'll come to the house and choose something from my store? You, too, Lord Hunterton. I insist.'

'I'd be honoured to have you dress me, madame.'

Her eyes flew to his, and she saw the deep amusement in the dark jade depths, even though his features registered nothing but polite acceptance. Carefully she extended her hand. 'I'll be leaving you, then.' She found with surprise that it was trembling slightly as it was carried to that mobile mouth, thinking, 'This one is much man. It's no wonder André stood no chance . . . and yet . . .' She lowered her gaze, thoughts racing, as she said her goodbyes and returned home.

'What do you suppose she is up to?' mused Jason, throwing his greatcoat on to the chairback that had received it before.

'Marie? Why do you ask? She wanted only to apologise and to reassure herself that I would help her to keep up appearances.' She came to him, allowing her hands the pleasure of sliding slowly up his chest to creep round the back of his neck as she moulded her body to his. 'I don't want to talk about the countess, or her son.'

'She isn't the friend she pretends to be!'

'I don't want to talk at all,' she cajoled him, feeling his rising need of her and moving her hips very slightly against him, bringing a gasp from his throat. 'Teach me to fly, Jason.'

With a groan he swung her into his arms, carrying her to the bed. 'When I get you home, I'll teach you to listen to your betters when they speak,' he stated with mock ferocity.

'I like it at the hotel. You can't beat me here!'

'Beating you isn't what I have in mind, and I intend getting you on to my own territory as quickly as possible. Now stop wriggling, or I'll never free you from these lacings.'

'You'd never treat the countess in such a cavalier fashion!'

'I'd never treat the countess at all! Now be still, woman!' Then, softly, 'At least for now!'

Later, her thoughts were able to return to the ball. 'And if I flirt madly with some exceedingly handsome young man, will you beat me? And whom will you allow me to flirt with?'

'No one.'

'Then whom will you flirt with?'

Jason kept his thoughts to himself, remembering the invitation in the dark eyes of the countess. 'Oh, I shall find a dozen or two, no doubt,' he said airily, certain that no woman of Blanche's age could understand the subtle wiles of an older woman, especially one as lethally feline as the countess. When he saw her again, he knew that he had not been mistaken.

It was the morning of the ball, and they had gone to the house as promised to choose their costumes. 'It must be a secret,' Marie insisted. 'You must not see each other's costume before this evening. You shall choose your costume first, Blanche, while Lord Hunterton takes wine in the grand salon. Then I shall get my driver to spirit you back to the hotel, Blanche, for it will certainly take you all afternoon to prepare, and you must rest. You will forgive me, *ma chère*, but rings are meant for fingers, not eyes! No objection, now. We must see a vision tonight.'

With the gracious patter of an experienced hostess, she settled the slightly bemused Jason into a comfortable armchair. 'A cigar? You don't? How wise. Come then, Blanche, we shall see what we shall see. I have hoarded the cast-off finery of most of the de Chauvenay ancestors, and when it fell apart, had it reproduced exactly—a little hobby of mine, having no ancestors of my own worth mentioning.'

It took less than ten minutes for Blanche to find her costume among the racks of satin cloaks and ball gowns, shepherdesses' flounces and Roman togas.

She opened a cupboard and there it was, almost as if it had been awaiting her. It took a little longer for Marie to make one or two minor alterations, and then to convince Blanche that she really should return with her prize and get Ellen to fit it properly before resting. 'I shall send my own hairdresser later, with precise instructions,' Marie enthused, recapturing the gaiety that had been between them before the unfortunate incident with her son. 'There must be no detail overlooked.' Finally, after wrapping the dress in a sheet and bundling Blanche into the waiting carriage before she was fully aware of what was happening, Marie returned to the grand salon.

Jason rose at her entrance, coming forward with the lithe gait of a panther, his size, his very bearing, dwarfing every other man she had ever known. 'So now we shall go to your room.'

'My room?' *Mon Dieu!* Had she been so obvious? There was a gleam in the green eyes and a quirk to the devil's eyebrow that told her that she had, but all he said was,

'Your store-room, madame. Were you not going to help me to choose my costume for this evening?'

Fighting for self-control, a feeling entirely alien to her, she led him upstairs, knowing that his eyes bored into her back, allowing her hips that extra swing. 'Have you any ideas?' she asked, adding, 'For your costume.'

'I am full of ideas, madame,' he said, still playing her game. 'But I had hoped for your guidance.' She turned at that, having reached the top of the stairs two steps above him, his eyes on a level with breasts obviously unconfined beneath the thin silk of that deceptively modest gown. He raised his head a little. She lowered hers. Both knew that she could give him more guidance than Blanche had ever dreamed of. 'The costume, madame?' he suggested softly.

'The costume, my lord.' She led him into the warmly-scented room where perfumes mingled, together with the slightly musky odour of a gown worn once and put away uncleaned, a carnal, elusive body odour. It caught at his nostrils and he wrinkled them, fighting its persuasive sexuality. 'Something displeases you, Lord Hunterton?'

He turned, seeing her as a part of that room, sensual, slumberous, very slightly decadent . . . and Jason Hunterton was nothing if not a man . . . or devil . . . or both, in equal proportions. 'Nothing here could possibly displease me.' Reaching for her, knowing already how easily she would come into his arms, he kissed her for a very long time—with precision and expert sensuality, with calculated passion and exquisite torment, until he found the response he sought, the ragged shuddering breath that preceded the deep moan torn from her throat. Then he released her, holding her within the hard circle of his arm until he knew she could stand alone. 'And yes, I am rich,' he stated softly. 'I am also in love with a very great lady. Please send whichever costume you choose to the Hôtel de Sully. Send it, madame. Please don't think to bring it.'

He had reached the door and begun to open it as the Spanish throwing-knife thudded into the wood beside his head. He froze, then removed it slowly and weighed it in his hands. 'An excellent choice, madame. I look forward to receiving the rest of the costume later.' Closing the door gently behind him, he had reached half-way down the stairs before he heard the muffled stream of invective from behind that door. With a smile, he shook his head. 'I never did believe the story of the Breton peasant girl until now. Blood will out!'

In the hall he saw a hovering, glowering André. 'You are leaving, monsieur.' It was not a question, nor a request.

'I am. I can see myself out, but I think madame la Comtesse may require your attention.'

A scream of pure frustrated rage rose from above. 'If you have harmed her . . .'

'Oh, don't be a fool! I haven't even offended her, and there is little you could do about it if I had.'

The young man took the stairs two at a time and, chuckling, Jason let himself out.

The tight black trousers, leather boots and white blouson open to the waist, accompanying the wide-brimmed be-feathered hat and scarlet sash of a pirate of the Spanish Main arrived at the Hôtel de Sully two hours later . . . together with the mate of the knife he had taken. 'Was there any message?' he asked the man who had delivered them.

His eyes clouded. 'Madame very sick. Stay in her bed one day, maybe two. She sends regrets, and hopes you will forgive.'

'Good!' murmured Jason, with only the slightest tinge of envy.

'Monsieur?'

'It's nothing. Convey my deepest felicitations . . .'

'Monsieur?'

'Tell madame la Comtesse that I understand very well.'

'You will forgive her?'

'Almost anything,' Jason laughed. Whistling softly, he put on the garb, pleased with his rakish reflection in the tall mirror, and, as an added touch, called for one of Blanche's gold chain necklaces.

'Are you male or female?' she laughed through the door.

'You'll have to wait and see!' He delighted in her gurgle of laughter.

'Oh, Jayce, I refuse to dance with a shepherdess! I absolutely refuse.'

'Unless you're going as a shepherd,' he countered. 'May I not see?'

'No!' With a shriek. 'Not fair! You'll have to be patient. Go on down, the music has begun, and Ellen tells me there must be a hundred people there already. Marie's hairdresser has not arrived yet, so I'll be another hour.'

'Don't count on her coming.'

There was a pause. 'Jason?' What have you done . . . or said?'

He adjusted the hat: somehow it did not appear quite so rakish. 'Nothing . . . nothing at all. She sent a message that she wasn't feeling well and wouldn't be coming this evening. She may well have forgotten the hairdresser.'

'Jason!' The adjoining door was flung open and Blanche stood there, eyes flashing dangerously— wearing nothing but the flimsiest of chemises. 'What have you . . . Oh, Jayce!' Voice going husky, looks scalding him.

Suddenly the hat felt exactly right, but was forgotten in the instant as he moved towards her, trying for sanity. 'You can't appear like that!'

She never spoke, waiting for him, then in a rush closing the gap, flinging herself into his arms, nuzzling at the length of bronzed torso revealed by the deep neckline of the blouse, murmuring his name over and over. A sudden muffled giggle. 'Those trousers are far too tight.'

'They weren't before!'

'Then get rid of them.'

'I've just dressed, woman!'

'Only the trousers. Keep the shirt . . . and the hat . . . especially the hat!' She was laughing, wriggling against him, tugging at the fastenings of the pantaloons. Suddenly not laughing, not tugging, hands moving tremblingly over the corded muscles of his back . . .

'The hairdresser is here, milady,' came Ellen's voice from the next room.

'Darnation!' muttered the Lady Davenport. 'Tell her I'll be another ten minutes . . .' Then, reading the dark eyes above her, 'Make that a half-hour!'

She made him go to the ball before her. 'I shall need another half-hour at least for my dress and my hair . . . and a further half-hour to calm myself,

Jayce, why do you do this to me? How can you do this to me?'

'You mean this? . . . and this?' His voice endlessly deep, his hands turning her blood to molten lava.

It was therefore very late when eventually he went downstairs, circulating, smiling, not for an instant losing sight of the gallery above until . . . at the top of that ornate staircase, halting for a moment, holding that pose until every eye was upon her, slowly descending . . . La Comtesse Angélique de Chauvenay. Not even the brush of Fragonard had been able to capture that dress—unless the replica exceeded the beauty of the original—the low, square-cut *décolletage* trimmed with lace, the wide panniers accentuating the tiny waist, and that high, powdered confection of hair curled and trimmed with delicate ropes of gold, giving her features the same cool aristocratic expression as that in the portrait—until she looked into Jason's eyes—and gave a low gurgle of laughter. Not Angélique, but Circe and Aphrodite, and Calypso who could keep a man such as Odysseus a willing captive of love for seven long years . . .

And Jason threw back his head and his laughter pealed out as he took the stairs two at a time, astounding the rippling audience still further, and with a low courtly bow, that almost brushed the hem of the fabulous skirt with its gold tassels reflecting the candlelight, held out his arm. 'My lady,' he said, eyes alight. Then, more softly, 'My lady . . . my love.'

CHAPTER TWELVE

IT WAS LATE MORNING, a damp and misty morning, and Blanche turned to run teasing fingers across Jason's chest. 'It's so much more civilised to be rich,' she murmured, a contented sybarite nestling beneath the thick quilt. 'I'm so glad we sent Ellen on ahead or I'd feel guilty lying abed at this time. Do you feel guilty, Jason?'

He gave a lazy smile, 'No. Exhausted!'

'Oh, Jayce!' Then, suddenly anxious, 'Am I a terrible woman to want you so much? I've heard that a true lady should treat these . . . activities . . . with patience and tolerance, and be thinking of her children and tomorrow's menu.'

'Perhaps that all comes with marriage,' he said, half jokingly, and saw her eyes darken.

'Then I shall never get married. Jason, I don't want to feel this way: I want to have fun and flirt madly and be free, make friends as I see fit without wondering whether you'll approve.'

Jason put aside his twinge of jealousy, recognising it for what it was, and accepting the need to control this small weakness in his character—a weakness hitherto unknown. 'Is that why you were kind to your Frenchman at the ball?'

'Kind? Was I? I thought that I was only polite.'

'I've seen your frosty politeness and your "delighted-to-meet-you" social politeness. You were not merely polite.'

Blanche watched the play of emotion on the tightly controlled features and allowed herself a tiny smile, reflecting that it was most satisfactory to be needed . . .

but utterly delicious being wanted! 'I suppose I could have accepted his apology in the midst of the ballroom, but it would hardly have been fair.'

'You said that you never wanted to see him again,' he reminded her.

'I was wrong.'

She remembered that she had been standing before one of the great mirrors, her dress reflected to full advantage, the rich satin gleaming in the light from the chandeliers. Jason had been drawn a few paces away by an exiled Englishman who, having caught their accent, insisted on hearing all of the changes made to his 'beloved homeland'. Blanche had seen André an instant before his dark eyes found hers, so that she had time to recover, having forgotten in her hours with Jason how incredibly handsome the young count was.

He was wearing the red damask toga and that rich Tyrian purple coat of Lorenzo de Medici, its sleeves and hem trimmed with leopard-skin so that it swung out as he moved. His eyes had widened as he saw her dress, then closed briefly in an instant of pain. Like a sleepwalker, as if no one milled and pushed about him, he crossed to face her. 'I know . . . why you . . . wore white,' he said, the pain rending his words into fragments, causing him to forget his carefully prepared speech as if it had never been. 'I had hoped that I would be the one . . .' His eyes went instinctively to Jason, and something changed in that burning gaze, something that, because of the angle of his head Blanche had missed, something dark and ugly as he took in the broad shoulders and raven hair and remembered the first time he had seen his rival in the carriage confidently taking this woman, the woman he desired above all, into his arms. But then André, as Jason turned, drew himself up a fraction. 'Won't you please introduce us, Blanche? Is it too much to ask?'

Blanche felt her heart reach out to him, and put light fingers on his arm, drawing Jason over with her other hand so that she stood between them as she made the introductions, feeling the tension in both as briefly they shook hands.

Her reverie was broken by Jason's voice demanding, 'Is it too much to ask that you listen to your lord and master when he speaks?'

Blanche returned to the present, hiding her tiny irritation at this game of his playing the master. 'I was thinking of poor André,' she revealed honestly, and saw his eyes darken.

'I don't want to talk of the other men in your life,' he stated shortly.

'I wasn't about to.'

'I had other subjects in mind.' Reaching for her, he found his hand brushed aside, and saw with surprise the grey eyes like flint.

'You can't control my mind with the same ease with which you control my body, Jason. There have been no other men in my life before you, but I've had—still have—will always have—friends, acquaintances and a variety of people in between of both sexes. You've met André, you know Jeremy . . .'

'I don't want a catalogue of names!'

'No, you're right. Until you accept their names, you can't really accept their existence.'

'I don't have to.'

'Mud!' exclaimed Blanche vehemently.

'What?'

'I said "mud" . . . A slimy, dark, all-encompassing substance that blankets all beneath it. I will not obligingly hide half my life under a layer of mud to suit you or anyone.' Deliberately she turned her back on him, gazing blindly at the tapestries on the wall, wanting to storm from the bed—and wanting to stay there for ever. Several minutes passed.

'I apologise.'

'Accepted.' But still she did not turn, the Paris streets beyond the window as cold as her heart. Why did it always have to be like this? Why could men never love without needing to possess body and soul?

Her mind returned to the museum at the de Chauvenays, and the case of butterflies. Why was it necessary to kill something so beautiful just for the pleasure of seeing it unchanging? She heard Jason's deep, ragged breath.

'If I don't stretch out my hand and touch you,' he said quietly, 'I think I'll go mad.'

'Oh, Jayce!' And she was in his arms, clinging to him fiercely, thinking, 'It doesn't matter. Nothing matters while I'm here.' But of course it did, and there was a terrible desperation in their lovemaking that only widened the chasm between them.

'I think I should go now,' he said softly, and she nodded, rising silently to dress, allowing him to help her with her back fastenings, wishing that she did not need this small service, not when the air was so chill between them. She vowed to change her whole wardrobe that very week, so that every dress fastened at the front. She felt Jason's chill fingers against her bare back and gave an involuntary shudder.

'Is it so bad, Blanche?' he asked, his voice husky with regret. 'Have we already reached a time when you tremble at my touch? I'm old enough to recognise the difference.'

She turned, shocked. 'No! Oh, no, Jayce! Your . . . your hands were cold, that's all.' Then, almost in tears, 'Has it come to a time when you should ask such a question? Only a few hours ago . . . Is it André? There was never anyone but you . . . Not in this way.'

Slowly he turned her to face him, jaw tight, eyes bleak. 'I love you. That is a fact I've had to face. I'm also a jealous lover. That, too, is a fact, though I've not come to terms with it yet.' His lips lifted in the semblance of a smile. 'If I help you to write your memoirs, with a list of your conquests for posterity, and never reproach you or question you about one of them, do you think you could lie just a little and convince me that I'm the last?'

Blanche bit her lip, but could not keep the tears

from overflowing. 'I can't help what you call my "conquests" other than by going into a convent. I can only tell you that you were my first lover, my only lover and, if God and the Fates will it so, my last.'

It was only later, lying warm and replete, head snuggled against his shoulder, languid limbs still entwined, that she realised that even then she had been unable to use the word 'love'.

And so it was late in the evening when the carriage drew up before the elegant town house typical of that area which Jason called the Marais. 'A little too close to the Bastille during the Revolution,' he informed her, 'so all the *haut ton* moved out. The area fell into disrepair from which, as you'll see in the morning, it still has not recovered. I purchased the house for a few *louis*, but the inside is virtually unchanged from the days when places like these saw glittering parties and names such as Molière, Racine and Voltaire.'

'May I perhaps see?' Blanche queried, and caught his apologetic smile.

They went into the candlelit hall, and as Jason banged the door shut behind them, closing out the tentative tendrils of mist that had sought to gain entry, a voice called, 'Is that you, milady?' and a beaming Ellen appeared at the top of the tall, curved staircase. 'I'm so glad you have arrived at last. I've unpacked, and told your other maid just how you like your clothes laid out. Good evening, my lord.'

'Good evening, Ellen,' Jason smiled, noticing, as Blanche had, her establishment of the pecking order between herself and the 'other' maid. 'Has cook prepared anything, since she wasn't too certain as the time of our arrival, or shall we survive on cold meat and cheese?'

'Your cook is a gem, my lord, a real gem. She put on a good thick soup—what she calls a "boolibase"—from down south as I understand it—with all sorts of fish and bits floating in it. When you didn't arrive, it was took off and made into a sort of sauce for whatever it was we had for luncheon today—a sort of fish, and a very tasty one, too. Not a drop wasted.'

Another woman had appeared, a slender, dark-haired gypsy-looking woman in her late twenties, and Jason greeted her with a familiar hand on the shoulder and a friendly '*Ça va*, Estelle?'

'Blanche, this is my indispensable right hand. Estelle couldn't be called a housekeeper exactly; in fact to call her a servant at all would be almost an insult. She runs the house whether I'm here or not, listens to my woes, puts a glass into my hand when I need it, and takes it firmly away when it shouldn't be there.' The woman gave a brief bob, and vanished as silently as she had appeared.

'Another gem,' agreed Blanche a little drily, but he merely laughed and led her upstairs, one arm about her shoulders.

'We've time to change, then supper and an hour to relax. *Mon Dieu*, it's good to be home!'

It would be, Blanche reflected, if I were home. The house is well run by an obviously devoted staff, but they are not my staff. Even Ellen, close as she has become, has not the intelligence and wit of Annemarie. For the first time since her arrival, she felt homesick.

The bedroom, with its large, dominant four-poster, had a quiet elegance, but was entirely a masculine domain and only fractionally softened by the neat row of Blanche's toiletries set out on one of the chest of drawers. 'We can change the velvet bed curtains for brocade,' he offered, reading her expression. 'Though I do put my foot down about pale pink muslin!'

'So would I,' Blanche smiled, feeling better for his sympathy. 'Let's change now, and think about the décor tomorrow.'

'Forgive me, then, while I go down and make my presence known. Ellen will undoubtedly help you to change, but if you need anything else, that bell-push goes direct to Estelle's quarters.' She gave him an enigmatic look and received a world-weary sigh. 'She's both housekeeper and friend, nothing more.'

'Doesn't say much, either! One might say the ideal woman—devoted, dependent and silent.'

He turned at the door, giving her a long look. 'If I didn't know you better, I would say that you were betraying signs of jealousy!' As she made to speak, he continued, 'Estelle is devoted because I saved her life, and she's silent because she was born mute. I rescued her from a band of gypsies who treated her like an animal, beating, starving and abusing her as the mood took them. That was nigh on five years ago, shortly after I began my search for the boy, so it is ancient history for both of us. We'll go shopping tomorrow, and I'll show you my Paris, since you've obviously had time enough to see that lovely face she presents to tourists and the rich.'

It was some time before Blanche could regain her composure enough to change, and even when Ellen brought her some cordial, she could not rid her mind of the thought that the boy they sought might be living among such savages. They must find him at all costs. Shopping could wait. She must talk to Jason the following day. She barely noticed the quietly luxurious décor in the high-ceilinged dining-room, and only when the piping hot soup had thawed her could she respond to Jason's words.

He was speaking of France's history, carefully avoiding the gory details of the Revolution, much of which England already knew from the desperate *émigrés*, avoiding, too, mention of the callous commercialism after Waterloo when the battlefield became a great tourist attraction and the ever-enterprising French set up souvenir stalls, carrying everything from buttons and bullets—to bones and pieces of hair. 'Yet I love her,' he insisted, 'for all of her faults.'

'A nation of fashion designers and revolutionary students . . . which seems to be the only thing that has come out of the glorious Revolution? Why, you've only to go on a long holiday and you return to a new government. Hardly a world power!' she suggested.

He smiled, deliberately lightening the subject. 'She is certainly a world power in female fashion. If a man wishes a happy wife or mistress he is obliged to buy French; the one who rules the boudoir rules the house, never doubt it! As for the students, surely it is their *raison d'être* to question.'

'But not to force change. The moment anyone comes to power, someone else will organise a cabal to bring him down.'

'A word invented by the British, I believe—the five ministers of Charles II, wasn't it?' The green eyes softened. 'But, of course, France has its faults, Paris more than most, but to me Paris resembles a mature and experienced courtesan. She has learned from a number of patrons, but is not averse to learning more. She is a languorous lady while retaining a touch of *cocotte*, a mother who will listen to your woes, a child who will tease them away. She is ever-changeable and whatever a man wishes her to be. No, I'm not averse to making my home here.'

Blanche felt a small, inexplicable tug in the region of her heart, but looked about her and forced a smile. 'It looks as if you have already done so!' She was considering the scattered treasures, Parian ware statuettes on the whatnot in the corner, a beaten pewter tankard amid the silver, its dented side begging to reveal a story, assorted memorabilia of a chequered past.

The cook had conjured a chicken from somewhere, and presented them with tender breasts braised in white wine with a delicate cream sauce, enabling Blanche again to change the subject so that the meal ended in a quiet harmony that they had not experienced in many days. They were to take their coffee in the drawing-room, where a small fire had been hastily built but which was still cool from being so long uninhabited. 'The staff have their own quarters, and come here only to dust a little when I'm away,' Jason apologised. 'You won't recognise the place tomorrow.'

'It's a beautiful room, but, as you say, a little on the chill side.' Then softly, 'Why don't we move to somewhere warmer?'

He set down his coffee and came to where she stood by the fire, his eyes smouldering. 'You were ever a practical woman, Blanche!' Lean fingers cupped her face. 'Shall I ever tire of you, I wonder?' He smiled in a way to melt the strongest resistance, turning her face upward, searching the soft grey eyes. 'Shall we make tonight a beginning, forget the tensions of this morning, vow they'll never come between us again, and start with my divesting you of your innocence one more time?' For answer Blanche twined her fingers into the softly curling hair at the back of his neck, drawing his head down to meet her kiss. When at last he raised his head, his breathing was as ragged as hers. Wordlessly he swung her into his arms, carrying her to their room as if she weighed no more than a doll.

Blanche awoke slowly to the sound of birdsong outside the window. For several minutes she lay with her eyes closed, attempting to analyse her feelings. Wonderingly, then, she looked down at her naked body. Strange. It appeared no different. She turned. He, too. He was just a man. No . . . never that! Almost angrily she rose, throwing on a high-necked *peignoir* and going downstairs to where a silently gesticulating Estelle was directing the laying of the breakfast table, not in the formal dining-room, but in an adjoining ante-room.

'Good morning, Estelle.' The woman turned with a polite smile, taking in the dark-ringed eyes and the love-bruised lips with knowing regard. She suddenly caught sight of an accidental error in the table setting by the maid who, at Blanche's entrance, had quickly finished her work and hurried out—leaving two knives carelessly crossed. The housekeeper's face turned grey, and she snatched up the offending knife, repositioning it. 'It's all right, Estelle,' Blanche hastened, seeing the woman's obvious distress. 'I'm not in the least superstitious, and don't for an instant believe that crossed knives portend a tragic event. Come, now. Pour some of that ambrosial coffee.' As an afterthought, she asked, 'Oh, I'm sorry. You do understand English, don't you?'

The slightly elongated eyes chided her. With gracefully flowing gestures, the gypsy pointed upward to where her master slept, then to herself, and twined her forefingers together, moving them to her lips, then again pointing upward.

'I see. You and Lord Hunterton are friends, and he has taught you to speak . . . forgive me . . . understand English,' Blanche translated. 'Well, that certainly makes life easier, for my French is strictly out of the schoolroom.'

'Not for long,' came his voice from behind them, and Jason entered resplendent in a dressing-gown of Indian silk. He greeted Estelle silently, laying his hand briefly on her shoulder, smiling into her adoring eyes, before turning his full attention to Blanche. 'You didn't wake me,' he accused softly. 'Did you fear we'd never reach the table?'

Blanche was glad that Estelle had immediately withdrawn to see to their breakfast. 'Would we have?'

'No, but since we are here, I suggest we take advantage of the meringue-light croissants that cook will produce and then take the carriage out. I want you to see every boulevard, every corner, every square, every park. I want you to know the *boulangeries* which make the freshest, crustiest bread, the *épiceries* which sell the cheapest groceries and freshest vegetables.'

'You expect me to shop and barter, then?'

He laughed. 'If it amuses you. I want only that you experience Paris to the full.' Then, more seriously, 'I want you to love it with all its faults, with its *clochards*—the vagabonds who often choose to live that way—and its *poules*, who rarely do.'

Over the following days Blanche saw much of these social outcasts, for there were few places one could drive without glimpsing them. 'All too familiar,' said Blanche, as the phaeton rolled on through the Bois de Boulogne, and Jason was telling her that it had once been a royal park but had been opened to the public by Louis XIV and now contained another kind of game, even during the daylight hours. 'For these aren't *la crème de la crème*; most are well past their prime and often diseased, but it is these people who will help us in our search. So, as in London, I must adopt the guise of Jayce Hunter or, here, Jacques Chasseur. They are quite unaware of the identity of the child I seek—I've told them only that he is the son of a friend.' There was a momentary hesitation, then, 'I must leave you behind when I go out this evening, however. I have a man to see whose morals make Black Jack resemble a saint, and to reach him I descend to Hades—or its Parisian equivalent, the sewers where he conducts his business.'

'Then you surely won't go alone?'

'He has stipulated that I do. He will be alone, but one false move, and he could lead me into those channels and lose me down there for ever. Yet, if there are gypsies, he will know; if a boy with a disfigured hand, he will know. I need his help above any other, so must take the risk.'

They had reached the house, and she had been firmly led inside. 'I can't stay here and wait while you go into such a place,' she insisted. 'Is there nowhere I can wait? Somewhere near by?' She caught his searching look, and turned away. 'It's not that I'm concerned about you; I simply want to be part your search.'

He gave a smile, understanding the eyes that belied her words. 'The main entrance to the sewer is at the corner of the rue Réaumur. Give me an hour, and then take the carriage to there. Wear something that a housewife might wear who has come from the market.' He put a warm hand on her arm. 'We'll go to a café afterwards, and I'll teach you how to eat fresh croissants without dropping a crumb. I must go now.'

'Good luck, Jason.' He nodded and left, but Blanche could not wait for him as calmly as she had promised, and after pacing the floor for a full ten minutes, went to change. If this man was as evil as Jason had said, she had to be with him, and armed. She had to stand by him, no matter what the danger. Wearing a long cloak, she made her way downstairs to Jason's weapons cabinet and rang for Estelle. 'I need the key of this cabinet. Lord Hunterton is going into danger, and I must be there.' Then, at the housekeeper's violent shake of the head, she snapped, 'I didn't ask, Estelle; I told you I wanted the key!' She held out her hand imperiously.

The dark eyes opened wide at the autocratic tone, but like many before her when confronted by the Lady Davenport, she did not argue and took a small key from the ring, extending it with a thrusting gesture, her lips in a tight disapproving line. There was no time, however, to make amends or give lengthy explanantions, and swiftly Blanche selected a beautifully engraved horse-pistol, beloved of a gentleman of the road—such as Jayce Hunter purported to be. Slipping it beneath the voluminous cloak, she hurried out and within minutes was driving out to the entrance of the sewer.

Heart beating erratically, she took a pace into the gloom, hefting the reassuring weight of the gun and wondering, not for the first time since she left the house, whether she had lost her mind completely. Picking her way over noxious heaps of refuse and black puddles of filth she moved forward, all senses tingling, waiting for the tiniest sound ahead that would tell her that she was moving in the right direction. She thought she heard a laugh, but it was down a branch off the main tunnel, and she knew

that if the men moved away she could well lose
herself, as Jason had said. Nevertheless . . . Throat
dry, she left the large passage and made her way to
the left, choking back a cry as a large rat slunk away
at her approach.

At her tiny cry there was a sudden silence, and she
froze, then a voice called, 'Who is it?', and there was
the sound of the filthy water being churned up as
footsteps hurried toward her. She wanted to turn and
run, but knew that whoever was there would catch up
with her before she had made more than a few yards.
Bringing out the heavy gun, she held it in shaking
hands and waited.

Suddenly Jason appeared round the bend ahead
and, as he recognised her, gave a harsh curse. At the
same time, a stranger appeared at his elbow, and
Blanche's breath was released in a gust of relief. This
could not possibly be the evil one that Jason had
spoken of! This was only a boy, possibly even younger
than she, and dwarfed by Jason's broad frame, smiling
up at him easily. He said something in soft argot and
Jason answered in kind, but Jason's voice was uneasy,
and Blanche held out a placatory hand.

'I'm sorry . . . I thought you might be in some
danger . . .' She forced a little laugh, gesturing toward
the pistol she held. 'Facing off a band of cut-throats
and waiting for rescue . . .'

'Be quiet, Blanche!' He turned and spoke quickly
and, to Blanche, quite unintelligibly to his companion,
gesticulating toward her. The stranger's smile never
faltered, but suddenly he turned and walked away,
and Jason broke off with a low curse, turning to
Blanche with a glare, moving past her and back
toward the entrance. Only there did he spin to face
her, eyes black with fury. 'Don't ever do that again!
They call him "Fantôme". He is invisible until he
wishes to kill—or, on rare occasions such as this, to
talk—and then he disappears again. If he so chose,
my life and yours would not be worth a *sou*. He
governs more men than the Prefect, and it is said

with some truth that he who governs the streets, governs Paris.'

'Jason, I'm sorry. I just couldn't see you in danger and not be there!'

Looking into that lovely anixous face, Jason drew a deep breath, realising the courage it had taken to follow him into the regions of Hades. His eyes softened. 'Very well. He does know of a boy with a scarred hand, though he doesn't know which hand or what form the scar takes. We'll go now, to a gypsy encampment just outside town. They've been there a month or more—unusual—and a number of children from the slums have joined them. The gypsy's life seems a glamorous one—until the first hard winter.'

The encampment was large, and more established than most, with gaily painted caravans, and dark-skinned people lighting up their own cooking-fires. Jason made his way to the largest, and a handsome, mahogany-skinned woman answered his knock. Blanche held back, fascinated by the camp life about her, the hordes of children chasing in and out the caravans, the women stirring richly aromatic cooking-pots or weaving baskets, making pegs and bead necklaces to sell, the men, shorter than the townpeople but broad and well muscled, cutting wood or tending their shaggy horses. Swarthy faces turned their way, then, obviously accustomed to the curious city folk, returned to their work.

'There is a boy here.' Jason's voice sounded beside her, and there was a subdued excitement in it that was difficult to suppress. But when the child was brought, even Blanche felt her hopes plummet and knew that the disappointment must be far worse for the man who had been looking for so long and so vainly. 'No,' he told the leader's wife. 'He isn't the one.'

The boy was in his early teens, with greasy blond hair falling to his shoulders, and pale blue incurious eyes. His right hand, extended on command, had at one time been terribly burned, the skin dark purple and wrinkled, the fingers twisted stiffly. Jason spoke gently to the child and brought an *écu* from his pocket, which disappeared faster than the eye could judge into the pocket of the other, and with no change of expression. 'Let's go,' Jason said, and there was a resignation in his tone that told Blanche far more than any explanation of the number of abortive journeys he had made.

In silence they made their way back to the Marais, but at the house they were met by Ellen, who advised them with a frown, 'A gentleman came to see you, my lord. Nasty bit of goods, if you ask me. He wouldn't stop, but gave me this note for you.' She handed Jason a sealed letter, repeating to Blanche, 'Nasty bit of goods. Can I help you to change, milady? Don't seem right, you in them clothes.' But Blanche had eyes only for Jason, who had paled and then, with a muttered expletive, crumpled the note into his pocket.

'Jayce, what is it? What's wrong?'

The green eyes were cold as the Atlantic, and his jaw tightened. 'It's unsigned, of course; a copy of the Decree of the National Assembly—the decree abolishing royalty in France in September of '92. In short, a warning, my dear, from someone who knows exactly what I'm doing, and where I live.'

'What will you do?'

'Continue as before, or course. It's not the first time, and probably won't be the last.' He raised a smile. 'One pays little attention to curs, apart from watching one's heels! Let us change and eat. Tomorrow we'll talk with some of the *clochards*, who have ears everywhere. I'll take a détour through the Bois, and you can communicate with one or two of the regulars there who will guard turf with tooth and claw, but have the tenderest hearts for an animal or a child.'

The following day came and went, and then another. With her gentle understanding and easy

charm, Blanche found an almost eager willingness to
help from the women of the Bois, to whom gentleness
was an alien experience. It was mid-afternoon of the
fourth day, an icy, blustery day that kept client and
poule alike in their homes, and Jason had insisted
they turn for home, when suddenly Blanche cried
out, 'Stop! Stop!' with such urgency that the driver
almost set the horses back on their haunches. Leaping
from the carriage without awaiting help, she ran back
to the blowsy, wind-blown creature she had glimpsed
. . . then pulled up a few feet away, shaking her
head. 'I—I'm sorry . . . I thought you were someone
else.'

'*Ce n'est Rien*,' muttered the scarecrow, turning
back into the undergrowth whence she had come.

'Blanche?' Jason murmured behind her, and she
turned with still shocked eyes.

'I thought . . . There was a girl I once knew in
London . . . on the stage. She always spoke of going
to Paris, to play at the Comédie. I thought . . .' She
gave a shudder, allowing him to lead her back to the
carriage, but it was only later that evening, beneath
his gentle probing, that she could bring herself to
speak of her past.

Jason was standing with his back to the roaring fire,
which cast a warm glow over the bronzes and copper
plate. It was a strange room, he knew, culled from an
incredible assortment of styles and eras; yet, as a
whole, harmonious and restful to the eye. 'You don't
have to tell me, Blanche,' he said gently, when the
subject was raised.

She searched his eyes and realised that he was
perfectly serious: he would accept a part of her past,
an undoubtedly shady part, without either question
or reserve. With a sigh, she went to look out of the
window, not that she could see more than the house
opposite, but the window reflected the face of a
woman, once a girl, never a child.

'I was Trixie Devine for almost a year,' she began.

'Before that, I was the unwanted, unloved, daughter of the Davenports. I don't mean that to sound self-pitying—I've long outgrown that—but when a man becomes obsessed with having an heir, a continuation of the name, and then has a daughter, the child is bound to be somewhat unwelcome, to say the least.'

She could not tell him of the way in which her birth had torn her family apart, of how her father had ranted and raved when the doctor told him that his wife should never have another child, of how he had moved to the top the house for over five years, speaking to no one.

'Was it not better when your brother was born?'

She turned, and he saw the pain behind the grey eyes. 'For them, yes. The situation as far as I was concerned was intolerable. My brother's birth had left my mother bedridden. Through guilt, my father lavished every luxury on her, but it was young Alex who received his love ... In all truth he was, and still is, a lovable person, handsome, bright, gay. It was no consolation at the time. I was a stranger there, and retaliated with a vituperative tongue and totally unfeminine behaviour. When I was fifteen, my father decided that he had had enough, so he sent me to an ancient and autocractic aunt and uncle in London.'

Jason gave a sympathetic nod. 'Just the thing for a rebellious child who needed only love.'

'It lasted two long and lonely years; then I ran away. There was a small travelling theatrical company playing in London, and I watched them massacre *Romeo and Juliet*. I was about to walk out, when I noticed the audience for the first time. They were loving every minute of it; but more, they were loving the players. Juliet was a scrawny, frizzy-haired girl with absolutely no talent for Shakespeare and a voice like a magpie. Her name was Leonie Peters, though she called herself Angélique Moreau and told everyone that she was the illegitimate daughter of a French aristo. That night I went backstage and asked if I could join the troupe.'

'They must have jumped at the chance of employing Lord Davenport's daughter!'

Blanche gave a frown. 'I may have hated my father, but there were still my mother and Alex, and I would have done nothing to bring disgrace upon them. No, the bills outside had advertised "the divine Angélique Moreau", so when they asked my name, I had to think fast. I used the diminutive of Beatrice and called myself "Trixie Devine".'

'So you made friends, and played Shakespeare.'

'Yes . . . and no. I made friends . . . A special friend who gave me all the understanding and love that I had missed before. Leonie allowed me to sleep in her room, which contained just one double mattress on the floor, but to a young girl with a head full of dreams it was a magic carpet. No, I didn't play Shakespeare. The manager said that the way in which I spoke was not dramatic enough. I couldn't "wring the customers' hearts", to use his phrase. I could dance a little, however, and sing, though my voice was more suited to a *chansonnière* than an opera star! My childhood habit—which you've noticed I still retain—of imitating my so-called betters enabled me to hold the audience's attention between acts, so I did well enough. I even held pretensions of fame, with my name in lights, so "Trixie Devine" seemed too dull by far.' She gave a lip-biting grin, finishing quickly, 'I called myself Boadicea Devine!' She was laughing even before Jason's choked cough dissolved into laughter that joined hers. 'So you can appreciate that when I saw that terrible creature in the Bois, and thought it might possibly be the dear friend who had given me so much of my youth . . .'

He nodded sympathetically. 'And your career on stage?'

'Not much of a career. I had a tongue like our Romeo's rapier and a wit to match, which was all very well while I was taking off the gentry and the government . . . the audience loved it. Then the manager became a little too interested in furthering my career—a fat man with six pairs of hands—so I'm afraid I turned my mimicry upon him. The customers lapped it up; the cast even more so, but . . .' Blanche gave a philosophical shrug. 'I was advised that my career was over.'

'A great loss to the theatrical world,' Jason agreed with mock seriousness. 'Now, however, I believe dinner is served, so perhaps we can continue this fascinating dissertation in the dining-room.'

Blanche laughed. 'I suggest that we forget the whole thing!'

Later, he observed, 'You know, you've been here for almost a week and you still haven't allowed me to take you to the shops. We have been invited to a ball by the Baron Duplessis and his new wife . . . the fourth, I believe. All of the *haut ton* will be agog to see her . . . and each other, so I think something a little special is called for.' Then, seeing the doubt in her eyes, 'Don't all women love the chance of shopping for a new wardrobe?'

'Or course, but . . . I don't feel right accepting that sort of gift from you . . .' She met his surprised look, and saw his eyes darken.

'Why others, and not me?' he questioned, his voice ominously soft.

Blanche had been dreading this discussion and took her time, sipping her tiny glass of port and rolling her napkin into a totally unusable ball before replying. 'Others have bought me a shawl, pairs of gloves, even a length of silk or velvet. If I accompany you to one of those houses in the Rue de la Paix, which is fast becoming the fashion centre of the world—with prices to match—I shall emerge in gowns of your choice because I'd not wish to offend you. They and I would completely bought and paid for.'

'Never that! Is that what you think I want?' He reached to grasp Blanche's hand. 'I own nothing of you, nor ever shall. Wear white for the rest of your

life, if you wish. Save and scrimp and buy your own.
I thought you'd professed a desire for change, but
was possibly wrong. I had thought we were close
enough for my money not to come between us as an
ulterior motive. I was undoubtedly wrong there, too.'
Angrily, his anger covering the hurt pride within, he
rose from the table. 'Nevertheless, you need new
clothes.' Reaching into his pocket, he threw a heavy
pouch on to the table. 'A few *louis* for *frivolités*, the
gowns you'll charge to my account. You may go
alone. I'll give the driver the addresses. Call it a loan,
since you won't accept a gift from a friend.'

He strode out, startling the maid as she entered to
clear the table, and slamming the library door behind
him as he gained that sanctuary, cursing all women
for their mule-headedness and Blanche in particular
for her, to him inexplicable, pride.

Blanche made to rise and follow him, then changed
her mind. Since their first meeting in Paris, Jason had
worked to undermine the wall of independence she
had erected about her, and she worked equally
assiduously to repair it. This business of her wardrobe
had to rear its ugly head sooner or later, for she had
been fast running out of excuses of late. 'I'm not a
Puritan,' she objected aloud. 'Far from it. But those
gifts should surely come between husband or wife . . .
otherwise I'd be no better than those woman
occupying expensive apartments and driving in the
Bois in sables and mink, with their *coco* on one arm
and another equally dumb animal on the other!' She
gave a deep sigh. 'I refuse to go to him now. I'll deal
with him tonight, when his hurt pride has cooled a
little.'

The following morning, however, Blanche wondered
who had 'dealt' with whom as she touched a
surreptitious finger to her bruised lips, unable to
restrain a tiny smile, remembering the steel in velvet
texture of the mouth that had caused the offence.
Jason had swept aside all her well-rehearsed objections
with unassailable logic. 'I refuse to make love to a

chattering woman!' Drawing her into bed, those expert hands drove every protest from her mind, created spirals of sensation that rose through her until every part of her was caught in a whirlpool of ecstasy, and she would have agreed to anything.

Silently he handed her into the carriage, eyes gleaming as they moved to her mouth.

'Are you sure you won't come?' she asked. 'I've said I no longer mind.'

He smiled at that. 'You said a great deal with your heart, but a Parisienne shops with her head. I should not wish to distract you. I, too, have business which will take most of the day. The carriage is yours; the driver knows where to go and will wait for you. Go and indulge yourself.'

This she did more than successfully over the next few hours, emerging from the overloaded carriage at the end of the day with one more shop to visit, a mountain of boxes behind her, and a feeling of utter contentment tinged with more than a little guilt, wondering whether she had indeed needed all that the sophisticated salespeople had talked her into.

She started suddenly as she caught sight of a familiar form across the street. 'Le Comte de Chauvenay,' she murmured, then with a deep breath, ignoring the tiny leap her heart had given at the sight of that elegant frame and Greek god's features, crossed the boulevard to where André was studying the contents of a gunsmith's window, putting down a twinge of conscience at knowing Jason's reaction.

'Blanche!' The long-lashed eyes lit up as he brought her fingers to his lips. 'You are alone? Without your . . . escort?'

'Jason is at business, and has been generous enough to keep me amused in his absence.'

He eyed the patient driver at the reins of the carriage and the heap of assorted boxes, and the fine lips tightened. 'Most generous! I had hoped to see you, Blanche. We must meet. Even as friends. Allow me to take you to a late lunch.'

'Thank you, but I have eaten.'

'Then an apéritif · . . You cannot say good afternoon and then at once goodbye.' His fingers were warm and firm about her arm as he pursuaded, 'My mother mentioned something about . . . a lost boy.' Her eyes flew to his. 'I may possibly be able to help you in your search.'

Unable to keep the excitement and hope from her voice, she said, 'I—I was given to understand . . . to believe . . . that you would not want him found. Marie said that she wouldn't mention it to you because of your views.'

He gave a mirthless smile. 'Did you not know? Both my mother and I have known the bitterness of rejection by two people who had eyes only for each other.'

'Jayce . . . and Marie?'

'Is it so unbelievable?'

'Yes . . . No. Marie's very attractive, but . . .' She felt a flash of anger at the woman who had pretended friendship and then betrayed her, but put down the very jealousy that Jason had accused her of and brought her priorities to the fore. 'You really will help me to find the boy?'

'Let us discuss it.'

'I can send the carriage home, but you'll have to drive me back.'

'Everything I have is yours,' he answered, unable to keep the gleam of triumph from his eyes. 'Where would you like to go?'

'Nowhere. Can't we just drive for a little while?'

'I, too, wish for discretion.' Signalling for his waiting carriage, he helped her in, then swung up to sit beside her in the dimly-lit interior, taking her hand. 'It has been so long.'

'A little over a week.'

'A lifetime of lonely days, wondering where you were and what you were doing—and lonelier nights . . . knowing!'

'André, please!'

A deep silence, then, 'The boy. Yes. It is important that you find him, *n'est-ce pas*? And the rich and generous Lord Hunterton, it is equally important to him?'

'You know the answer,' Blanche stated, feeling a sudden chill that had nothing at all to do with the wind that beat at the leather hood and probed inside to ruffle her hair. 'Will you help us, André? Can you?'

'I can, of course. Friends of my father hold the same misguided ultra-royalist beliefs, and would gladly cross palms with silver for such a cause. Unfortunately they would assume that I held the same high ideals, and would therefore see no reason to cross my palm.'

She understood, then, and stared at him in disbelief. 'You want Jason to pay you?'

His eyes moved over the lovely face in which the colour came and went, lingering on her mouth. 'It would please my mother if the grand salon were to be re-furnished.'

'She'd never accept . . . Never be a party to blackmail!'

'Frenchwomen are notoriously practical, *chérie*, and you know how she adores her home. For myself I care little for my surroundings. A small gift—say two thousand *louis d'or*—would ensure my passing interest in this lost boy king of yours. Of course the degree of my personal interest depends not on the generous Lord Hunterton but on yourself, and no one . . . no one but you and I need ever know how great that interest would be.'

Blanche felt the anger, the shame, the betrayal rise within her. To think she had once called this monster a friend, blinded by the all too beautiful shell that contained the viper within. Ice crackled across her words as she stated softly, 'I once called you a cur. I was wrong, for at least a cur walks on four legs. You, monsieur le Comte, must surely have crawled from the slime of the sewers, where once I had cause to go.' She took the cane from his fingers, and before he could prevent her, rapped for the driver to stop. 'I shall find my own way back, for I'm sure that if I had to spend one more minute in your company I would surely be contaminated. I'll say nothing to Jason, for I'd not want even your death on my conscience!'

The handsome features became ugly. 'Yes, I'm sure he would object to sharing what he has already paid for. You won't lose me so easily, Blanche. I still have influence.' But already she had stepped to the pavement unaided, and was striding purposefully away, putting as much distance between them as possible. 'No,' he reiterated. 'You won't lose me so easily.'

It was only when she saw the carriage disappear round a far corner, felt the wind tear at her skirt and realised that her breath was coming in short sharp gasps that she allowed her pace to slacken. How dared he! She cursed aloud, then, cutting through the man's proposition and reaching to the root of her reaction to it, 'Jason hasn't bought me! He hasn't!' But the thought nagged at her all the way back to the Marais, even though she had decided to walk, allowing the blustery wind to sting her cheeks.

It stayed with her even as she prepared for the ball, glad than Jason had not returned before her and that Ellen was ensconced below stairs. Her new wardrobe had been carefully hung, and running her eye over the rich billows of material, she felt a coldness within her. 'I shall think of it only as a loan,' she informed her mirror-image, but knew with something akin to fear that she was in no small way tied to Jason—owned in part by him. 'A little late to think of that now,' she realised, then with a tiny smile, 'and they are quite beautiful!'

When Jason finally returned, he echoed her sentiments fully . . . to the degree that they almost never appeared at the ball. 'If you look at me like that,' she blushed, 'everyone will know. Oh, please allow me to dress!' The gown was of midnight blue satin, the deep *pélérine en coeur* and large beret sleeves edged with seed-pearls that were also scattered over the skirt. She wore no jewellery, but a pearl-studded comb held the tall Apollo knot, giving her height and a cool elegance that was totally belied by the expression in her eyes as she watched Jason dress. She had decided to say nothing of her encounter with André, but still could not forget his remark about Jason and his mother, and felt the warmth and pride within her as she basked in the loyalty of his love.

The ballroom was ablaze with light, and guests milled and circled in perpetual motion, so that Blanche lost track of all the names and faces that were presented. There were quadrilles aplenty, but it was the waltz which was the firm favourite, once danced by Napoleon and Joséphine non-stop for three hours, a feat which made the little Corsican's military skills seem pale by comparion. 'I wonder,' Jason said, holding her breathlessly tight and smiling into her eyes, 'whether anyone has thought to dance this at half tempo?'

The delicious decadence of the thought brought the colour to her cheeks. 'We could always try it when we return home.'

'Shall we?'

'Now? Leave all this? Could we?'

For answer, he swung her expertly to the edge of the floor and like two children they gathered their cloaks and ran, hands clasped, for the door.

CHAPTER THIRTEEN

Not every evening was as happy, however, and with Jason's long absences and no one but Ellen for company, Blanche became increasingly homesick. 'I go out day after day,' she confided to Ellen one evening, 'meeting every range of society from prostitutes to princes, prising every scrap of information possible from drunks and dukes alike. The language-barrier I have overcome to a great extent, but it's the sheer frustration that depresses me. And to think that Jason has been doing this for five long years! There is not even a chance to relax, to blow away the cobwebs. A carriage ride in the Bois can never be compared to the feel of a good horse and the wind of the Heath in one's hair. We don't know for sure that the boy is in France. I could just as well be in England . . . or Spain or Italy, searching for him. Heavens, there are no frontiers for the gypsy bands! Oh, Ellen, I'm so homesick at times, I could scream!'

'Why not have a word with his lordship?' Ellen suggested, but Blanche shook her head.

'He has enough to worry about without having to think of my silly moods. Forget it, dear Ellen. I'm just babbling.'

But Ellen loved her mistress far too much to forget such unhappiness and, as casually as she could, brought it to Jason's attention that evening when Blanche was in her room writing to Annemarie and Alexandra. Jason gave a nod and a smile, but his thoughts were obviously elsewhere, and with a sigh Ellen returned to set out her mistress's dress for dinner, muttering about the unfeeling indifference of men in general and his lordship in particular.

For the next three days Jason was rarely at home, but the following morning stated, 'You need a breath of fresh air, Blanche. I've decided that we should take a ride towards the Bois, and for once have time to ourselves.' Then, at her polite, though distinctly unenthusiastic, smile of acceptance, he teased, 'If you don't come, you won't see what I have to show you there!'

Puzzled, her senses tingling with excited curiosity, she allowed him to help her into the carriage and settle the rug about her knees. They went at a brisk trot into the park, passing the glistening lakes and skirting the cool woodland. Finally, 'Here we are,' he said, pulling up before a small farmhouse and helping her down.

Blanche held back. 'I thought you said that we would be alone . . . I'm hardly dressed for company!' But he merely smiled, and led her to the rear of the building where bales of winter feed were piled into a tidy stack and, beside them, pulling at wisps of hay . . .' Oh, Jason!'

'I call her Étoile,' he said, meeting her incredulous glance before she moved slowly, disbelievingly, toward the Arab mare who reached out a questing nose, shaking her silky black head on which a clearly-marked white star lay between large, velvet-soft eyes. 'She's yours to name whatever you choose, but it seemed appropriate.'

'Oh, Jason!' she whispered, eyes brimming. Then, running back to fling herself into his arms, 'Oh, I love you! I love you!'

Jason became very still, not breathing, just looking into that lovely face, seeing it change, seeing the eyes widen in realisation, seeing the distress and—in their deepest depths—the fear. 'Jason . . . I don't want to love you.' Barely audible.

'Would it be so terrible?'

'Yes.' Her eyes were brilliant. Then, desperately,

'Oh, don't you see? I'd be captured, pinioned, imprisoned in a beautiful glass case like André's butterflies. I'd never know freedom, never be whole again.'

He spoke her name, not understanding the panic within this wild spirit, but she shook her head, clinging to him, anguished.

'Kiss me, Jayce. Make me forget I love you. Please kiss me!' Her pain was in that kiss, and his anger and despair and frustrated love, tasting the salt tang of her tears beneath his punishing mouth—until she broke away breathlessly, the fire in her eyes dying as she whispered, 'Forgive me.'

'I have no choice. I'm the fool that's in love with you, remember?' Then, more gently, 'I suggest a long hard ride through the park. My own mount, purchased at the same time, is stabled near by, but first you need a riding-habit.'

Blanche raised a shaky smile. 'You're good to me.'

'I could be!'

'Jayce . . . Are you very angry with me?'

'No . . . not angry.' But he did not elucidate, leading her back to the carriage and helping her into the well-padded seat. 'Rue de la Paix,' he directed. He could give her that, at least. He could shower her with gifts, give her every comfort that life could hold. He could give her pleasure, of that he was very sure, telling his love through his body and his hands. He could not give her the promise that he would never claim her heart and mind and soul—for he wanted nothing less.

The subject was not raised again for several days, though he often caught those troubled grey eyes on him—in the reflection of a mirror, when she thought he had not seen, on a ride through the woods, when he turned unexpectedly. 'Do you realise,' she said one afternoon as they were resting the horses, her back against the ancient copper beech in the park, 'that when I look straight ahead, like so, my eyes see only your mouth. Is it a wonder, then, that my mind's eye is, every moment of every day and always, filled with thoughts of your mouth?'

'Do you realise,' he answered, 'that what you have said is quite irresistible?' He used that mobile mouth with an expertise that only a man who has known women from all strata of society could possess. They broke apart reluctantly, interrupted by the distant sound of a violin carried on the wind. When they exchanged glances, Blanche felt her heart beating faster. 'Come,' he said, his voice betraying none of the excitement she felt, but only a weary resignation that this was undoubtedly yet another false trail. 'Let's investigate, anyway.'

'If the boy is there?' she had to ask, not daring to hope.

He turned, giving her a long look. 'Then we take him.' There was a frightening matter-of-factness in his statement that boded ill for anyone attempting to stop him.

The gypsy encampment, a temporary affair ready to be moved on by any over-zealous official, consisted of an assortment of roughly-made carts and tents, with two wagons, one containing a cage of dejected-looking monkeys and the other holding a listless scrawny lion. A group of brown-skinned children stamped and jigged about an ancient fiddler who smiled at them, baring toothless gums, and it was they who saw the newcomers first, ceasing all movement to cluster in wary curiosity about the old man.

'Dammit!' Jason cursed. 'It's the same thieving vagrants I bought Estelle from!'

A thick-set man with elongated eyes, hooked nose and olive skin betraying Moorish blood shouldered his way through the tight group that had appeared as if by magic, and now regarded the visitors sullenly. 'The *gorgios* are welcome,' he said, though his smile was not reflected in the glinting eyes that moved over Blanche avariciously.

'Where's your *sher-engro*?' Jason demanded without preamble. 'The one I met before, many journeys ago, the one they called Lobo.'

The gypsy's smile hardened a fraction. 'I'm *sher-engro* now. Your business with Lobo is now with me.'

'And Lobo? What of him?'

There was a ripple in the crowd, and it parted to allow a man through—if one could call that horrendously deformed creature a man. The Moor's lips tightened in contempt. 'There is your great wolf that once all feared.'

The creature looked up at Jason from its lopsided position, dragging a twisted broken left leg that barely supported it and moving its head painfully on misshapen shoulders. 'How do you know me, *gorgio*?' The voice was a harsh grating from a torn mouth.

Jason's old anger, his long-held desire for vengeance, died. 'I once purchased a girl from you—when you *were* Lobo. She was nought but a sick and ill-used animal then. I came to take any others you may have brutalised in the same way. I'm wiser in the ways of trade, now. I'd not have paid you in gold but in steel this time . . . But I see that someone else has already paid you as you deserved.' Then, to the Moor, 'Why do you keep him here?'

An ugly smile and a shrug. 'One day, I'll feed him to the lion. For now, like you, I am repaying a debt. I made this carrion as you see him, catching him when he was drunk, taking him to a place where he would not be heard or found. It took many days, *gorgio*, and gave me great pleasure, as he had taken my sister for many days and my wife after that. I keep him alive and feed off his hatred.' The black eyes went to Blanche, and she felt a shudder run through her. 'Your woman is beyond compare! Mine was to me. You understand.'

Jason tore his eyes from that wreck of a man. 'Yes, but take care the flames of his hatred don't become fanned beyond your control, *sher-engro*.'

'What could he do?' Dismissively, he replied.

Blanche looked at the huge arms and massive fists that clenched and unclenched as the cripple glared at his torturer, and did not want to consider a situation where, crippled as he was, those hands might find his victim's throat. 'Let us ask about the boy, and leave here,' she begged.

Jason gave a nod. 'If the child's here, I pity him.' To the leader, 'We came looking for a child, about ten years old.'

The smile was knowing. 'We have several to suit all tastes . . .'

'No!' Jason stopped him, sickened. 'No, not that kind of child. We're looking for a runaway, a boy with a scarred hand. He is the son of a friend, who would pay well for his return. The father took too much wine with some gambling friends and beat the boy, so the child ran away.'

Decisively the gypsy shook his head. 'There are no runaways here, *gorgio*. I know other tribes take them, but they are always trouble, police trouble, and we want none of that, but I will pass the word.'

Jason threw him a coin, thanking him, but already Blanche was riding away and the *sher-engro's* eyes followed her—as did the darkly burning gaze of the one they called Lobo. Jason followed her at a brisk trot back to where they stabled the horses, but not even the warm, sweetly-scented interior of the stable could dispel the chill in her heart. 'I wish they'd move on.'

'They will,' he comforted. 'They rarely stay more than a few days in any one place.'

Blanche vowed to stay away from the Bois for the next two days at least, content to accompany Jason to other areas of the city where they had formed a chain of informants glad to receive the price of their next meal just for keeping eyes and ears open. Of the man they called Fantôme, they neither saw nor heard anything. Neither did they notice the closed black carriage that was to be found turning away when they arrived home, or pacing them in the dismal back streets, where no such expensive conveyance should be seen.

On the fourth day, Blanche heard from one of the servants who had been, like many others, to see 'that poor lion' and donate a few *centimes* for its feed, that the troupe was leaving, and she felt safe to ride out again.

'I've business to attend to, this morning. We'll go this afternoon,' Jason decided.

'I see no reason to wait,' argued Blanche mildly. 'I have no need to see the banker friend you mentioned you had an appointment with. I can give Étoile a good warm-up and meet you at the stables at one. You can bring a basket luncheon with you.'

A slight frown creased his brow. 'No,' he said. 'I don't want you to ride alone. Étoile will be frisky after so little exercise . . .'

'Are you telling me I can't control a frisky horse? You had no such qualms over Saladin.'

'You weren't alone.' And, impatient to be away, 'For once, do as you're told, woman!'

'You don't own me!' Blanche exploded. 'I shall ride what I please when I please and where I please! I take orders from no man, and though loving you is something apparently beyond my control, liking you is something I have to work hard at, especially at times such as this!' She stormed upstairs to change. 'No one dictates to me,' she fumed, pulling on the striking black and white velvet riding-dress, throwing a furious glare toward the window as she heard the front door slam.

'I'll drive myself,' she stated, her tone brooking no argument as she allowed herself to be helped into his lordship's second carriage, a light cabriolet, then set the reins to crack with unnecessary force over the equally surprised roan's neck. By the time she reached the park, however, and set the carriage along the trail to the stables, her black mood had dissipated and she looked forward eagerly to the prospect of a brisk canter. It was the only thing she had sorely missed since leaving London—it seemed a lifetime ago.

She called the horse's name softly as she entered the stable, noticing only in passing that the door was open and gave a fleeting thought to reminding Pierre, the young groom they had hired, to be more careful. The mare could be heard stamping and blowing restlessly, causing Blanche to hurry to the stall. 'It's all right, my impatient darling! We'll have a really good gallop, even if it's not the South Downs, and get all that fire out of you.' She slid into the stall to reach for that tossing head, then, 'What on earth . . .?' as she noticed that her own snaffle had already been fixed in place, a lead rope falling from the mouth to the floor. A sound behind her caused her to start to turn, before the world exploded at the back of her head and she crashed into darkness.

When Blanche regained consciousness, Étoile had gone. With a groan she attempted to rise, feeling nauseous, head throbbing painfully—only then realising that her wrists were tied. She closed her eyes for an instant, forcing herself to think rationally. Someone had stolen Étoile, and she had disturbed them in the act. Someone had known that she and Jason rode in the afternoons, that both horses were cleaned out, then curried and brushed to gleaming perfection before nine. What of Jason's horse? She called him, and was relieved to hear an answering whicker, but then realised with a shiver that the horse-thieves might well be coming back for the other, both being perfect thoroughbreds. She must get help.

Attempting to rise, she found that the rope that secured her wrists were also tied to the metal ring that secured Étoile to the back of the stall while the groom worked on her. She could stand; it was obviously long enough for her to lie down, but a pace away, and she was pulled up short. Blanche cursed roundly, then, more out of frustrated anger and no little fear than in any real hope of being heard, she screamed for help. After what seemed an eternity, she gave up and sank to the warm straw, fighting her tears, assuring herself that in an hour or two—three at the most—Jason would come for his mount to meet her for luncheon—unless he was so angry with her that he decided to return home. She knew that half an hour at the most could have passed since her arrival, assuming that she had been unconscious for only a few minutes, so settled herself to wait.

Suddenly she heard the soft creak of the stable door. 'Jason? Pierre? Oh, thank heavens! I'm over here in Étoile's stall.' No answer. No rush of booted feet. 'Jayce?' Hesitantly, 'Don't play games, now. I'm tied up!'

'Good,' came a husky whisper. 'That makes it far better.' To her horror, the deformed shape of the gypsy, Lobo, slipped into the stall and stood, balanced lopsidedly on his good leg, gazing down at her.

Blanche could only stare at him in disbelief, frozen by the menace in that twisted frame, whispering foolishly, 'What . . . do you want?' Then, cursing herself for the weakness that caused her heart to pound and limbs to lose all strength, she ordered more strongly, 'No matter. Untie me immediately, and I'll see that you're well paid. Find my horse, and you'll receive a higher reward.'

The man snickered. 'I know where the horse is— the chief has her. We broke camp at dawn, and we're headed south. He wanted both of you when you and your man first came into camp, but he's soft—says he knows what your man would do if you was took, but the mare—now that's another thing. A man could afford to lose a horse, and the tribe will get a good price at market. The chief said he'd left you tied and safe. No one notices me around anyway, unless they want someone to kick, so I left the wagon and came back.'

Blanche looked about her wildly—knowing that no one would hear her screams unless they were passing

near by—but . . . she screamed at the top of her
voice . . . then cried out as his great hand cracked
against the side of her head.

'Enough of that! There's no one about at this time
of day. Afternoons is popular. We gypsies know
that—know when the babies are taken for walks and
the ladies for rides—know who'll buy the bunches of
flowers we've already stole or the pegs we make.'

Stalling desperately for time, Blanche asked, 'I've
no doubt the tribe has many skills, the women making
pegs and baskets, but what of the others? What do
the men do?'

She knew she had failed when he grinned, 'We
steal horses, like your mare and this other one that
I'll take with me . . . after I've had my little bit of
fun . . . Don't get much fun nowadays with the new
sher-engro there.' And he spat out the name viciously,
his black eyes hate-filled. Then they turned to the
woman half sitting in the straw, her back propped
against the back of the stall, legs drawn up sideways,
taking her as far away from this monster as possible,
and their expression changed.

Dropping to the straw, favouring his crippled leg,
he began to edge toward her, the travesty of a smile
twisting the broken mouth. 'Now, you take it easy,'
he said in what was meant to be a reassuring tone. 'I
don't want to hurt you, because you are so very
pretty, and I believe your man would try to come
after us if I was forced to hurt you. He'd find us, too,
since we're only down the Versailles road, but then
we'd be expecting him and have to kill him.'

'He won't have to come after you. He'll be here
any minute,' Blanche cried. 'If you touch me, he'll
kill you.' Then, seeing no change of expression, 'If
you touch me, your chief will kill you!'

'Enough!' he ordered, his fearful memories making
his eyes ugly. 'One more word, and your mouth'll
look like mine—and I've other plans for that mouth.'
He had been slowly easing his great bulk towards
her, and with a sudden dive grabbed her skirt,

dragging her down, in the same movement tossing the full riding-skirt up—to reveal the tight black pantaloons beneath, and the fashionably spurred boots—which cracked into his jaw as Blanche drew back her knees and kicked out with a force born of terror. He screamed in agony as his jaw broke.

'Nicely done, my dear!' came Jason's cool voice, belying the ashen, cavernous features and the burning fury in the deep jade eyes.

Lobo scrambled crab-like to his feet, his agony, blind hatred for all *gorgios*, for all aristos, for all tormentors, tearing a formless cry from that shattered mouth as he launched himself at his judge, jury and executioner . . .

With quiet, calculated ferocity Jason took two paces forward and with fist and boot reduced his victim to raw meat.

'Stop it! Jayce! Stop it!'

He stepped back, breathing heavily, not from his exertions but from the agony of mind that had prompted him to commit murder. 'He'll live!' Then, for the first time since he had walked into that scene of horror, he took time to allow his shocked mind to register the state of the woman he loved . . . and felt anger. 'Get up!' A whipcrack. 'Dammit, get to your feet!'

Shock, fear, terror—and then an anger that matched his. 'Well, help me, then! Get these ropes off if you've nothing better to do! What took you so long?' Finally, as his tearing fingers loosed those cutting bonds, 'And deal with *that* . . . You almost killed him!' But, before he could turn, 'Oh, Jayce!' and she collapsed sobbing into his arms, saying his name over and over like a litany.

'I never got to my business,' he growled holding the trembling frame in a crushing embrace. 'I couldn't let you ride alone, couldn't bear to see you so angry, so . . . apart from me.' His lips moved over her temples, her eyes, her cheeks damp with tears and then, almost savagely, her mouth, punishing her for the fear within him.

Finally released, Blanche's first thought was for her horse. 'We have to find Étoile.'

The quirk of a smile lifted the corner of his mouth. 'We'll find her.'

'Lobo said they were on the road to Versailles. They couldn't have gone far. We must leave immediately.'

'No.' Then, as she opened her mouth to protest. 'This time, you'll do as bid. If this one,' he gave the still groaning gypsy a nudge with his foot, 'says they're taking the Versailles road west, then we must look to the east and north.'

Blanche frowned. 'He was hardly of a mind to lie!' A shudder ran through her.

Jason put her gently from him, holding her gaze steadily. 'The man wasn't thinking of murder, but of rape. He knew you'd be found eventually, and that I'd follow him. That's how I know the band are headed north or east.' He gave a grim smile. 'My life among the—shall we say—lower orders of society can stand me in good stead upon occasion, but I need to make the contacts. I want you to trust me, Blanche.'

Even while her heart cried out for speed, her head ruled caution, and she knew that she had no choice but to do as asked, so she gave a brief nod. 'What of him?'

'I'll call on the Prefect of Police. He doesn't deal leniently with horse-thieves, and has a Frenchman's gallantry toward the fair sex. Under the circumstances, I don't think this animal will surface for a very long time. Now, I want you to return home. Can you bring yourself to do that? Do you have the strength, my love?'

When he said it like that, hands firm and warm on her shoulders, voice deeply caressing, Blanche felt able to walk through fire. He read her eyes, giving a brief nod. 'I'll be at the house in three, maybe four, hours. Tell Ellen to set out a simple dress and cloak for you. Wherever they've taken Étoile, they mean to sell her as quickly as possible to the highest bidder—which means an auction or fair or anywhere they can move undetected, therefore so must we. An honest merchant, horse-trader, or farmer and his wife will attract far less attention than a couple of aristos looking for a stolen Thoroughbred. Go now. I'll be with you as soon as I'm able.' The lean brown hands, which a moment ago had unleashed a power that could kill, cupped her face tenderly. 'We'll find her,' he promised, allowing his lips to brush hers, light as a butterfly's wing, before turning back to the gypsy. 'First you, my friend, and a few questions.'

Blanche left, hurrying to her carriage, closing her ears to the cry of pain that escaped the stables as Jason began his interrogation. She could feel no sympathy, knowing the man's history of violence and the anguish he had caused others, yet still did not wish to think of his condition when eventually brought before the Prefect.

Making her way to her room, she stopped by the kitchen to ask that a cool cordial be brought to her and a bath be heated. She had given Ellen the day off, and Blanche was privately glad that she would not have to put up with the woman's scolding on her condition. 'Hurry, Jason,' she murmured. 'I'll never forgive myself if anything happens to Étoile.' She saw that the bedroom curtains were blowing, and made a mental note to tell the maid to close the window after she had finished cleaning and had aired the room—then suddenly she froze.

The softest noise, and a voice commanded, 'Do not make a sound, mademoiselle.'

She spun, and her hand went to her mouth, cutting off the instinctive cry as a shadow stepped from the deeper shadows of the bed curtains. 'Quiet!' he said, and she looked into the smiling eyes of Fantôme, the king of the underworld. Unable to speak in the moment it took him to cross to the open window with the silent glide of a cat, she saw him take a stiletto from his pocket and lay it on the table there. 'This one was for Jacques,' he stated—and as her eyes flew wide, 'No, not at my hand, The *bête* who was to deliver this feeds the crabs. His master feeds on crab. It could be poetic, *non*?'

Recovering slowly, first from the shock at the Bois, and now from this intrusion, Blanche asked, 'Who?... How?' Her voice emerged barely above a whisper.

The ever-smiling Frenchman swung a leg over the sill, and something in Blanche's subconscious registered that it was all of twelve feet to the ground. 'The man moves in high places, but you have a mutual friend, I believe. The Comtesse de Chauvenay collects beautiful things about her . . . jewels, pictures, men. She does not take it well if something she desires cannot be bought.'

Blanche shook her head in disbelief. 'Not this!' She flung out a hand towards the glinting weapon.

'No. Poison is a woman's weapon, but la Comtesse is angry with Jacques' rejection of her—so angry that she has spoken of the one thing she thought would hurt him. She wished to stop him finding the boy.'

' "Hell have no fury . . .",' murmured Blanche.

'*Exactement*. But she would not wish him dead. There are those, however, who would kill to stop such a child being found.'

Blanche felt her heart turn to ice, not daring to speak that name.

The man gave a philosophical shrug. 'What Jacques does now is up to him.'

As he went to leave, Blanche regained her voice. 'Wait! Why did you come here to warn him? I thought you were angry at our last meeting, and I feared for him. Do you now owe him some kind of favour?'

'I owe favours to no one, mademoiselle. It was you I came to see, knowing that Jacques means something to you.'

'I . . . don't understand. You don't know me.'

'Ah, but I do! I knew you when you came into the

world of *le diable* himself to stand beside your man,
knowing he might be in danger. I know you from *les
poules* who speak of you as "La Douce," and *les
clochards* who talk of "Le petit Ange". Mademoiselle,
life means this much to me,' and he gave a sharp
click of his fingers. 'I love no one but myself, and
hate no one at all—for if I did, they are no longer
alive. I have met few men I respect—and fewer
women—but from now Le Fantôme is your man.'

At the sound of a light knock, Blanche turned to
the door, startled, having forgotten the cordial she
ordered. 'Oh . . . yes . . . just a moment.' A barely
perceptible shuffling noise brought her about again.
He was gone. A shudder ran through her as her eyes
fell upon the knife that he had left, remembering
Jason's words. 'He is invisible until he wants to kill—
or on rare occasions to talk—and then he disappears
again. If he so chose, my life and yours would not be
worth a *sou*.' She drew in a deep unsteady breath,
glad that such a creature had decided to favour them.

It was mid-afternoon when Jason returned, and she
ran to him immediately, telling him of her news. He
gave a frown, and the firm lips tightened. 'So, the
countess has released the Hell Hounds!' For still she
had been unable to bring herself to mention her
meeting with André.

'I'll go to her, and ask her to retract her words.
Tell them that she lied in a fit of jealousy . . .'

'It would do no good, my dear. The Chauvenays
and I have set a course that we cannot steer away
from.' She wondered how much he did know, how
much he had guessed, but then he put an arm about
her, drawing her close. 'I refuse to find fear in
shadows, when there are more important things at
hand.'

'You've found Étoile!'

'I know where she will be. There is a fair tomorrow
near the forest to the south-east just past St-Maur,
with bands of gypsies coming in from all over France

for the horse auction in the afternoon. We have twenty-four hours to relax in.'

'Relax!' Blanche cried. 'How can you talk of relaxing? Étoile means everything to me . . . the most wonderful gift you could have given me . . . but where there are gypsies, then surely the boy may be there also. We must go down there and search for him . . . Someone must have seen something of him somewhere, some time . . . and we must find Étoile before the auction. We must take her by force, if necessary, and the boy too. The men who took Étoile will surely be expecting us. You can't hide so distinctive a mare; a dealer would recognise an Arab a mile off, and that blaze would stand out as brightly as the star it resembles. They won't dare put her up for auction; they'll sell her privately beforehand. Oh, Jayce, can't we go now?'

'No, though we will go early.. You aren't familiar with the gypsies, my dear. They may well sell her at auction—though I doubt it—and you'd never recognise her. We'll not be searching for an all-black Arabian with a white star, but a black mare with a blaze and two or three white socks, or an all-black with chestnut lights in her coat or a cropped mane and tail. She could be bloated out with water and drugged to appear listless; she'd fetch a lower price, but it would also cut the risks.'

'Stop it! I don't want to hear any more! Poor Étoile. It's all my fault: I should have gone to the stable earlier.'

'That might have had even more disastrous results. Don't forget the thief didn't mean you to discover his identity; had you seen the *sher-engro* at work, he would undoubtedly have taken you with him. You'd be travelling with the tribe and Lobo by now.'

Blanche gave a shudder. 'But what are we to do?'

'Have dinner,' suggested Jason practically; then, seeing her expression, 'I'm not being callous or unfeeling, so don't glare at me like that. We can do nothing until early morning, and I've not eaten since

breakfast. Come now, Blanche, where is that calm
rational lady I knew, the one with the brain of an
abacus and the heart of a lion?'

'She isn't hungry!' Tempted, however, by a
beautifully presented meal, Blanche found that it had
indeed been a long fast from breakfast. 'We will
leave early?' she still had to ask. 'Very early?'

Jason gave a reassuring nod. 'Quite early enough.
We would look suspicious if we were the first arrivals,
so we need a fair crush. That will be the time when
the children emerge to help with the stalls and mingle
with the crowds for other kinds of profiteering. We
must be fresh and alert with eyes everywhere. As for
Étoile . . . I promise you that we shall find her.'

CHAPTER FOURTEEN

FINDING ÉTOILE, thought Blanche despairingly an hour after their arrival, was akin to finding the proverbial needle in the haystack. Spread over nearly four hundred acres, the fair was not so much a fair as a market, its packed stalls and booths selling everything from pins to ploughshares. It had an area where pens of cattle, sheep and pigs raised such a cacophony of sound that she had to cover her ears in passing. There were sheep-shearing competitions, log-splitting events, donkey races, dog-and-monkey races, and the inevitable games of boules.

Everywhere there were children; farmers' sons leading in calves to sell, town-dwellers with faces covered by chocolate smears and carrying boxes of white rats they had cajoled their parents into purchasing. There were boys, of all descriptions, but not one of them bore a scar on the back of his left hand. Jason made discreet enquiries; some met with carefully blank expressions and averted profiles, others with helpful suggestions. No one had seen or heard of the boy, though one thought he had heard talk of a band that went to England the previous year. 'Yes,' said Jason tiredly, 'I know of that one, but they did not have him.' Blanche knew then how it was that he had been in England at that time.

She gave him a sympathetic smile, her own spirits low, seeking an elusive horse, and an even more elusive gypsy boy who could rule France. Taking the object of greater hope, she said, 'Shall we ever find Étoile before the auction?'

'We'll find her.'

On they went, she in a simple grey wool dress, her hair hidden beneath a green-checked scarf, a serviceable and somewhat old-fashioned cloak pulled up about her face, Jason in brown leather-patched jacket and drab breeches tucked into dusty Hessians. Walking through the wilderness of wagons and caravans, tents and marquees, Blanche wondered at the incredible number of black and partially black horses they encountered, from great Normandy Percherons to delicate jennets far from their Spanish origins; but no Arabs, and no Étoile.

Suddenly Jason stiffened. 'That music!'

'Music? Heavens, it's everywhere, though I'd use the term loosely.' But already he was striding through the maze of canvas, ropes and pulleys to where a laughing group were gathered, clapping and dancing to the lively jig played by an old man with a violin. It was the ancient fiddler at the encampment in the Bois de Boulogne.

When Blanche would have rushed forward, Jason's fingers closed over her arm. 'But it's him!' she whispered. 'He *must* know where Étoile is.'

'Of course, but there are only the two of us. I'd just as soon wait a few minutes more to ascertain the whereabouts of the other gypsies. My business is with the *sher-engro*, and I've a feeling he'll be very near. Where he is, there we'll find Étoile. Have patience; we're almost there.'

It was still chance alone that brought them to their goal, for in passing the tent of "Sheikh Hamed Ben Saadeh, *Mage Extraordinaire*," they almost collided with two women emerging from the gloomy interior. '*Pardon*,' apologised Blanche. One woman smiled politely and made to move on, but the other took Blanche's arm and rattled off something in a dialect, frowning and gesturing back toward the tent before joining her friend. Blanche looked askance at Jason, seeing, with a prickle at the nape of her neck, his rigid jawline and narrowed eyes.

'The woman suggested that you do not go in there,'

he translated. 'She said that the so called wise-man was a fake, and there was a terrible stench of horse's ordure from behind a screen at the back of the tent.' He took a deep breath, turning to pull the placard from beside the entrance, reversing it. 'We want no interference,' he stated grimly.

Sheikh Hamed Ben Saadeh rose from behind the table on which were spread a crystal ball, an impressive-looking leather-bound book and several parchment scrolls. 'So!' said the Moor softly. 'You came—you and the incomparable one.'

'Did you doubt it?' Jason said, his tone deceptively mild.

Blanche had not hesitated, but had gone immediately to the heavy red curtain at the rear of the tent, wrenching it aside. 'Étoile!' And she flung herself at the Arab's neck, hugging and petting and calling her foolish baby names. 'Come, we'll have you out of here. He was right: they did black out your beautiful star, but we'll have it back in no time, my lovely.'

'You realise,' stated the *sher-engro*, 'that I've only to raise my voice, and none of you will leave!'

As if by magic, two lethally glinting throwing-knives appeared in Jason's hands still held negligently at his sides. 'I can throw just as well underhand,' he advised conversationally, his smile deadly. 'So that by the time you opened your mouth, you'd have no voice to call with.'

'You are a man who does not make empty threats.'

'Never.'

'Nor I.' Suddenly he, too, smiled, moving his left hand in a sweeping, graceful gesture. 'But there are other horses, *gorgio*, and my tribe need their *sher-engro*. Mademoiselle, I regret my treatment of you, but your man obviously found you in good time.'

Blanche gave a shudder of revulsion. 'Your pet wolf found me first!' She saw the black eyes sharpen. 'If my man had not found me in good time, you'd not be conversing so amicably now, I'll warrant.'

'I hope you suffered no harm? For if he returned, I assure you, Mademoiselle, he would suffer far more.'

Jason moved to Blanche's side, the knives vanished as mysteriously as they had appeared, and he put a warm hand on her shoulder. 'Lobo is alive, though he had time to wish otherwise before being taken into custody at the Prefecture.' Then, losing patience, 'I suggest you leave this area and take your tribe with you. Not all gypsies are thieves, I know, nor all *gorgios* honest men. But when a man steals that which is mine, he walks a dangerous path. There are dark shadows in both town and country, *sher-engro*!' He stepped round the horse, and there was a rending sound, then he led both Blanche and the mare out through the long slash in the canvas, not deigning to look back.

Blanche was trembling with delayed reaction as she followed Jason back to the carriage. 'Where in thunder did you learn to use throwing-knives? Not in the salons of London, I'll be bound!'

Jason took one of the gleaming weapons from beneath his jacket, holding it consideringly in one hand, then gave a short laugh. 'Props.'

'I beg your pardon?'

The jade eyes sparkled with laughter. 'I used them as an actor uses his props. Borrowed from an acquaintance whom the Prefect really would like to meet.'

'You were bluffing!'

'All the way.'

'I don't think that's funny! You might have got us killed . . . or at least beaten to a pulp!'

Jason retained that infuriating smile. 'I think not, my dear.'

Blanche shook her head in disbelief. 'Take me back to Ellen,' she commanded. 'She is the most eminently sane person I know, and I'm sorely in need of sanity just now.'

'You're right. I think we must accept that the boy is not here.'

Tying the mare behind the carriage, they made a leisurely journey back to Paris and the warmly elegant house in the Marais. 'Strange,' Jason mused that evening. 'For all its brevity of ownership, this house more than any other feels totally my own.'

'You've filled it with enough tangible evidence of your life's memories; you've a positive treasure-trove of serendipity.'

He smiled a little ruefully. 'Too much. I never travel light. Yet I've dragged a fair amount of it over hundreds of miles and into dozens of temporary abodes. Only here does it feel *right*.'

'I wish I could say that about my home,' Blanche smiled. 'I never bought it to begin with, and it has taken me years to impart a sense of ownership on it. I don't want to feel permanent. I imagine that's the basis of it. The house is filled with both the practical and the beautiful, but there's nothing there that I couldn't leave. Only people are real—Lexie, Annemarie and the children . . . Why, what is it, Jason?' For he had risen almost violently from his chair, crossing the room away from her, and when he turned, the handsome features were drawn with deep emotion.

'I'm not going to ask you to leave it, Blanche. I'm not going to ask you to bring Annemarie and the children to Paris, to make it your home here. I'm not going to ask you to marry me, even though everything that's in me cries out with wanting you here beside me for the rest of our lives.'

'Jayce, I . . .'

'No, don't say it. There's no future here, not with me. A woman needs security, safety; she needs a home in which to raise children and an assortment of pets—without worrying whether they will be kidnapped or harmed in any way simply because their father is searching for some politically suicidal Grail.'

'You know I'm not afraid of that.'

'I am!' He came to her then, lifting her from the deep armchair, one arm loose about her waist holding her gently against him, his free hand lifting her chin

so that she was forced to look into the deep jade
depths of those pain-filled eyes. 'You are everything
to me. You're the laughter and the tears, the comfort
and companionship, the very breath I take each
morning, the wonder I feel with you every night . . .
And because of that, I want you to leave me. I want
you to return to England.'

The silence drew out like the gossamer strand of a
spider's web hung with dew or the ephemeral fragility
of a snowflake, destroyed by a breath. She said
nothing, dying a little inside, knowing that to say yes
would mean the end of all that she had come to love;
to refuse him would mean the end of gaiety, of
freedom. It would mean being hunted by day and
haunted by night. 'If I go, I'll hate you for making
me.'

'I'm sorry.' Harsh. Guttural. Pain-filled. Then,
'Hate me then! Hate me!' His grip tightening, mouth
descending, anguished, wanting her to leave, yet
loving her, wanting to beg her, torture her with
pleasure so that she could never leave. And his
fingers, tearing, rending until he felt her flesh beneath
his hands—that warm, velvet-soft, yielding flesh that
filled his arms by night and his mind by day . . . And
then his lips against hers softening, tasting the salt
tears, his hands slow-moving and caressing. Mouths
as one, savage, yet strangely tender. Bodies swift-
moving now, giving more than receiving with a
passion that left them spent, cleansed, devoid of pain
or fear. 'No yesterday,' he said. 'No tomorrow. Only
today.' His fingertip lifted a tear from her cheek and
transferred it to his lips.

She gave a tremulous smile. 'The servants will be
talking! I suggest that we adjourn to a more socially
acceptable location.' For one whose life had just
shattered, Blanche reflected, her voice had remained
remarkably even.

The following afternoon, Pierre Boucher arrived. 'An
artist and old friend from the Place Pigalle,' Jason

introduced him. 'I think the drawing-room needs a portrait of you.' And Blanche knew that it was over. He would send her to safety in spite of her own desires, now that the danger was real, loving her too much to allow her a part of it.

'What would you like me to wear?' She *could* have asked him, 'How do you wish to remember me?'

He gave a slightly twisted smile. 'You'll always be my White Lady, in spite of all that has transpired to change that. There was a ball gown, the one you wore on New Year's Eve.'

It was appropriate, she thought, the night that he had realised his love for her, the night she had run away from her love for him, she knew that now. The night that the goddess Fortuna had thrown her dice and changed the whole future for both of them.

Each afternoon from then Blanche stood at the window 'as I've seen you so often,' with the folds of the curtains bringing the eye to the deeper folds of that exquisite dress, her face turned a little toward the view, the shaft of sunlight that broke through at that time of the day creating a halo of her hair. At first she had been stiff and self-conscious, but beneath the little artist's empathetic guidance she allowed her body to relax and even, at times, forgot his presence entirely. It was at those times that the Frenchman held his breath, prayed, and worked on the face, capturing the dreaming of the soft grey eyes and the memories in the slightly curved lips.

During the warm spring mornings of that following week, she and Jason would take the carriage to a secluded park or garden, not to the formally beautiful Jardin du Luxembourg, but to quiet squares of chestnuts and plane trees, where they would sit for an hour or two, carefully talking of nothing at all. They would cross the Pont-Neuf, lingering for a moment on one of the stone bays to watch the grey-green water drift beneath so slowly that the slightest wind made the surface of the water appear to move upstream.

Most of the time, however, they rode, and it seemed to Jason that Blanche was indeed riding as if there was no tomorrow, putting Étoile at hedges and streams that she would have skirted before. Finally the day came when he caught her in the soft, warm shadows of the stable, sobbing into the mare's silken neck. 'Blanche! My love!' He gathered her to him, holding her strongly, rocking her, stroking that bright honey hair until, with a final quiver, she was still.

'Oh, Jayce!' Softly and despairingly. 'Monsieur Boucher says that the portrait will be completed by Wednesday. In three days. I have told Ellen that we'll leave on Thursday.' Then, as the silence drew out beyond bearing, 'Please help me, Jason. You know I don't want to go.'

He drew a deeply ragged breath as the knife twisted slowly within him. 'You must. Neither of us has a choice. I can't work here, knowing that you may be in danger.' Then, for love of her, he relented. 'We'll go to Versailles, to the Palace of the Sun King, tomorrow and take a basket with some crusty bread and cheese and pâté as only cook can make it, and I shall tell you the story of our merriest monarch. She'll make some profiteroles too, filled with her own ice-cream which will undoubtedly melt on the journey.'

Blanche managed a smile. 'I shall have the chocolate sauce all over my fingers.'

'And I shall lick it from each one . . .' A moment of stillness. 'No profiteroles, then. And the day after tomorrow?'

'I shall go shopping. Something for Fleur and Jean-Luc, and gifts for Estelle and the others.'

'That isn't necessary.'

'It is necessary. Will you accompany me, and help me to choose something appropriate?'

'I think not, though I'll take you to La Colombe for dinner. We can eat the little puff pastry doves they use to adorn every dish, and listen to the music of a century ago.'

She knew that he was attempting to leave her the

very best of memories that would appeal to every one of her senses, but they both knew that she already held those. She wanted him to take her to bed and not set her free until the final day dawned. She also wanted to plead that he not touch her at all lest her tight-held, tenuous resolve crumble into a million pieces.

That resolve was threatened even more by the events of the following evening—and proved beyond any doubt that Jason's decision to remove the woman he loved from the field of battle had been one born of experience. They had passed an idyllic day at Versailles, even forgetting for a moment here and there why they were visiting that tranquil spot. 'I don't want today to end; not ever.' Blanche sighed, nestling into the curve of Jason's arm as they drew up before the house.

'Shall we issue a royal decree that this day should be frozen in time?' he smiled, swinging her down from the carriage, twisting her round and catching a corner of her mantle in the process.

'Clumsy!' she laughed, her eyes moving about her, attempting to capture every door, every window, every stone in her mind's eye to keep for ever. Suddenly on the far corner appeared a shadow that was not a part of the scene, a glint of metal. Jason bent to adjust her mantle. She recognised a firearm. 'Jayce!' she screamed. A crack, and the bullet passed within inches of her—where his head had been a moment before.

'Get inside!' he shouted, pushing her toward the front door.

'That corner!' He was off, racing toward the sound of running feet. 'Jason, no!' Imagining the fleeing man firing again, and without thought of safety, she ran after him. She heard a faint cry. 'Oh, no!'—but, as she rounded the corner she saw Jason stooped over something—a man. When she reached them, she cried 'It's one of Marie's men.'

Jason rose, a frown creasing his brow. 'Dead.' He

indicated the pistol still clutched in the man's hand—and the knife between his ribs. 'He was obviously the would-be assassin, but who in heaven's name killed him, and why?' He turned to Blanche, and his frown deepened. 'I thought I told you to get into the house!'

'You might have been hurt.'

'You could have sent for help. Ye gods, woman, this isn't a game! There are no prizes for bravery. You can't go charging about the back streets and sewers of Paris like some Donna Quixote.' He gave her a little shake, and his eyes reflected his frustration and concern and love. 'You are going back to civilisation, my lady, and as quickly as possible. In the meantime, I've a call to make on the Comtesse de Chauvenay.'

'It—it isn't her, Jason, It's André you have to see.' As they made their way back, she told him the whole story, finishing, 'I knew how angry you'd be, so I was going to try to forget it.'

'Angry!' Jason exploded. 'I'll have him horsewhipped. He's not worth calling out. What's left of him afterwards will be thrown into the first coach out of Paris, and heaven help him if he returns!' They had reached the carriage, and he said to her, 'Tell cook to delay dinner. This may take a while.'

'No, I'm coming with you. Please, Jason? For Marie's sake. I'm sure she's guilty of no more than a fit of jealous pique.'

'You have a remarkable gift for understatement, considering the consequences. Very well, but André is mine.' There was a deadliness in his tone that brooked no argument.

At the de Chauvenays', Jason's strong double knock was ignored for several minutes, and angrily he slammed down the knocker again. This time the door was opened to reveal a frightened-looking maid who was wringing her hands in her apron. 'Oh, Lady Davenport, Madame la Comtesse is in the library. Terrible! Terrible! Please come.' Mystified, they followed the woman to where Marie de Chauvenay rose from behind the desk—but a Marie that was almost a stranger. Dark rings circled her eyes, and her once-elegant hair fell in loops and tendrils about her ashen face.

'Blanche! Blanche! What have I done? He . . . he's dead.' She crumpled to the chair again, burying her face in her arms.

With a glance at Jason—how on earth could she have known?—Blanche hurried to take the bent shoulders in a comforting embrace. 'Marie, tell me.'

Reddened eyes were raised to her face. 'An hour ago. The grand salon. André had been drinking heavily. He never used to be like this, but since you left . . . Oh, I don't blame you. He fell in love with you, and could not live with your belonging to another man. He was standing at the open window, boasting of how he would refurnish the room . . .'

'André?' Suddenly Blanche understood. 'André? Dead?'

As though she had not spoken, the countess continued, 'He told me of your meeting. What he had said. He was laughing and leaning outward. "All Paris will be mine," he laughed, and there was a wildness in his laughter that made him a stranger to me. "I'll find the brat myself, and they'll pay a king's ransom . . . That's good . . . A king's ransom." I asked him who, but he said that when Lord Hunterton had been disposed of, all would be settled. "Do you hear me, Paris? Do you hear me, my soon-to-be bride?" he shouted, and then suddenly . . . suddenly . . .' The shocked gaze moved to Blanche's face. 'He . . . he cried out, "No!", and then he just . . . fell forward over the sill. I thought he had passed out with the drink, but when I pulled him back into the room . . . Oh, Blanche . . . It was terrible. His throat . . . Blood . . . I—I saw nothing, heard nothing . . .'

Sharing her pain, Blanche drew the sobbing woman into her arms, holding her tightly as her eyes met

Jason's. He gave a brief shake of the head. This was not the time to tell her of her servant. 'Someone moved fast,' he commented, and Blanche felt an icy chill as she remembered,

'From now, the Fantôme is your man.'

'I'll stay with her at least for tonight,' she decided. 'She shouldn't be alone.' But Marie pulled away, shaking her head.

'I shall be with André. I will stay at his side.' Nothing they could say would move her from that decision, so that finally they left to return to the Marais.

'It's over,' murmured Blanche, but Jason shook his head.

'André de Chauvenay was only one link in the chain. I must find the boy before they do, and you must return to England. Rebuild your life. If you love me, take up your old butterfly ways.'

'How can I?'

'With determination . . . and the knowledge that you must never see me again . . . if you love me.'

The portrait was completed, the brocade of the dress dappled with sunlight and shadow from the window, the richly diverse texture of the Valenciennes lace collar contrasting with the satin-smooth curves above it. As on that first night, Blanche wore no jewellery except the pearls in that intricate coiffure, and her skin gleamed as if the artist had wrung life itself from the canvas. It was the face, however, that held them, for without any doubt it was the face of a woman in love and thinking of her lover, cheeks flushed, eyes softly dreaming, lips parted a little, curved upward in a tiny knowing smile.

Blanche turned to find Jason's eyes on her, but was unable to answer the damning evidence of the artist's brush and turned aside almost angrily. 'He idealises me.'

'Not at all, mademoiselle,' Pierre expostulated. 'It was a work of love, *oui, certainement*, but no exaggeration.' He turned to Jason, hands palm upward in a beseeching gesture. 'You do not think I exaggerated such beauty, *mon vieux*?'

'Impossible,' Jason assured him, but his eyes were bleak.

'I—I must make final arrangements with Ellen,' Blanche said, and without awaiting his reply almost ran from the room, telling the cook that a light omelette would suffice for dinner, before making her way upstairs.

Ellen was putting the last few knick-knacks into a portmanteau, one of the three new ones they had purchased to accommodate the surfeit of memorabilia they had acquired on their travels, together with four large trunks already filled with Blanche's new wardrobe. 'We'll certainly be leaving with far more than we came with, milady,' she observed.

'Yes.' That one word spoke volumes.

That evening, Blanche knew, would be the longest of her relatively short life. She moved the truffle omelette about her plate, tasting not a thing, answering Jason's vain attempts at conversation with monosyllables until he, too, lapsed into silence, but the worst was yet to come. Coffee was served in the drawing-room, where her portrait now hung above the fireplace. Brandy occupied another hour, and Blanche took a second one, hoping it would make the world go away, or time stand still. Eventually, 'It's almost midnight'.

And finally it was over, that heart-rending, crushing, time before dawn. Jason lay watching the moonlight marionettes on the ceiling, and listened to the sobbing of the woman beside him until even that ceased.

When Blanche awoke, it was to an empty space in the bed beside her and an even greater void in her heart. She moved her hand to the indentation where his head had lain, then withdrew it as if burned. 'No!' she remonstrated. 'Too late. It's all too late. I'm going home. Hearts can mend. I'll be me again. In a year, maybe two . . .' But she had never lied to herself, and was not about to start now. Without waiting for Ellen, she dressed herself, and it was only when she went downstairs that her gaze fell on the side table by the window on which her gloves lay.

A small silver basket stood by the gloves, filled with forget-me-nots, but then, going closer, she realised with a small gasp of wonder that each flower was made of velvet, and in its centre was a tiny yellow sapphire.

'You won't, will you?' came that beloved voice from the doorway.

She raised swimming eyes. 'Forget you? How could I . . . ever?'

'You know that I'm right, don't you? You have to leave.'

'Knowing doesn't make it any more acceptable.' Then, with a deep breath, 'I can at least watch for strangers from the Continent.'

'You would put yourself in danger. No, I forbid it.'

'You'll have no control over my life once I'm there. Oh, Jayce, won't you change your mind? I don't ask for marriage or for evers. I don't even ask for tomorrows. Just let me be with you for today . . . and then again today.' He shook his head, but said nothing. 'And you won't even escort me back to England!'

'No. In the Revolution they used the guillotine. A quick death. Cleaner by far. That's the way it must be. I must not even think that I shall see you again, and you must not consider it.'

Blanche drew on the ivory kid gloves. She knew that he would not touch her; he would not kiss her hand; she would not kiss his cheek; and most definitely they would not say 'Goodbye.' One last look, and he opened the door for her. One long look, and she passed through. She wished that it did not seem as though she was running away. She tried to think of home, of her villa and her friends, of the soirées and parties, and rides in the park, but at that moment she gained the distinct impression that she was running away, not to. The click of the door that he closed gently behind her seemed to have an echo of finality about it, but not half as final as the inaudible crack of a heart breaking.

CHAPTER FIFTEEN

ALEXANDRA GREETED HER with open arms. 'My dear, you just can't imagine how desolate London has been without you!' Then she took in the rich Burgundy travelling gown with its cream lace-and-muslin cravat and the modish wide-brimmed matching bonnet set at a jaunty angle and lavishly decorated with ostrich plumes. 'Why . . . Whatever have you done with our White Lady?'

A tiny smile touched Blanche's lips, not quite dispelling a certain sadness in the fine grey eyes. 'I left her in Paris,' she stated with a finality that allowed no questions, but then her smile widened and she took her friend's hands in a warm clasp. 'But now I'm home again, and Beatrice, Lady Davenport, is going to take London by storm! How I've missed it all! Dancing at Almack's, the plays at Drury Lane, an opera at the Garden, and above all my friends. Oh, Lexie, you must give me a welcome-home party!'

Even while agreeing and planning for a glorious homecoming that London would not forget for a very long time, Alexandra Fitz-Hugh registered the high colour and too bright eyes that—none but a friend would have noticed—sparkled with unshed tears. There had been far more than her innocence left in Paris, the woman reflected, but this was not the time to pry. 'I knew, of course, that wonderful as your holiday may have been, you would most certainly have been back this week at the latest.' She deliberately prattled on, revealing none of her doubts or fears, certain that the holiday had not been entirely 'wonderful'—far from it! 'I said to young Jeremy only last month that you hadn't missed the Derby for the last three years, and once the season had started, one could wager on your presence.'

'How is Jeremy?' Blanche enquired, not wishing to admit that the challenging mile-and-a-halfer had quite escaped her mind.

'Oh, he pined most dreadfully, and there was talk of a suicide attempt after that shameful Croydon race. He confessed all, you know, and no one would receive him—definitely *persona non grata*—for ages.'

'Poor Jeremy!'

'Both the suicide attempt and the confession failed of course to expiate his act, so he returned to the bosom of his mother, who consoled him with lavish gifts and an introduction to her new neighbours, the de Bienvilles who brought that old Marchmont place. You know, the one that no one but eccentric and exceedingly rich *émigrés* would want.'

'I don't think I've heard of them.'

'Not at the top of the tree, but a charming couple for all that. They've a daughter, Luciette.'

'Aah!'

'A perfect little doll and ideal for young Carlysle . . . sweet, docile, child-loving and without a single opinion that isn't an echo of her mama.'

Blanche's vanity suffered the very slightest pang that she had been replaced so quickly in the heart of one who had professed undying devotion but with a little self-admonitory laugh, she said, 'I wish them all happiness, and I'm glad to see that he finally took my advice.'

'I, too,' her friend laughed. 'You'd have eaten him alive! Come now, let's discuss who I'm going to invite to your homecoming party. This season's eligibles are rather thin on the ground, I'm afraid, though there are one or two quite dashing whips among them.'

'I'd not take a man who couldn't handle the ribbons or take a five-bar in his stride,' Blanche stated, then in her mind's eye came a vision of that frosty gallop over the Downs, of broad shoulders and sure hands at the reins, of powerful thighs encased in buckskin, and laughing jade eyes holding a challenge that she could never resist.

Alexandra saw the fine-boned features tighten.

'Well, you leave that to me. Now, how did you find the house? I called twice and was received most graciously by your Mrs Baines. Of course, I only wished to reassure myself that all of your silver was safe!' she admitted quite unashamedly.

Blanche had to laugh at the picture her friend's confession conjured up. 'Oh, I had no doubts at all about the silver, and I can well imagine Annemarie's reaction to your less than subtle questioning and surreptitious snooping. She has, of course, worked miracles over the past weeks to turn the place into a real home with assorted knick-knacks brought from heaven knows where—though I must confess it felt a little alien.'

'You've been home only two days!' Alexandra patted her hand. 'You wait until you've got into the deadly dull progression of parties and pic-nics—you are coming to Brighton with us, of course?—you'll soon feel as if you'd never left. Naturally you'll become a travel bore, stretching every yard of your journey to a mile, and turning every stone into a diamond.'

Memory. Ellen in Paris. 'Given time, even stones can become diamonds.' 'No, I don't think so,' Blanche said quietly, inflexibly, causing Alexandra to wonder how many more doors would be closed gently but firmly in her face.

Annemarie found an identical problem. 'You must tell me all about Paris,' she had begged. 'Have they finished the Arc de Triomphe yet or, like poor Marie-Antoinette, did your triumphal entry into the city pass under a carefully balanced and disguised arch of cardboard?'

'There was no triumphal entry,' Blanche had told her. 'Nor exit either.' She had skirted round the various tourist sights, telling her of Ellen, whom

Annemarie had never met. 'You'd have liked her. I was sorry to lose her, in a way, though I could never have afforded to keep her on. She had the choice of staying here for a few days but elected to visit her parents and sister in Gower Street—not the area I'd have imagined her coming from. I've given her excellent references, of course, so she should do well.'

'And the boy?' Annmarie asked, when she realised that Blanche was going to say nothing. 'Has Lord Hunterton found any lead that will reveal his whereabouts?'

'No. Nothing.' The subject had been cut off with the precision of a fine-honed knife.

It was a fortnight later, on the eve of the homecoming party, that Annmarie gathered a further idea of the events leading up to Blanche's precipitous return from Paris. She had taken the white brocade ball gown from the wardrobe. 'Will you wear this? I know you don't generally wear white now, but this is so beautiful, and you've worn it only once, at Hunterton Hall.'

'Twice,' corrected Blanche. 'When Jason decided that I should leave Paris, he had a portrait commissioned. He wanted to . . . to remember me in that dress.' She turned away quickly from the creation that Annemarie held over her arm. 'No, I shan't wear that; put it in a box with tissue and a lavender bag. I'll not wear it again. I don't think I'll wear the blue with the seed-pearls either—Jason taught me to waltz in that one.'

'But you waltz divinely! Lady Fitz-Hugh says that the exquisites simply clamour to fill your card, and you wear each one of them into the ground.'

Again one of these sad, secret half-smiles that bore no resemblance at all to the gay insouciance of five months ago, and Annemarie wished with all her heart that her friend had never met Jason Hunterton. 'It's less tiring at half the speed,' she remembered, then changed the subject pointedly. 'I'll wear that dark gold satin with the new sleeve shape. The most daring designers in Paris are flattening the sleeve at the shoulder, no more stiff linings with down-stuffed pads but one or two little puffs to the elbow—so much more comfortable. Which necklace do you think? The gold one with the garnet drops or the diamond one with the emeralds?' Then a deep sigh. 'It really doesn't matter, does it? Everyone will say exactly the right thing whatever I wear!'

Alexandra had indeed excelled herself, with half the *haut ton* of London turning to applaud Blanche's entry. 'Lexie, thank you! You're a miracle-worker. How an earth did you persuade all these to appear at such short notice?'

The older woman led her into the mêlee, highly pleased with Blanche's delight. 'Bribery and corruption work wonders,' she laughed. 'Though most of them came when I told them that our White Lady was no longer wearing white, so I warn you, you'd better have some deliciously decadent reasons to spread about. Look! There's a new one for you, very high on the list of eligibles—Baron Gravelly's son, the Honourable Tristram, a little wild from his year in Sydney Town—actually thought of settling in New South Wales! He says that convict labour's cheap and land even more so—but I think sanity's slowly returning, and he'll divert you for a while.'

Blanche allowed her friend to lead her forward, and her heart gave a lurch at the sight of broad shoulders and black hair, but the hair did not catch blue sparks from the chandeliers, and when he turned, the appreciatively widening eyes were of a bright cornflower blue. She let out a sigh of relief as he bent low over her hand. This one was no threat at all to her bruised heart, and she was able to switch on her brightest smile. 'I want to know all about New South Wales!' she commanded

'I'm afraid you'd find it a little dull, Lady Davenport. No balls, at least none like this: only a tiny theatre and very few shops. One can ride for

ever, though, to the blue of the hills if you so desire
. . . Oh, but I'd not wish to bore you . . .'

She smiled into his eyes, the lovely face upturned
and shining with interest, making him feel as if they
were completely alone in the room and the crowd
about them mere shadows. 'Nothing you could say
would bore me!' She thus assured herself of another
devoted admirer, and a few minutes' monologue in
which her thoughts could drift.

As the evening progressed, Blanche found herself
relaxing a little and actually enjoying herself; thanks
in part to Alexandra's careful choice of guests and in
greater part to several glasses of excellent champagne.
Once or twice her hostess was obliged to extricate
her from what she termed 'a situation', but on the
whole all went smoothly. The first was when Blanche
got into an argument with a landowner who had
bought a new stallion. 'Vicious brute, but I put him
on a running martingale and stopped his antics in no
time. Still pulls badly, though.'

'What do you expect?' Blanche exploded. 'I'd like
to see you try one on and not pull to escape the
pain.' Alexandra moved in as she launched into
telling the man exactly what she thought of him, and
with smiles and pretty prattle separated them. 'Put
the animal into a rubber snaffle,' Blanche stated, as a
parting shot. 'If you take away the pain the poor
brute's trying to run from, he'll calm down, I'll
warrant.'

'Now, Blanche dear, you must meet Charlotte
Bellwood—a little scatty, but definitely amusing with
a treasure-house of gossip.' An hour later, however,
she saw Blanche with a slightly inebriated young
blade, and recognised the baring of the teeth that her
friend used for a polite smile when politeness was
teetering on the edge of truth. She was side-tracked
momentarily as she reached them, but overheard the
over-ardent suitor declare, 'If you don't, I'll give up
on life completely. I'll not breathe until you agree to
be mine!'

'Then you'll undoubtedly expire,' Blanche agreed unsympathetically.

'I'll wait. I'll wait for the next hundred years if necessary!'

'You'd certainly have problems with a cotillion, let alone a waltz at that age, so why not settle for one now and forget all this nonsense?'

'But why won't you allow me to take you away from all this? I'm rich, some say I'm handsome, I know everyone there is to know. I'm not afraid of the truth, if it comes from those coral lips.'

Blanche gave a sigh, bored to tears. 'It's quite simple, your lordship. You have as much substance as that delicious sorbet you've just brought me—and leave me just as cold!'

'Blanche!' cooed Alexandra. 'Forgive me for dragging you away. There is someone in dire need of advice. Forgive us, your lordship.' Before the gaping exquisite had time to speak, he found himself suddenly alone.

'Thank you,' Blanche smiled in relief as they moved to the buffet table.

'He'd have amused you immensely before Christmas, as would all the others you've none too delicately demolished this evening.'

'A brace of bucks! I had rather a brace of pheasant!' Then, seeing her friend's crestfallen expression, 'Oh, Lexie, it's a wonderful party and I'm having an unforgettable evening, truly I am. I'm just not yet ready to jump on to the marriage-go-round. I think I'll go down to Hove next week. The sea air will do me the world of good and blow away some of the cobwebs.'

'It will take more than sea air to blow away your memories, my dear, nor can you dance them away, nor ride them away.' She gave a gentle smile. 'I've heard rumours this evening of a French count and a Spanish gypsy. There were even a couple of poets and artists tossed in for good measure. I've not heard a word of a certain English lord with the manners of a prince and the face of Pan.'

'An apt description. Neither will you. I left Jason in Paris with a number of unforgettable memories and—though I'd admit it only to you—a moiety of my heart. I'm not trying to forget him, Lexie, or the wonderful turbulent times we shared. I'm simply attempting to recover from them and rebuild my life. He made the decision himself as an alternative to marriage. Now, I'd really rather not talk of it any more. Introduce me, won't you, to that grey-haired gentleman with that sparrow Miss Beddoes? I saw him at Epsom last week. The young lady with him at the time was sporting an ostentatiously large diamond racehorse brooch with the jockey enamelled in the most garish crimson and gold which quite detracted from the stones. His racing colours, I assume.'

Within minutes of the introduction, all others were forgotten as Blanche and her companion, whose quick wit and bright mind totally belied his years, engaged in absorbing discussion on racehorses in general, the Derby, and winners in particular.

Worse by far were the long nights when she both longed for sleep, that she might escape her memories, and dreaded it for the dreams that haunted her. Jason's body above her, beneath her, enfolding her, his eyes laughing, gleaming, afire with his hunger for her, and those hands, those magical, wondrous hands, the memory of which caused Blanche to roll the sheets between her teeth to muffle the whimpers that rippled up from her stomach and to keep from calling his name while she waited for the dawn.

'You look *ravissante*, my dear!' cooed Dorothea Wendel-James as Blanche was led into the sumptuously decorated drawing-room. 'You have lost pounds, and are finally quite fashionably pale. Hove is so horribly bracing, but I shan't let you out at all. We have so much to discuss that you'll not leave this room for a week—you can stay at least a week, can't you? I've been so solitary, so *malheureuse* since my dear Henry died—though he was considerate enough to leave me the small consolation of this house and a hundred or so thousand—that it will cheer me no end to have you here.'

Blanche had forgotten how exhausting her friend was, or had never been so affected by it. 'And you've taken up French.'

'Been *taken* up, my dear! He is so *gentil* , this little tutor of mine. Twice a week he comes and sits right where you are now. He has the most wonderful brown eyes that look deep into mine. He is not tall, you understand, and a little . . . *dodu* . . . no, more than a little plump . . . But so masterful, so strong! Not at all like dear Henry, who might have been most fashionably languid or half asleep—one could never be sure.'

Blanche allowed her to prattle on, wondering how quickly she could diplomatically bring her visit to an end, when a name caught her ear, and she stiffened.

'You know the Huntertons?'

'Oh, intimately, my dear, intimately . . . or at least my very best friend—next to you of course—Adeline Barrington does. She and I went to Epsom—doesn't absolutely everyone? and she introduced us.'

'I never saw Hector and Becky there,' Blanche mused, then seeing her friend's face, 'Oh, I don't know them half as well as you obviously do. I was introduced by Lord Hunterton's brother Jason, and . . . well you know how friendly they are . . .' Then, with a flash of pure genius born of desperation, 'In fact that is one of the reasons I came south. They were kind enough to invite me to the Hall on my return from France, so I thought how much nicer it would be to spend a day or two . . .' She saw the hurt expression. 'Or three, with you. I hardly know them, whereas you and I will cheer each other immensely and you can tell me absolutely everything about your *gentil parfait* knight.' Ye gods! Blanche thought, catching back a hysterical giggle, I'm even beginning to sound like her!

Since Blanche had arrived on the Brighton stage, Dorothea insisted that she use the Wendell-Jameses' carriage, an elegant landaulette with silver embellishments, to take her to Hunterton Hall. There was, therefore, no way out. 'One simply cannot drop in on people like the Huntertons in a hired carriage,' Dorothea had protested, and Blanche, who had originlly entertained no such idea, was forced to accept her friend's mandate. It was therefore with mixed feelings that she approached the comforting solidity of Hunterton Hall and pulled at the great iron bell which seemed to echo throughout the house.

'I'm only passing by,' were her first words to Rebecca as that familiar bundle of dynamite strode from the drawing-room to greet her.

'Your coachman seems to have other ideas. Not to worry. We'll send a search-party for him in a day or so. No, better make that a week or so. You're looking awful. A few days with Saladin on the Downs will bring the colour back into your cheeks.' There was no mention of Jason.

Blanche took a deep breath. May as well face it, get it out into the open. 'Becky . . . Jason isn't with me.' Stating the obvious—start again. 'I left him in Paris.'

'Sensible girl! You promised to visit us again. Hector's in the drawing-room; he'll be as delighted as I to see you again.'

'Becky . . .'

'I can guess. My arrogant, charming, over-powering, dictatorial brother-in-law asked you to marry him, and you declined the honour. Am I correct?'

'No . . . He refused to ask me to marry him, and ordered me to leave.' Then, at the incredulous disbelief in the shocked eyes, 'It's not what you're probably thinking. Oh Becky, he has had threats to his life! One attempt, while I was there, from people who want to stop this endless search for a boy who may well be dead anyway. I begged him to let me stay.'

'Of course you did, because you're in love with the man—and he refused you for the same reason. What now? Will he send for you when he's had time to miss you or when this immediate danger has passed? It's not the first time he's been in a like situation, both here and in France, over the past five years.'

'No, it's quite finished. I shall do all in my power to find the child if he is here. Some rumours say that he is not with a gypsy band but with some French *émigrés* in London, but then among the royalists the rumours fall thicker than a Siberian snowstorm. I'll send a message to Jason if I find any truth or, pray God, if I ever find the boy. But I couldn't go through all that again, and I honestly believe that the child must be dead. Oh, Becky, you should have seen some of those people they say he lived with. No child of aristocratic blood could possibly survive such a life. As for Jason . . . Yes, I'll probably love him for the rest of my life . . . but I'll never see him again.'

The older woman gave her arm an understanding pat. 'I've enough problems in thinking of tomorrow. "Never" isn't in my vocabulary. Come and see Hector now, and after luncheon you can have a long rest in your room or rejoin us for a game of cards. We've invented a new game where we gamble for the rooms in the house, the furniture and the servants! He's a far better player than I, but at present I own the kitchen staff, the entire master bedroom and the wine cellar . . . not to mention his beloved horses and the dogs . . . Yours, incidentally, are as large as small ponies now.'

Blanche had to laugh, feeling a great burden lifted from her. 'I'd say you were the better player by a long way.' Then, taking the other's hand in a tight grip, 'Thank you, Becky.'

They were halcyon days that followed. Hours spent in the saddle with a respectful groom following or Hector trying vainly but goodnaturedly to keep up, good food and easy conversation at the table and 'a little something . . . an old herbal remedy . . .' taking care of her nights. Jason's name, if mentioned at all, was brought into the conversation quite casually and only briefly, but in those moments Blanche learned a considerable amount about the man she loved.

'Jay was always the wild one,' Hector laughed once. 'Now me, I was the quiet one . . .' And, with a glance at his wife who was only half listening, 'Quiet and gentle, handsome, intelligent, loving, witty . . . sophisticated . . .'

'Modest, too!' finished Rebecca.

Another day he had taken her to see the mastiffs, pups no longer but boisterous, rangy young dogs whose fraternal battles often ended in genuine snarls and the occasional slash from lethal fangs over an apparently uninterested female of the pack. Blanche made to run forward as they came in sight of two such contestants, one obviously getting the worst of the battle, but 'Watch!' cautioned Hector, and at that moment there was a flash of fawn, and the largest of the dogs erupted into the group, knocking the victor aside and running him off with fearsome growls before returning to his brother, giving him a sympathetic lick before dropping down to stretch out in the sun at his side. 'Just like Jay and I,' Hector smiled. 'I hated school and loathed university, but there was always Jay to take care of me and see off the bullies when the going got too rough.'

Blanche knew that, however casual these odd tales of Jason, they were were still not conducive to the rebuilding of a life without him, so she announced her intention of returning to London. 'Even though I've been wonderfully happy here, and totally spoiled.'

'It's always your home from home,' insisted Rebecca. 'Whenever you tire of London, you know where we are.'

'Come down for the weekend every month or two,' Hector suggested. 'Bring Annemarie and the children with you: they'd love the country, and we'd enjoy having them, wouldn't we, Becky love?'

They exchanged a long look. Uncharacteristically, Rebecca blushed. 'It would accustom me to the problems to come,' she said evasively.

'Rebecca?' Then, seeing the shining eyes, 'You're not! . . . You are!' Hugging her. 'Oh, you've said nothing all week! You'd have let me go without telling me!'

'Well, it's not absolutely certain . . .'

'Of course it is!' Hector denied proudly. 'Women always know these things.'

'I am rather long in the tooth for such folly!'

'Nonsense!' Blanche laughed. 'You're just the perfect age, young enough to bear children and old enough to cope with them. Oh, Becky, I'm so happy for you!'

'I never thought you liked children.'

'Not for myself, but if a couple want them as much as you, and have such a perfect atmosphere to raise them in, then they have my warmest blessings.' A picture flickered across her mind of a young boy, raven-haired, tall and straight as a spear with deep jade eyes—but she brushed it aside with a decisive shake of her head. 'All the more reason for me to return to London. You'll have a thousand things to do, and I've a present to buy. I want to be the very first to do so.'

'It's only two or three months old. You really don't have to rush into anything,' Rebecca laughed, warmed by her guest's enthusiasm. She and Hector had agreed to keep the news from Blanche under the circumstances and it was only a last-minute impulse that had made Rebecca confide in her. Now she was very glad that she had. 'She is still very small,' she protested.

'So will the present be! Are you certain it's going to be a she? I thought everyone wanted boys.'

'Not I,' stated Hector firmly. 'I want a girl that I can dress in ice-blue velvet and pale pink silk, who'll have ringlets down to her waist and who will still put her arms round my neck when she's eighteen.'

'My, those years flew by!' said Rebecca with a touch of her old dry humour, and the subject dissolved in laughter.

At the villa once more, Blanche found herself watching the children with new eyes: Fleur still reserved, though apparently content, humming to herself occasionally and holding long serious discussions with the two dolls Annemarie had made and dressed; Jean-Luc growing in confidence as his carved horses sold as fast as he could make them, buying new tools to make his work faster and easier. He had discovered the work of George Stubbs, and used the artist's anatomical sketches as a bible. When the painting came from Paris a month after Blanche's return, however, Jean-Luc said only, 'Thunder!' and put George Stubbs aside for ever.

'I thought that this might please you,' the accompanying note said. It was signed with a tiny blue forget-me-not.

The painting, bearing the unmistakable brush-strokes of Pierre Boucher, showed Étoile in a restive mood, head tossing, one forefoot pawing impatiently, nostrils flaring, eyes challenging. It bore all of the accuracy of Stubbs with the fire and passion of the Parisian taking Paris by storm that year, Eugène Delacroix.

Blanche looked at it for a very long time in silence, then went to her room and sobbed for over an hour, rising late in the afternoon to tell Annemarie, 'I'm going to a party.'

The Frenchwoman took in the puffed eyes and swollen lips where Blanche's knuckles had rubbed away the memory of his kisses, and gave a nod of acceptance. 'Of course. May I ask where, that I may choose the right gown?'

'I don't know. Anywhere. There must be a hundred parties in London at this very moment with an ocean

of champagne between them. I shall start at the
furthest away and work my way back.'

It was said by some who had mourned the passing of
the White Lady that Blanche Davenport was most
certainly in need of care and attention, a flame about
to burn itself out, an angel in danger of singeing its
wings. Over the following weeks, there were others
who had seen the White Lady as a challenge and
Blanche Davenport as a beautiful feline that defied
belling. These—young bucks and middle-aged *roués*
both—were astounded by the creature who now
greeted their most boring sallies with trills of laughter
and their most clumsy advances with blushes and a
fluttering fan that only revealed the promise in those
once cool eyes.

July came and went. In her new role as Lady
Protector, Annemarie opened a letter that came up
on the Brighton stage—of late there were letters and
gifts appearing from all over the south of England, it
seemed—and read of the confirmed existence of
Rebecca Hunterton's child—'causing more problems
than Hector ever dared, so it must be a girl!' She
hurried to Blanche with the news and saw her friend
tear off the exquisite ball gown that she had just
purchased and hurl it into a corner. 'When that idiot
Sunderland arrives, tell him I've a headache . . . or
the plague . . . It's certainly hot enough!' She sounded
for the first time in weeks like Blanche Davenport.

The floribunda roses were out, crimson melting
into gold and the butterflies in profusion supping at
the heady nectar. The fair was on the Heath, the
gypsies with their pots and pegs and bunches of
heather, the stalls and booths with dripping honeycomb
and shell-games that no one could beat, and the
famous Barnum Brothers' Circus. 'How the children
would love the circus!' Blanche exclaimed to Alexandra
as they toiled side by side in that bleak hall in St
Giles. 'It seems a million miles away from here. If I
had unlimited wealth, I'd gather every one of these

poor urchins here today and take them to breathe fresh air for a change, just to see the colour in their cheeks and the sparkle in their eyes. The only thing they know of the country here is this fresh bread and cheese and fruit that we've been lucky enough to get today. They need something to make them forget this terrible summer.'

The elder woman nodded sympathetically. 'At least we stayed—and tried. Had we had any sense at all, we'd have gone into the country like most of our friends—like all right-minded individuals.'

Then she saw her friend's face, and reached to squeeze her hand. 'I know that you'll not leave while you are looking for this boy, this runaway son of Lord Hunterton's friend. But you've gone into areas where they've had the plague, even, endangering your very life. Why, you fainted last week and have been sick twice since; I'm quite worried about you overtaxing yourself. You never stop.'

Blanche smiled. 'I'm all right. There have been very few plague victims this year. Typhus and smallpox have carried off more, but what can you expect in the flea-ridden, fly-infested, overcrowded conditions in which these people live? And there's the typhoid fever, too. Cesspits are hardly ever cleared, and the majority of the houses simply have porous drains that carry the waste directly into the river. The Thames is no more than an open sewer, and from it the water-companies pump the so-called drinking water straight into domestic cisterns. It's bad enough now, but God help us if this new disease they call cholera hits the rookeries.' She passed a weary hand across her forehead, filling the extended plates automatically. 'I can't stop now, Lexie. I've made this crusade of Jason's my own, but there is so much to do, so many who need my help. I know that the gypsy bands are on the Heath, yet I haven't been able to go to them. I know I should give up everything to look for this boy . . . He is so important to so many.' Then, realising that she was revealing too much, she improvised, 'Jason tells me that he has quite a large family. Yet when I see these children here, I become the White Lady again and find I just can't desert them. I'll go to the Heath tomorrow. The fair leaves at the end of the week, so I must try. Perhaps one of my genial giants will go with me . . . I'm so glad that the very ordinary Lady Davenport warranted the same care as the White Lady.'

Her friend laughed. 'Well, it was only for a few weeks, not years, and you've really not changed at all. You're still devilish hard to cope with!'

Blanche gave an answering smile and one of the instant quips that was expected of her, but in her heart knew just how much she had changed—how little of the White Lady remained. Stretching her aching back, and glad that it was only an hour before a bath and clean sheets, she scraped the last morsel of bread and cheese on to a waiting plate. 'Fanks, miss!' 'You're very welcome. I wish it was more.'

'*Merde*!' exclaimed a familiarly accented voice, and a calloused hand threw an empty plate on the table. 'It is three times this week I don't get 'ere in time. Does a man 'ave to turn to crime to get a crust of bread?'

Blanche had almost cried out as her mind registered that disfigured hand an instant before her eyes flew to the face of the boy confronting her. Long-lashed cynical eyes, dark like his mother's, auburn haired— as his grandmother had been before the Terror had turned her white—the unmistakable Bourbon nose. Very carefully Blanche retrieved the boy's plate and handed it back to him. 'I know a place where you could have all the bread and cheese you could eat.'

The street-wise regard assessed her, and made a decision born more of hunger than trust, and he gave a nod, gauging his credit. 'And an apple?'

'And cake, too, if you're good,' she promised.

Still he did not smile, and she wondered whether he had forgotten how. 'I've walked all the way from the 'Eath. My shoes they fall apart last week—I don't make them so good yet. Is it far to this place?'

'No . . . Though the end of your journey may be much further than you think. Does your . . . mother know where you are?'

'She's dead.' There was little emotion there. 'I run with the others. I get fed or beaten, depending on how fast I am. I get to be pretty fast. Do we go now?'

She caught Alexandra's wide, questioning gaze as her friend stood absorbing this exchange, not daring to ask the question. 'I'll be taking this one home, Lexie. Can you cope?'

'Someone special?' Already she had read the answer in the brilliance of her friend's eyes.

Blanche felt a warm glow deep inside, all her previous vows forgotten as if they had never been. There was much to do but in a week—two at the most—she would be facing her future and whatever dangers it held—with a child that would be cherished and protected, and with a man that was all of her life. 'Very special,' she answered with a smile, and taking his hand, led the gypsy king out into the sunlight.

CHAPTER SIXTEEN

IT WAS ALMOST midnight, and the city streets were finally quiet. Blanche leaned her head back against the lace-trimmed antimaccasar and gave a deep sigh, regarding the woman in the chair opposite with a tired smile. 'Do you think he'll come?'

Annemarie nodded, returning the smile and brushing a strand of hair from her forehead. 'I'm certain he will—given a day or so of acclimatising to civilisation!'

'And bath-water!'

'He certainly put up a fight! I swear if you hadn't insisted on scraping off some of that dirt before you allowed him to eat, we'd never have got him clean. At least it tired him out. I went up a moment ago, and nothing would have woken him.'

'And I imagined it would be so easy! He would come docilely, act as a king in disguise, and agree to all my suggestions with touching gratitude.'

Annemarie gave a low chuckle. 'Instead of which, we were confronted with a ravenous wolf-cub whose favourite word appears to be "No", but he'll come round.'

'I hope so. Will you miss England at all? Will you fear old memories, old reprisals, if you and the children go back with me?'

'England has held few good memories, and I've been so many years away from France that we'll be strangers when we meet. Are you going to sell the house . . . or keep it for a while?'

'In case Jason doesn't want me in Paris any more than he did before? No, Annemarie, I'm burning my proverbial boats and have decided to leave England for good. There will be holidays, of course; just as he will always return for long visits to his brother, so shall I miss Alexandra and, yes, Rebecca Hunterton also, but I'm determined to make Paris my home now.'

'With or without Jason?'

Blanche felt her heart give a leap, and there was a burning sensation in her throat. Surely he would not turn her away if she appeared with the boy. He could not take the child beneath his wing and leave her outside . . . Could he? She bit her lip, and Annemarie saw the gesture with a wave of sympathy, but then those grey eyes met hers and Blanche gave a decisive nod. 'With or without him. Come, it's after midnight, and I've a feeling that tomorrow is going to prove even more exhausting than today. Somehow I must contrive to present Jason with a gypsy royal, not a wolf-cub in lamb's clothing.'

A full month had passed, however, before a buyer was found for the house, a generous widower who was delighted to retain the servants and even purchased Blanche's matched greys, together with coach and groom. It was a month of exhaustive legalities, and even more exhaustive schooling of the gypsy boy, who appeared to take a fiendish delight in confounding their best efforts. One day he would appear tractable, even eager, making a perfect leg, holding both knife and fork at the same time, and submitting to the now gleaming auburn hair being coiffed into fashionable waves. The next he would turn into a circus, playing clown, performing bear and snarling tiger in sequence, until all and sundry were about to commit either suicide or murder. Only Annemarie, with the weary resignation and endless patience of a mother, would return to the fray unbowed. 'He's a boy,' she would smile. 'A ten-year-old boy,' as if that said it all. Perhaps it did, but a distinctly jaded Blanche saw no end to the battle—

and when it came, was equally as surprised as the others.

Louis, as they had appropriately re-christened him, appeared at breakfast one morning with his usual bright smile and ravenous appetite. 'What shall I have for breakfast in Paris?' he asked. 'We are still going, no?'

'Yes, of course,' Blanche replied warily, knowing that his acceptance of the impending trip varied with his volatile and totally unpredictable moods. 'We shall be ready in a few days. Are you looking forward to seeing Paris?'

'You forget. We have come . . . came from Paris and camped in the environs of Paris until summer. I shall not be camping this time, eh? I live in a big house with servants and rich *vêtements* . . . clothes.'

'Perhaps . . . Yes, probably,' said Blanche, wondering whether Jason would look after the boy in that warmly beautiful house in the Marais or put him into the care of wealthy royalists. She rose and went to put a reassuring hand on the childishly thin shoulder. 'Don't worry. You'll be well taken care of.'

The dark eyes widened as they searched her face. 'I don't want to be . . . taken care of. I want to be with you.' Then suddenly, unexpectedly—for he had shown no trace of affection before—he threw his arms about her, burying his head in the hollow of her shoulder. 'You must keep me! It is right. You have no son. I have no mother. It is *right* that you keep me!'

Blanche felt an unfamiliar tightness in her throat, and gently released herself from that clinging embrace. 'I shall try, Louis. I swear that I shall try, but as I've told you before, you are an important person to a number of people, all of whom can give you so much more than I. I'm far from rich.'

He spun away from her, eyes stormy. 'I don't want your money!' And he let loose a stream of quite incomprehensible French argot, liberally laced with invective, that told her exactly what he thought of

being bought and sold like a prize bull, finishing, 'So!
We go to Paris, and I tell the same to this Lord
Hunterton, who already I do not like!'

'Louis, my dear . . .' But he had turned, running
to his room, hiding the threatening tears that a 'man'
does not shed. Blanche met Annemarie's distressed
gaze. 'So!' Then softly, 'We go to Paris!'

Paris was unchanged. It should not have surprised
Blanche, but somehow it did, for having changed so
much herself in the past months, she fully expected
the world to change with her. The letter she had sent
ahead to warn Jason contained but three words: 'We
are coming.'

She had suggested to Annemarie that she and the
children stay at a near-by hotel while Blanche went
to confront Jason alone, but the Frenchwoman had
shaken her head in firm denial. 'No, I do not agree.
Jean-Luc and Fleur can stay behind—we shall hire a
nanny for them as soon as we reach France—but you
and I and the boy shall go together. You must
introduce Jason and Louis immediately, and only
then, when he has seen what a perfect gentleman
Louis has become and how close he is to you, only
then should you talk. I shall wait in another room to
take Louis at that time. We Frenchwomen understand
such things. One does not go into the lion's den
unarmed.'

Blanche smiled, thinking that with that rich mane
of sable hair he could well be likened to the King of
Beasts. 'Perhaps you are right,' she agreed; then,
with a twinkle, 'I shall need a very special dress for
the occasion, don't you agree?' and saw her friend's
answering smile.

'*Now* you are thinking like a Frenchwoman!'

The dress was of the palest oyster satin, its huge
sleeves and full puffed skirt accentuating the tiny
waist held by a wide ribbon sash that matched the
close-fitting pastel blue bodice. It clung low on her

creamy shoulders and, as was her wont, she wore no jewellery, but her appearance of crushable fragility was totally offset by the determined gleam in the lovely grey eyes as she was admitted to the house in the Marais that held so many memories.

They had sent a message from the hotel and Estelle was awaiting them, her dark eyes lighting up as she siezed Blanche's hand in a joyful clasp, leading her into the hall. Her gaze went past Blanche to where Annemarie and Louis stood uncertainly in the doorway, and she gave a wide welcoming smile as Blanche said, 'This is Madame Baines, a very dear friend and a French *émigrée* returned home, and this is Louis, the boy we were looking for. Perhaps you would show Madame Baines to the small salon, while Louis and I meet Lord Hunterton. He is at home, I assume?' The housekeeper nodded, gesturing toward the drawing-room, but when she would have gone ahead, Blanche forestalled her. 'No . . . We shall go in alone. I'm sure we are expected, even though we gave no precise time of our arrival.' Heart pounding, she took Louis by the hand and went to open the wide-panelled door . . . and then her heart stopped altogether.

He was standing before the fireplace, staring up at her portrait, which dominated the room. He had not yet dressed for their arrival, and the white *blouson*-style shirt tucked carelessly into tight-fitting black trousers accentuated the breadth of shoulder and slimness of hip to the degree that it brought a dryness to her throat which she had to clear with a little cough.

He turned round with a muffled exclamation—and then became very still as their gazes locked. The room seemed to fade and the noises in the hall to disappear, as did the crunch of carriage-wheels in the street. She had meant to play every role from coquette to sophisticate. He had determined to be coolly polite. Prepared speeches forgotten, they each took an involuntary pace forward—then stopped, a chasm

of indecision between them, longing held leashed by
logic.

Louis stared from one to the other in growing
disbelief and impatience. This had gone far enough!
Stepping forward, he faced the stranger with straight
back and rigid shoulders. 'I am Louis,' he enunciated
clearly, certain that these two were *complêtement fou*,
and thrust out a stiff hand. 'I will shake your hand,
monsieur, but I do not think I like you.'

Jason returned to reality with some difficulty,
tearing his gaze from the vision before him towards
the boy. He took in everything at one sweeping
glance—the auburn hair, the eyes, the Bourbon
nose . . . and the birthmark on the back of the hand
clenched at his side. His eyes flashed back to the
woman's, and received a short nod of confirmation.
So it was true! His long years of searching were at an
end! Several seconds had elapsed, and swiftly he bent
to shake that already descending hand. '*Bienvenu*,
Louis. I have been expecting you. I am Lord
Hunterton, and . . .' As the boy's last remark sank
in, he gave a slight frown. 'Why do you dislike me?'
But his interrogative glance went to Blanche, and he
saw her stiffen as the boy stated,

'Madame Blanche is not rich, but she tells me that
there are rich people like you in France who will wish
to take care of me. She say that you will give me
better things than she can, but I do not believe that.
More, I do not wish that.' In his anger and stress he
had lapsed into French as he finished, 'I do not want
sheets of silk. I have slept on the ground or mattresses
of straw all of my life! I do not want this so big, so
beautiful house, with servants I do not know putting
me to bed. I want a caravan again—small and warm—
but with Madame to hug me and tell me great
adventures that I can dream about. So now you will
buy me from Madame, that I know, but you should
know, monsieur, that I do not like you for it!'

'Louis!' Blanche cried out, feeling the colour drain
from her face as she went to him. 'No one is going to

buy or sell you. I never would. That's a terrible thing to say!'

The dark gypsy eyes glittered as he flung off her hand. 'There is nothing more important to grown-ups than money. I learn that with the tribe. You do not have money, but you have me. *Enfin*, I am worth selling, *non*?'

'That's enough!' Jason's voice rapped out, bringing their attention to bear, seeing the fear and anger in the boy's tight features and the sick despair and repudiation of such a terrible charge in the other. 'Louis, you will go at once with Estelle to your room which has been prepared for you.' Then, more gently, 'We shall talk later of this nonsense of putting you up for sale, and I can assure you that there will be nothing done against your will. Nothing that is not in your best interests. Do you understand?'

'*Bien*! Then I will stay with Madame!' So saying, he stalked majestically from the room.

Blanche turned, one arm outflung in desperation. 'Jason, I swear . . . There was never talk of money.' The jade eyes were as chill as that ever-cold stone as he raised an eyebrow, causing her to add, 'You should know me better!'

'You've been away a long time, my lady.'

She felt the burning of threatening tears at the back of her eyes. This was not at all as she had planned, and it was worse, far worse, than she had ever dreamed. Her anger at his injustice boiled up within her, and then she exploded, 'Damn you, Jayce Hunterton, you do know me better!' Eyes flashing, she faced him squarely. 'I've sold everything, given up everything, uprooted Annemarie and the children, and for what? To be insulted, humiliated, and, for the second time from that glowering look, rejected. I've brought you the one thing you wanted above all, with no thought of personal safety or undying gratitude . . . and most certainly no anticipation of reward. How dare you!' He went to speak, but she cut him off with a sharp gesture. 'I'm here to make

Paris my home, if possible to be near the boy, who, I can assure you from long experience, will not take kindly to being used as a pawn to your king's knight.' The long-lashed grey eyes were suddenly misty as her anger faded. 'But he *is* only a boy, Jayce, and can't fight all of you . . . As I can't.' She turned away. 'I'll tell Annemarie we're leaving. Since you don't want me here, I . . .'

'*Want* you!' His exclamation was choked by his emotion, and she felt hard fingers dig into her arms as he swung her to face him. 'Want you? Ye gods, woman, I've wanted you from the first moment I saw you, dreamed of you every night and thought of you every day from then till now!' His hands were bruising her, and his eyes reflected all the torment he had suffered since the day he had watched her leave, taking his heart, his soul, and all of his life with her.

'Oh, Jayce!' And then she was in his arms, the lips ravaging hers telling her far more than any words could of the depth of his love and loneliness. She clung to him, feeling that old familiar drum-roll of her heart and the fire that threatened to engulf her. Stars burst behind her lids as she returned his kisses with a passion that matched his own, and when finally they broke apart, their breathing emerged raggedly from their throats.

'God, how I've missed you! How could I have let you go? Danger or no danger, you're here now, and I'll fight both heaven and hell to keep you.'

Blanche smiled suddenly very sure. 'I'm not afraid. I've never been afraid with you beside me.'

'Then you'll never be afraid again, for I'll be beside you for the rest of my life . . . If you'll let me.' Suddenly there was a note of uncertainty in his voice that she thought never to hear from this man of all men. He took hold of her hands, studying them for a long moment before finally saying, 'You've been everything to me: mistress, friend, confidante, protector, companion, adviser, a love beyond all loves . . . But, for me, that still is not enough. No . . .' as she went to speak, 'hear me out. I know how much your independence means to you. I know, too, that you've said that you never want children. I swear that I'll never force you to give up either belief, but, Blanche, I want you to be my wife.' He gave a tiny smile. 'You'll say that I'm old-fashioned, that we have everything now that marriage can offer and possibly more; probably you are right, but, my love, I believe in the sanctity of marriage. I believe that the vows made do set a seal on love.' He raised her fingers to his lips, brushing his mouth across her knuckles. 'I love you, and I want the world to know it. I want the totally selfish pride of saying, "This is my wife." Am I a fool?'

Blanche was unable to speak for several seconds and her eyes were misty as she nodded with a tremulous smile, holding on to her secret a moment longer. 'We both must be. Yes. Yes, I'll marry you, Jason.' She could say no more as she was again swept into his arms, his kiss dispelling any doubts that either might have entertained.

'I'll never tie you down,' he vowed again, but she laughed, shaking her head.

'Yes, you will, and I shall always fight to be a pace ahead of you rather than a pace behind, but the glorious battles we'll undoubtedly have will be based on trust and security and an abiding belief in a future together. As for children . . .'

'No, Blanche, that must be your choice entirely. I know how you feel, and I'd rather have no heir at all than gain a son and lose your love.' He glanced upward as a series of thuds from overhead signalled a battle royal between the gypsy and the housekeeper. 'That particular heir will, I hope, outgrow his dependence on you before he demolishes the entire house, and I've a good family in the country who have offered to bring him up as their own. They have twin boys of a like age, and the world will never know for certain that he existed at all. In the meantime, however . . .' and he laughed a little ruefully, 'we must keep him here. I've always wanted a son, but never quite envisaged a ready-made brat that actively disliked me from the start!'

Blanche drew a deep breath, asking . . . a little too casually, 'Would you mind if it was a daughter?'

'Almost as acceptable, though I'd not be as over the moon as I hear Hector is . . .' Then he broke off, and those sharp eyes swung to her face. 'Blanche . . .?'

She felt a delicious glow at his sudden indrawn breath and the dawning realisation in his face. 'I shall try to arrange a son for you, Jayce . . . But will you be terribly disappointed if this first one is a daughter?' With an inarticulate cry of joy he swung her up, spinning her round until she clutched at him, dizzy, laughing, begging him to stop.

Instantly contrite, he set her down, searching her eyes anxiously. 'Did I hurt you? Here, sit down . . . I'll call for some tea . . . coffee . . . a cordial? You must rest . . .'

'Jayce! . . . Jason! I'm perfectly normal, completely healthy, and there is absolutely no reason for you to panic!' The grey eyes sparkled up at him as she allowed her fingers to move through the thick curls at the back of his neck. 'In fact . . . resting was the last thing I had in mind!' His searching gaze reflected his doubts even though every nerve vibrated at her closeness. 'Jayce . . .' she smiled, 'I'm only a little bit *enceinte*!'

His burst of laughter dispelled any lingering uncertainty as to her fragility and eyes alight with love, he lifted her again and carried her effortlessly to that room at the top of the stairs that already held so many memories.

'We shouldn't! Annemarie is waiting for me . . .'

'She'll wait.'

'But . . .'

'And she'll understand. After all, she is a *French*woman!' Setting her down, he turned her gently to face him. 'My love, this will be a first time,

I promise you: the first moment of the rest of our lives.' Slowly he eased the oyster satin off her shoulders, moving it down her arms until the high full curves of her breasts were revealed in all their glory. She wore no undergarments at all. 'You came prepared for this!' he said huskily, wonderingly.

'I came hoping for this.'

'And yet you would have left . . . gone away alone . . .'

'You had to want me for myself . . . for always.'

His hands, those lean, gentle, yet strong hands, moved over her and the dress fell to the floor as he held her eyes with his. 'There is no end to my hunger for you,' he said softly, 'and longer than that will last my love.'

Blanche drew off his shirt and revelled in the feel of the bronzed skin beneath her fingers. 'Love . . . Yes, my own, but just now, after so very long, it's the wanting, the needing . . .' She felt his arms drawing her close, his lips crushing hers, yet with a new tenderness, a first-time worship that revealed his awareness of what was now between them.

When he took her, it was more than those other times, more wondrous than anything she had imagined possible as they soared in a heart-stopping flight to the heights, then plunged, and up again until she sobbed his name aloud, and again as a litany . . . and again, more softly, as the whirlwind stilled and the gentle breath of their loving mingled, mouth to mouth, flesh to flesh as, finally, they lay still, limbs entwined.

One finger rose to take a single tear from her lashes, as it had so very long ago, to transfer it to his lips. 'My lady,' he murmured, smiling into those lovely mist-grey eyes. 'My lady . . . my love.'

Happy Mother's Day.

This Mother's Day, instead of the usual breakfast in bed, why not ask your family to treat you to the Mills & Boon Mother's Day pack. Four captivating romances to enthral you.

THE EMERALD SEA by Emily Spenser

A marine biologist finds herself out of her depth on an Italian film set — and with the director.

THE MARRIAGE BED by Catherine George

A holiday in the Algarve becomes a nightmare when the heroine is kidnapped in revenge for an injustice she knows nothing about.

AN IDEAL MATCH by Sandra Field

Despite two broken engagements, a young woman still believes in marriage — she comes to love a widower left with three children but finds he had lost his faith in love.

ROUGH DIAMOND by Kate Walker

Can a successful businesswoman and a garage mechanic really bridge the gap between two such different backgrounds?

FOUR UNIQUE LOVE STORIES IN A SPECIAL MOTHER'S DAY PACK AVAILABLE FROM FEBRUARY 1987.

PRICE £4.80.

Bewitched in her dreams she awoke to discover the face of reality

The same dark hair, the same mocking eyes. The Regency rake in the portrait, the seducer of Jenna's dreams had a living double.

But James Allingham was no dream, he was a direct descendant of the black sheep of the Deveril family.

They would fight for the possession of the ancestral home. They would fight against desire to be together.

Unravel the mysteries in
STRONGER THAN YEARNING,
a new longer romance from
Penny Jordan.

AVAILABLE FROM FEBRUARY 1987. PRICE £2.95. **W✷RLDWIDE**